THIS YEAR, TRY A YOUNGER MAN ON FOR SIZE

"Look, Devin, this is cute," I said, standing up and walking back toward the front door. "But you and I both know that this is a bit much. You're way too young for me. Not to mention you're my girlfriend's son."

"I'm your friend's son, that part is true. But who said that I was too young for you? I like you. Hell, you're fly as hell and I wanna get to know you." He walked over to me and stood so close that I backed up and hit my head against the door. He placed his hands above my head. "You really want me to leave? Or do you want me to stay and get snowed in with you?"

Damn, I can't stand that the flesh is weak. "You can stay and we'll talk. But I *will not* be having sex with you."

"Who said anything about sex?" He smiled. "When the time comes for me to hit it, it'll be after you beg me to."

—From "Whatever It Takes" by Tu-Shonda L. Whitaker

KISS THE YEAR

Goodbye

BRENDA L. THOMAS

TU-SHONDA L. WHITAKER

CRYSTAL LACEY WINSLOW

DAAIMAH S. POOLE

POCKET BOOKS

NEW YORK LONDON TORONTO SYDNEY

POCKET BOOKS, a division of Simon & Schuster, Inc.
1230 Avenue of the Americas, New York, NY 10020

This book is a work of fiction. Names, characters, places and
incidents are products of the author's imagination or are used
fictitiously. Any resemblance to actual events or locales or persons,
living or dead, is entirely coincidental.

Whatever It Takes copyright © 2005 by Tu-Shonda L. Whitaker
Every New Year copyright © 2005 by Brenda L. Thomas
Dangerously in Love copyright © 2005 by Crystal Lacey Winslow
My Boo copyright © 2005 by Daaimah S. Poole

POCKET and colophon are registered trademarks of
Simon & Schuster, Inc.

Manufactured in the United States of America

ISBN: 0-7394-6107-9

Contents

KISS THE YEAR

Goodbye

Whatever It Takes

TU-SHONDA L. WHITAKER

I sat on the edge of my bay windowsill and looked down from the third floor of my Society Hill town house at the snow-covered cars and blinking Christmas lights. I blew an O of smoke from my cigarette, crossed my thick cocoa thighs, and said to nobody in particular, "Fuck Santa Claus! This'll be the last year that I pray for his fat ass to drop off Prince Charming. I know it's only Thanksgiving weekend but I'm starting early. And guess what? I ain't cooking no black-eyed peas on New Year's Eve." I took a long drag and tapped my foot. "Won't be no collard greens, and damn if I'm waiting on some man to be the first one who comes through my front door. I'ma be just like every other old broad. Go to church, make eyes at the pastor, and wait on midnight. Then I'ma come home, pull out Chocolate Thunder, and masturbate myself into a silver bullet convulsion!"

I hopped off the windowsill, mashed the remains of my cigarette in the ashtray, went in the bathroom, and prepared to shower. It's three o'clock in the afternoon on Black Friday and I've been frumpy long enough. Me looking out the window in mis-matched pajamas is not going to change anything. I'll still be thirty-six with no man, no prospects, and no hint of an orgasm ever returning. I swear, if I stay home this New Year's Eve, Dick Clark's ball will be the only one I see drop. And believe me, my four months of involuntary celibacy has been more than enough punishment. Punishment for being in my twenties and too hot in the ass. I was a single ho for way too long. Now I'm paying for it. I should've listened to my mother, married the square, David, and been a housewife. At least by now I would've had a baby and a dog. But nooooo, not me. I had to complain about him. *I don't like fat men. And I don't like how he always says yes. I need me a man that can say no sometimes.* Well, I had John, Kaareem, Malik, and Sharief. And they all said no. No, I'm not cheating on you, she's just a friend. No, she's not *really* my wife, we just live together. And no, I'm not breaking up with you, I just want to see other people. Believe me, I got a shitload of no's, and now I'm thirty-six with ovaries that look like Frosted Flakes and three fish that I *absolutely* can't stand.

I turned on the hot water and stepped into the shower. Then I closed my eyes and let the jet streams roll all over my body, splashed Victoria's Secret Apple bath oil on my mocha skin, and started singing Jill Scott's new song "Whatever." "How about some chicken wings . . . I'll hurry and go get it."

Now that's what I'm talkin' about, a mofo that makes me wanna buy him some sneakers!

Ten minutes passed, I stepped out of the shower and onto the towel lying on the floor. Then I stood in front of the full-length mirror that hangs behind the bathroom door and stared at myself. Ever since I entered my thirties I've been checking out my naked body from head to toe. I have to make sure nothing starts sagging or magically appearing. The last thing I need is for liver spots or varicose veins to fuck up my Tina Turner legs. Hell, if nothing else, I must always be cute. I'm five-six, a size sixteen, and I have no complaints. I often wonder why people think if you weigh more than a buck fifty, have wide feet, or can pinch more than an inch that you have to complain. Shit, I'm fly, and I don't need Oprah or Dr. Phil to lecture me into believing it. Not to mention how a Sears one-piece girdle does wonders for the extra fifteen minutes placed on hourglass curves. Let me be the first to tell you, when I've been blessed to get my freak on, my brick-house hips have turned tricks, don't get it confused! Needless to say, India Talani Parker can rock with the best of 'em.

I let my hairstylist talk me into a Farrah Fawcett flip. He swore to me that this hairstyle should do the trick and I would have Mr. Right knocking on my door. That was two weeks ago and several men have knocked on my door. The mailman, UPS, and Fed Ex, each delivering care packages from my mother in Murfreesboro, North Carolina. She seems to think that I must be miserable staying in Jersey all alone. Well, I'm not alone. I have two miserable-ass girlfriends to keep me company: Joan and

Tracy. As for my hairstylist, I got half a mind to cuss his ass out! That'll teach him never to lie to a horny old lady.

Seeing that nothing new had grown or changed on my body, I grabbed the lotion and slipped on my terry-cloth robe. Afterward I headed into my bedroom, and no sooner than I flopped down on the corner of my four-poster bed did the phone ring. I peeped at the caller ID. *Oh no, it's Joan. I got my own problems. I can't deal with the complaints about your husband. His ass has been cheating for years, so get used to it.* I let the phone ring and decided to pour lotion into my hand instead.

Goddamn! The phone was ringing again. This time I didn't even look at the caller ID. I simply snatched the receiver off the base. "Yes, Joan."

"It ain't Joan, ho. It's Tracy. I'm ducking Joan's ass too. She just called you?"

"Uhmm hmm," I said, rubbing lotion into my legs.

"Yeah, she just called me too," Tracy said, sucking her teeth, "and she left a message with Ju-Ju that if I speak with you to tell you she wants her digital camera back."

"Why does she need her camera all of a sudden?"

"She says she gon' squat in the bushes over at the Garden State Inn on Route 22. She claims her husband got a hoochie up in there."

"A nasty hoochie if she's laying up in the Garden State. Tracy," I said, placing the receiver in the crook of my neck, "Joan is a sick bitch, I swear she is."

"Well, she did hear the hoochie on his voice mail calling him Big Daddy. Humph, what would you think?"

"She shouldn't have been listening to his voice mail."

"Oh ho, don't try to act like you ain't never broke the code on a brothah's phone."

"Yeah, when I was twenty. Joan is forty-two years old."

"When you were twenty?!" Tracy screeched. "Paleeze, remember Jamil? Oh, you were checking his messages every five minutes. You were riding that machine like a dick, so spare me. And *that* was just last year."

"Whatever. Call her back and tell her to give me an hour."

"Just go over there. You know she'll be waiting. Goodbye."

"Uhmm hmm."

I can't stand that I'm knocking forty in the ass; because once Joan turned forty she lost her fuckin' mind. I met her six years ago when I'd moved to Newark and started teaching at Harriet Tubman Elementary. She was one of the nagging teachers that hung out in the teacher's room, diagnosing badass kids with ADHD and complaining about their retarded-ass parents. Joan was divorced, had a boyfriend and a son who lived in Brooklyn with her ex-husband. I liked Joan because she said whatever was on her mind, and although she complained, she really cared about the kids. No child in her class ever went home hungry, and for those who couldn't afford to go on class trips, she always paid their way. Eventually Joan and I started eating lunch together. Soon after that, she confided in me that her boyfriend was actually her ex-husband.

"Your ex-husband?" I asked her with my eyebrows raised and lips twisted. "What's the point?"

"I can't leave him alone," she confessed, taking a pull off her cigarette.

"Why not?"

"He's got a possessed penis."

"What?!"

"India," she sighed, "it's got a crook in it and I swear it be whippin' spells on me!"

Two years after that she remarried him, and now she swears he's cheatin' on her.

I met Tracy the same year I met Joan. Tracy is the school's secretary and knows everybody's business; therefore, it didn't take long for us to click. Tracy is five-four, the color of butter, has freckles and big breasts, unlike Joan, who's an A cup, five-ten with cinnamon-colored skin. Tracy *is* ghetto fabulous and acts like Boomquisha from the fifteenth floor, but no matter what, she's still my homegirl. She's thirty-four with a five-year-old daughter, Jasmine, and Ju-Ju, the "rent-free live-in." I told Tracy that I would've put Ju-Ju's black ass out a long time ago! Damn if he would be dickin' me and doggin' me. And I'm footin' the bill while he does it? Oh, hell no! Not India. Knowing me, that mofo would wake up one night with hot oil dripping down his ears.

I stood up and put on fresh undergarments. Looking through my closet, I decided that I would throw on a pair of tight black jeans, a black V-neck sweater, and black Gucci loafers. And, of course, a diva has to do what a diva has to do, so I threw on my three-quarter-length red-fox coat with the matching head wrap and stepped out the door. Damn, I almost forgot the digital camera for Joan. I went back in the house, grabbed the camera, came back out, and hopped in my gold 530i.

I slid in Jill Scott's CD, listened to my newly claimed favorite song, and sang about fixing a man some chicken wings for puttin' it down! Damn, I gotta give it up. I'm being downright pitiful. Every other word is about a man. You know what? This is going to be my updated constitution for the New Year: *I'm doing me. Period.* I'm not going to worry about dying a lonely old lady, I'm not going to worry about if God is punishing me for having an affair with some chick's husband, or if I'll ever get any milk to bring my dried-up ovaries back to life. I'm done with that shit! You know what? Forget the New Year, I'm starting my constitution today.

I rummaged through my purse and pulled out a cigarette, popped the lighter in, and turned this damn CD off. I lit my cigarette and took a drag. The next thing on my list is to stop smoking.

I parked in front of Joan's house and rang the bell. I waited three minutes and nobody answered. I rang the bell again and started tapping my foot. *Let me call her and see where she is. I swear, one day Joan is going to be hiding in those bushes and get arrested for trespassing!*

Just as I started walking toward my car, I heard Joan's front door open. I turned around with a screw face on, ready to cuss her ass out for having me ring the bell forever. As I turned around, her son was leaning against the door. He had on a pair of baggy gray sweats with matching boxers peeking up from the waist. A tight and crisp-white wife-beater on; one that appeared to be massaging his defined pecks. And from what I could see, as soon as he stood up straight, he would be at least six-one. *Wait a minute; is the onyx color in his eyes sparkling? Oh, this lil' niggah gon' cause somebody some problems.*

One of his hands was tucked into the waist of his boxers. My eyes caught glimpses of smooth black hair encircling his navel and running down his stomach in a straight line, leading my eyes directly to the imprint of dick. He took his other hand, caressed the waves in his dark faded Caesar to the front, and ran his fingertips slowly over his face. Then he licked his lips, stood up straight, and just as I thought, he was six-one. He yawned a little and said, "I'm sorry, I was sleeping. I was out late last night. What's up?"

He better stop asking me what's up. What is he, like seventeen? Humph, I'll fuck around and be going to the prom with his ass. "Hey," I said, biting the inside of my jaw, "I didn't know you were home from school."

"What do you mean school?" He chuckled, folding his muscled biceps across his six pack. "I've been out of *college* for a little over a year."

"Really?" *Oh, he must've dropped out, 'cause ain't no way he's grown enough to have a college degree . . . unless he has an associate's.* "Are you working now? Did you graduate?" *I swear I couldn't remember.*

"Did I graduate?" He looked perplexed. "Of course I did. And I do more than work, I have a career. I'm a graphic artist. I design online ads for Time Warner in Manhattan."

Well, damn, he has a real job. 401K and shit. I know it's time for me to leave. "Give this to your mother for me, please."

"Wait a minute." He grabbed my hand as I handed him the camera. "Ms. Parker, you mind if I call you India?"

"India? Boy, I'm almost old enough to be your mother."

"Boy? My mother?" He frowned. "I'll let the 'boy' part go for right now. But as far as you being old enough to be my mother, I doubt it. I'm twenty-three, and you?"

"Thirty-six."

"Naw." He smiled. *Wait a minute, does he have dimples? Oh shit, my panties are wet.* I took a deep breath as he continued, "You're not old enough to be my mother. You're young enough to be just right."

Is he flirting with me? He massaged my hand with his soft thumb and I thought the thumping in my coochie would send me into cardiac arrest. "D.J.—"

"India, my mother is the only one who still calls me D.J. It's Devin."

"Boy, you better stop playing before I leave here and go buy you some sneakers. What you want, some Jordans?" I laughed. *I can't believe I said that.*

"Oh, you got jokes. You're cute though, but just so you know, I usually wear Tims on the weekend and Prada loafers during the week. Therefore you should've bought those Jordans a few years back . . . and, India, stop calling me boy."

Did he just read me? "Did I give you permission to call me India?" *Hell, I didn't know what else to say.*

"When would you like for me to call you?" He smiled.

"Tonight—wait a minute—don't ask me trick questions."

"All right, would it *really* bother you if I called you India? It's such a beautiful name."

Am I blushing? Shit, I think I am. "Okay, Devin, India is fine." *I know I'm sounding stupid.*

"Thanks, I would like that. I have to admit, you look good as hell."

"Thanks for the compliment," I said pulling my hand from his embrace. "But I really should get going."

He let my hand go and smiled. "Would you like to come in? My mother should be back in a minute. She just ran to the store."

"No-no. Just tell her to call me." I almost tripped my fat ass down the walkway trying to get away from this lil' boy. *Oh my God, wait until I call and tell Tracy this shit.*

"Why would I lie, Tracy?" I said, with the cordless phone tucked between the crook of my neck and shoulder blade. I was standing over my double sink, cubing boneless chicken. "He really was trying to get with me."

"What do you mean 'trying to get with you'?" she asked, almost in disbelief. "Was he like, 'Hey, that's a nice outfit you got on? Your hair lookin' ai'ight?' Or was he like, 'What you got poppin', Shortie-Roc?"

"He was like, 'You look good as hell, girl!' "

"You sure he said that?" Tracy asked.

"Uhmm hmm."

"That's the same shit he said to me the other night."

"For real?" Instantly I stopped cubing my chicken. Suddenly I felt deflated.

"Psyched yo' mind!" She laughed. "Hold on, India. . . . *Jasmine,*" she yelled away from the phone, *"say excuse me. And how come every time I get on the phone you got something you wanna tell me? Go sit yo' ass down!* . . . India," she said, getting back on the line, "a bitch just playing with you. I ain't never seen him look at me. But word is bond; he was kickin' some hood shit to you. *'You look good as hell, girl.'* That's that bullshit Ju-Ju laid on me, fucked around and got me pregnant and shit. Now look, he got his feet propped up, scratchin' his balls, and he's so nasty that he keeps a nose full of buggers."

"Oh my God, Tracy, T.M.I., for real. That's entirely too much information. As long as he's there don't you bring me any more food from your house."

"Girl, please—I'm puttin' him outta here! But anywho, Ms. Parker, you about to have a lil' jump-off. Robbin' the cradle and shit. Girl, just so you know, Joan gon' kick yo' old ass!"

I started cubing my chicken again. "I'm not thinking about his young ass. I need me a grown man, not a lil' boy toy."

"Hell," she said, "my motto is, 'if he's outta high school and over eighteen, it's all good.' Plus, it's a lot you can do with a boy toy."

"I don't think so." I pushed the sleeves of my sweater over my elbows and dumped the chicken in the wok. Immediately it started sizzling. "How would Joan find out?"

" 'Cause an old bitch's pussy got a distinct smell," Tracy said, barely getting the words out because she was laughing so hard.

"Fuck you," I chuckled, "I guess your old ass would know."

"An old bitch's pussy!" she screamed in laughter. "I love ya, girl. You know I'm just playing with you. But if you don't tell, I won't tell."

"Please, Tracy, there won't be nothing to tell," I said, mixing Chinese vegetables in with the chicken, " 'cause I'm not messing with him."

Just then, my doorbell rang. "Wait a minute, Tracy—let me see who's at my door." I turned down the fire under the wok and pressed the talk button on the intercom. "Who is it?"

"It's Devin."

"Tracy," I said into the phone, "he's at my door."

"Who?"

"D.J. I mean Devin."

"Doesn't he know it's supposed to be a snowstorm?"

"I don't know. What the hell is he doing here?" I was in shock.

"Hell if I know, open the door."

I walked into the living room and cracked the door open. I could see that snow was starting to fall. "Yes," I said to him, through the crack.

"Hey!" He held up Joan's digital camera. "My mother asked me to return this. She said thanks for letting her use it."

"Use what?" Tracy whispered into the phone. "Tell him to talk up, I can't hear him."

He was pressed so close to the crack of the door that I didn't know what to say right away, so I said, "Tracy, let me call you back." I hung up before she could start complaining.

"I promise not to rob you if you open the door a little more." He smiled and his dimples started glowing. Shit! The heart in my coochie was awake. I opened the door and he stepped inside. He looked around at my red leather living room set; my mud cloth print area rug with matching pillows; wicker trunk, brass floor lamp; and large cherrywood Ethan Allen entertainment center; with a 36-inch TV, books, and fifty-disc CD changer.

Grover Washington Jr. was playing lightly in the background and Devin started moving his head a little. "Grover Washington?" he asked, pointing to the CD player.

"Yes." I was still standing by the door.

He took off his butter-soft brown leather jacket and placed it on the arm of my couch. He had on a gray hoody, the same sweatpants he had on earlier, and a pair of beige Tims. "It smells good in here. What are you cooking?"

"Chicken stir-fry with Chinese vegetables. . . . Devin."

"Yes, baby."

Baby? Please don't let me start blushing. Damn, it's too late. I folded my arms across my breasts and sat on the arm of my couch, next to his jacket. I could smell his Dolce & Gabbana cologne. "What . . . are you doing here?"

"I came to return your camera." He was still looking around my living room.

"What are you looking for?" I asked him.

"Your man."

"I don't have one."

"Not yet anyway."

Before I could comment or erase the stupid smile off my face my phone started ringing. "Hello?"

"Damnit, India!" Joan yelled. "Where the hell is my camera?"

"What do you mean?"

"Tracy told me that she told you I needed my camera. I would've caught this dirty dick ma'fucker today, if I had my camera."

"What was the camera going to do?" As soon as I said that, Devin looked directly in my eyes and smirked. He must've known that I was talking to his mother because he took his hand and waved it under his chin, as a sign for me not to mention him.

"India, are you listening to me?" Joan grumbled.

"Yes."

"Well then, Devin Senior is the type of man that I have to tap on the shoulder, breathe in his face, and say, 'You know I see yo' ass!' And the camera would've allowed me to take pictures of him, shoot some video of the girl, and play it all out for him tomorrow night at dinner. I would've cooked his favorite meal and all the while have his shit packed. Hold on, India . . . *D.J.! D.J.!*" she said away from the phone. "Where is this boy at? I need me some cigarettes. You know he asked me about you the other day."

"Really?"

Devin walked over and stood directly in front of me. Don't ask me why but I opened my legs, so he could stand between them . . . and he did.

"Remember the night you and Tracy stopped by for martinis?" Joan continued. She must've found a cigarette, because I could hear her taking a pull.

"Yeah."

"Well"—she paused and blew out the smoke—"apparently D.J. saw you when you were leaving and thought you looked pretty good. He had the nerve to ask me were you single."

"Really?" My eyes lit up. "And what did you say?"

"I told him that you were too goddamn old for his ass, so not to even go there. I had enough problems with his daddy and the neighborhood skeezers, I didn't need any with him."

"I beg your pardon."

"Girl, I didn't exactly mean you were a neighborhood skeezer. I was just making a point."

Devin bent down and whispered into my neck, "Tell her you'll call her back." The tip of his broad nose felt warm and his breath felt as if it were heating up the chocolate in my skin. I wanted to tell him to stop it, but all I could do was open my legs wider. Truth be told, I really wanted to throw one leg over his shoulder. "Look, Joan, my food is burning. I'll call you back."

"Wait a minute, India. Did you go to the grocery store?"

"For what?"

"It's supposed to be a snowstorm. You better go to the store and hurry back home. Girl, let me call and find D.J. and tell him to get his butt in here."

"All right, Joan. I'll talk to you later." I placed the cordless phone back on the base and pushed Devin slightly, enough so that he would no longer be standing between my legs. In order to fight my desire to reopen them, I crossed my ankles. Before I could tell him how he needed to leave, his cell phone rang. "It's my mother. One minute." He said, "Yeah, Ma." He was still looking in my eyes.

I could hear her yelling in his phone. "Why are you yelling?" he asked her. "Ma, don't worry about me. Didn't we have this talk about me being okay when I go out and for you to stop worrying? If I need you I'll call you. . . . I love you, Ma." I could hear her still fussing as he hung up.

"Look, Devin, this is cute," I said, standing up and walking back toward the front door. "But you and I both know that this is a bit much. You're way too young for me. Not to mention you're my girlfriend's son."

"I'm your friend's son, that part is true. That just means you'll get along with your mother-in-law." He chuckled. "But who said that I was too young for you? I like you. Hell, you're fly as hell and I wanna get to know you. For real."

"But, Devin, I just don't know about this."

He walked over to me and stood so close that I started backing up and hit my head against the door. He placed his hands above my head. "You really want me to leave? Or do you want me to stay and get snowed in with you?"

"Boy, please."

"I already told you to stop calling me a boy."

I took a deep breath and shook my head no. This could not be happening. "You don't even know me like that and vice versa."

"What better way to get to know each other?" He took one of his hands and started massaging my cheek.

Damn, I can't stand that the flesh is weak. Good Lord, I feel cheap. "Your mother will call you all night long," I said.

"I know how to take care of my mother. Now I need to know how to take care of you."

Why did that comment make me think about the size of his dick? "You can stay and we'll talk. But I *will not* be having sex with you." *Dear coochie, please don't make me out to be a liar.*

"Who said anything about sex?" He smiled. "When the time comes for me to hit it, it'll be after you beg me to."

"Please, I think not."

"You will." He moved his head toward me for a kiss. I turned my face to the side and his lips landed on my right cheek. He kissed me from my cheek down to my neck. I know he felt my nipples get hard.

"I'll make a bet with you," he said, looking up at me. "If you don't want to be bothered, after tonight, I'll leave and won't come back. But if you do, and you will, then you give me a chance and no more slick shit about our age difference."

I didn't agree one way or the other. I mushed him in the head and ducked beneath his arm. He turned around and pressed his back against the door. "If I tell you something, I want you to take it the right way, okay?"

"What?" I threw over my shoulder, heading toward the kitchen.

"You got a fat ass." He laughed. "That's the first thing I noticed."

"So you like me for my ass?"

"I like you. I'm just happy your fat ass is a part of you."

"Uhmm hmm."

"So have you always tried to hit on old women?" I laughed, wanting desperately to take my fork, stick it in his plate, and begin to feed him. *This is a hot-ass mess, that I've resorted to children.* I took a piece of chicken from my own plate and stuck it in my mouth.

Devin had a serious look on his face. The corners of his lips curled up, causing his smooth mustache and shadow beard to wrinkle. "You have an issue with being thirty-six, don't you?"

"No, I have an issue with you being twenty-three."

"I don't think so." He smirked.

Despite me having a fork in my hand, he pushed my plate from in front of me. Pushing his plate to the side, he grabbed my hand and said, "I think the issue lies with you. Now check it. Either we converse about you and me, without continuously talking about our age difference, or I go home. Snow and all."

"That's on you." I snatched back my hand and rolled my eyes. *If he thinks I'm sweating his ass he's got another thing coming.*

"Call me when you get your attitude in order," he snapped. He pushed his chair away from the table and stood up.

"Uhmm hmm. Bye." I waved my hand. "See ya." I gave him a salute. *Damn I need a cigarette.*

He walked in the living room, grabbed his coat, and opened the door. I stood in the kitchen doorway. From what I could see, it was at least two inches of snow on the ground. "So you're leaving here in all that snow?" I asked.

"Don't be concerned about me and the snow. I'm good."

"Take care then."

He slammed the door behind him.

I decided that the Rocky Road ice cream, with the extra nuts, should help melt the foot in my mouth. . . . I'ma go outside and see if he's still here. . . . No, I can't do that . . . I'll look desperate. He's too young for me anyway. He needs to be dating my oldest niece and not me. I took my spoon and dug into the gallon of ice cream. I walked back into the living room and sat down on the couch. As I stuffed the spoon in my mouth, there was a knock on the door. I practically broke a fuckin' kneecap sliding across the floor. Before I turned the knob, I made sure my clothes were nice and neat. I took a deep breath and cracked the door open.

"Hey, Indian." Mr. Marcus, my next-door neighbor, smiled, with the gold caps in the front of his mouth shining. I felt like pimp slapping the shit out of him. *How many times do I have to tell him my damn name is not* Indian? *I hope he's not coming to borrow any sugar, because I'ma tell him no.*

"Ya got any sugar?" he asked, rocking from side to side.

"It's In*dia*, Mr. Marcus. I'm fine, and no I don't have any sugar."

"Ya wouldn't lie to an old man, now would you, Indian?"

"In-di-a, Mr. Marcus . . ." I took a deep breath. "Just come in and let me check."

He closed the door and followed me into the kitchen. I could feel his beady eyes checking out my ass. When I turned around to quickly confirm my suspicion, he winked his eye, clicked his tongue, and made a gun motion with his hand. "Anytime, anyplace," he mumbled.

"What did you say, Mr. Marcus?"

"Nothin'," he said, squinting his eyes. "Nothin'."

I took some sugar out of my Annie Lee canister and poured it into a Rubbermaid cup. "You can return the cup tomorrow."

"What you cookin'?" he asked, taking the cup but looking toward the stove.

"I'm not cooking," I snapped. *I wish he would get his bald-headed, suspender-wearin' ass outta here! I would like to get my misery on in peace!*

"You got a lil' attitude, Indian? I mean if you want me to leave"—he frowned, while pulling at his suspenders—"tell me to bust a move. I'ma grown ass man, dawg. Ain't no need in you being all nasty and er'thang. Gon' tell me *you ain't cookin',* and I see the food sittin' right there." He pointed to the stove.

Should I tell him now or later that I fight old people?

"Ain't no need," he continued, "in lyin', ya heard? It ain't like I'm starving. It's just that ever since my wife died I ain't had no home-cooked meal. Usually I eat food right out the can, go to the soup kitchen or the food banks. It's all good though." He turned to leave.

"Mr. Marcus . . . ," I sighed. "Have a seat."

He turned back around smiling and sat down at the kitchen table. I started fixing him a plate. "Indian, you got a cigarette?"

he asked. I really wanted to smack him upside the head. I reached in my purse and handed him a cigarette. Before he could ask, I handed him a lighter. He tucked the cigarette behind his ear and the lighter in his pocket. Then he started eating. He pointed to his plate. "Next time cook some collard greens." He frowned. "This taste like it got MSG in it. This the type shit that give ya the runs. By the way, I could use a lil' somethin' to drink."

The runs? Oh no he didn't! "Juice or water?!" I snapped.

"You got soda?"

"Juice or water!" I snarled, giving him the evil eye.

"Whooo, look at you. You a pretty lil' mean thing. I'll take ice-cold water. You know, I'm having a private New Year's party over at my spot. We could rent some smoke machines, dim the lights, and get two thousand and six started off right!"

"Have you lost your mind?! I wish I would rent some smoke machines with you."

"I wish you would too." He grinned, picking up a toothpick and sucking food from between his teeth.

"Mr. Marcus, please stop doing that. I can't stand the noise."

"Well, if I can have some water, I could wash it out."

He's a nasty ass, no wonder his wife died. I was careful not to bend over while I reached in the refrigerator for a bottle of springwater, I didn't want him looking at my ass again. I slammed the water down in front of him and just as I did that my doorbell rang. *I swear, I can't be miserable for five fuckin' minutes! Don't these people know it's a snowstorm?* I didn't even press the intercom, I simply walked into the living room and opened the door. It was Devin. My heart started skipping beats.

"I had a flat tire." His deep voice was sounding like jazz to my ears. His hair and his jacket were sprinkled with snowflakes. I wanted to lick off the ones that were melting on his face.

"Really?" I smirked, fighting back a blush. "And you didn't have a spare?"

"I did."

"Well . . . why didn't you change it?"

"I did."

"Okay . . . and . . ."

"I didn't like the way things ended between us, so I came back." He hunched his shoulders slightly. "Problem with that?"

"Did I say there was a problem? And furthermore, I didn't know there was an us."

He tilted his head to the side. "India, cut it."

I sucked my teeth. "Truce." I opened the door wide enough for him to come in. He walked past me. As I turned around to close and lock the door, he slapped me on the ass. "Stop being so mean." I couldn't help but laugh. *Damn, I want to fuck him.*

"I hope my food is still on the table," he said, taking off his jacket and handing it to me. "On the real, I'm hungry as hell." He walked in the kitchen and before I hung up his jacket, I buried my nose in it. *It smelt so good.*

As I started walking, I heard Mr. Marcus say, "Yeah, she gotta lil' thang for me."

I hurried my ass in the kitchen. Devin was leaning against the center island, with his arms folded across his chest, looking at Mr. Marcus. Mr. Marcus was reared back in the kitchen chair, smoking the cigarette I gave him. "Your neighbor . . . Mr. Marcus, right?" Devin said.

"You right." Mr. Marcus grinned, flicking ashes into the ashtray next to his plate.

"Well . . . he was just telling me," Devin continued, sounding sarcastic, "how you cooked this big dinner for him." Then he twisted his lips. *Wait a minute . . . if I'm not mistaken, he has the nerve to have a smirk on his face. Is he jealous . . . of Mr. Marcus?*

"I always cook for Mr. Marcus." I smiled, winking my eye at Mr. Marcus, who I really could've choked.

Mr. Marcus laughed and crossed his legs. "Sho'ly do. She luvs Big Daddy!" He took a drag off his cigarette and began swinging his foot. "Tell him about our private New Year's party with the smoke machines."

"Smoke machines?" Devin asked, taken aback. The vein in his neck was starting to stick out. *He was really jealous . . . oh my God.*

"I'm tellin' you, Youngblood. Ain't no party like a Marcus Robinson party!" Mr. Marcus started waving his cigarette from side to side. "Wave ya hands in the air and party like ya just don't care."

"Sounds like fun." Devin looked at me and cut his eyes.

"It will be, won't it, Indian?" Mr. Marcus looked at me and curled his lips.

"Indian?" Devin mumbled to himself.

Mr. Marcus looked back toward Devin. "Youngblood, if you gota lil' honey then who knows, maybe we can get a lil' swingin' goin' for the New Year and straight up set this ma'fucker off! I might be an old man, but I'm a freak to the core."

"A freaky old man? Well, hell." Devin chuckled. "You should be right up her alley."

He's jealous. Damn, I got his ass! "All right, Mr. Marcus," I said, taking his plate from in front of him. "Would you like the rest of this to go?"

"To go?"

"Yes, I need to speak to Devin . . . alone."

"Oh, it's like that? Keep ya food. How you gon' use me, abuse me, and throw me out in the night air, in a snowstorm at that?"

"Night air? Mr. Marcus, it's just seven o'clock . . . and in a snowstorm? Hell, you live in the town house next door."

"Ain't no problem," he grumbled, getting up. " 'Cause Sandy Jones, in the town house over, cooks way better than you do anyhow!"

"*Sandy Jones?* Bye, Mr. Marcus." I walked his ass to the front door and locked it behind him. I wanted to kick him in his back, but I didn't wanna go to jail for fuckin' up an old man.

"So that's ya type, huh?" Devin said, as I walked back into the kitchen. He was still leaning against the center island.

"Why? Are you jealous?" I asked, trying not to smile.

"Me? Please, never that."

"Yeah sure." I walked over and stood in front of him. He held his arms out and I walked into his embrace. To hell with it, I couldn't fight it anymore. I placed my head in the center of his chest, took in the sweet smell of his cologne, and exhaled. *I don't know what the fuck I'm doing . . . but it feels so good.*

"India"—he kissed me in the center of my head—"I know I can't compete with Mr. Marcus, but let's just play it by ear."

"Be quiet," I chuckled, my head still lying against his chest, feeling his heart beat. "I just don't know, Devin. I feel a new type of baby-mama-drama coming from this. Not to mention some young ex-girlfriend bullshit."

"I can take care of my mother . . . and as far as ex-girlfriends, I'm good. All of my ex-girlfriends are checked." He started rubbing my back.

"Yeah sure. Your mother told me and half of the teachers' room about the nineteen-year-old chick she had to check for you—"

"Let me stop you right there. I'm a man; my mother didn't have to check anybody for me. I put the girl in her place; she didn't catch the hint, and kept calling the house."

"Yeah, and that's when Joan got involved. And if I'm not mistaken, Tracy even told the girl how she would stomp a mud hole in her ass. I . . . don't have time to be battling with a nineteen-year-old lil' girl. At nineteen you're still breaking out car windows and shit. Trust me, my things are expensive, and if she's tries to get fly and break up my shit, I'ma drag her ass."

"Damn"—he kissed me again—"I ain't fuckin' wit' yo' gangstah." He laughed, "But naw, baby, it's not like that. She's in check." I could feel his warm fingertips massaging my waist. I closed my eyes because as confident as I was with my body, a part of me still wished these love handles didn't exist.

"You feel so good, India," he said, acting as if my love handles were no problem. "I have to be honest with you," he said, now feeling on my ass. "When I saw you the other day I was checking for you hard as hell."

"Really?"

"Hell, yeah. I went as far as asking my mother were you single."

"You did?" I said, faking my surprise. "What did she say?"

"She said . . ."—he hesitated—"that you . . . were a sweet young lady."

"She didn't say I was too old for you?"

"Not really, but let's not talk about that. Let's talk about us right now."

"Devin," I said, looking up at him and stepping out of his embrace, "this is the second time you've mentioned 'us.' What 'us'? Let's be for real. I'm thirty-six years old. I'm single and I have no children. I'm tired of being alone and I don't wanna be like this for another ten years, while I wait on you to be the right age to be settled with a baby. I'm not trying to satisfy myself for the here and now. And I don't want my heart broken again. Hell, I did that shit already. It's about to be a new year and I have to be true to myself, and playing around, screwing you, dealing with a nineteen-year-old ex-girlfriend, and hiding out from your mother is not exactly what I had planned for two thousand six."

"First of all, India, how are you going to plan my life? Have you asked me what I want? Have you asked me if I want children, want to be married, or are you assuming that because I'm twenty-three with a big dick that I wanna fuck all the time.

Give me some credit. I'm young, but I'm grown and I'm diggin' the hell outta you. I can't marry my mother and I don't want a baby with a nineteen-year-old freak. Any brothah you meet, you'll have to spend time with him . . . well, give me that same opportunity and get to know me. Don't be so scared, I might turn out to be who you've been looking for."

He reached for my hand and pulled me back into his embrace. He started running his fingertips up and down the small of my back, whispering in my hair, "Just take a chance . . . this once . . . I promise not to disappoint." Oh God, I was melting. I looked up at him and what I saw was a man. A man that I could one day call my own. . . . He held his head down and started sucking on my bottom lip, pulling it in and out of his mouth. My nipples were hard and my legs were trembling. I could feel my juices soaking my panties and I swear to you, I felt like the sky in a thunderstorm. *All of this thumping in my coochie cannot be healthy!*

I'm not sure how my pants became unzipped, but I know that his thumb was causing me to spasm as he pressed it against my clit.

"It's so warm and thick," he whispered, bending his head down lower and kissing the cleavage showing through my V-neck. Don't ask me why, but I started standing on my tippy-toes, making sure he was able to kiss all of it. My whole body was throbbing. I couldn't believe I was doing this. "It feels so good . . . baby." I moaned.

"You want me to stop?"

I couldn't breathe. He was circling his fingers in and out of my slit. I thought I would die. This has to be illegal . . . I think its called jailbait . . . but in a minute I'ma be climbing the wall.

"You want me to stop?" he asked, softly, while pulling my sweater over my head.

My mind kept saying, *You need to stop . . . ,* but my body said, *Fuck that, we've been horny for months.*

He pulled my pants down and I stepped out of them. He picked me up and placed me on the center island. Gently, opening my legs, he said, "I've asked you twice if you wanted me to stop." He was standing between my legs and looking me in the eyes.

"Don't stop," I moaned, my legs shaking and my head feeling as if it would explode. "Please don't stop."

"What do you want me to do . . . to you?" He was bending down, taking his tongue and teasing my clit with it. "Tell me."

"I want you . . . ," I said nervously, "to make love to me. . . ."

"You sure?"

"Yes . . . only if you want to . . ."

He took his tongue and pushed it inside of me. Taking his tongue out and sucking on my inner thigh, he asked, "Do you want me to make love to you?"

"I think so . . . Just don't stop . . . Don't ever stop. . . ." *I can't believe that I'm being this easy. . . .*

"I won't stop, baby, I promise I won't." He started kissing me and I pulled his hoody and wife-beater off in one sweep. His pecks were hard, chiseled, and buffed, resembling fudge mountains, and his nipples, their beautiful peaks. He pulled down his pants and his dick was a chocolate log. Long and thick, with a slight crook at the tip. Immediately chills trampled through me. I could only imagine the callaloo of pain and pleasure that was to follow. I lay back on the counter, threw both of my legs over Devin's shoulders . . . and I swear 'fore God, I was dick-delivered to the moon. . . .

By the time the night ended, my ass had been stretched all over the center island, the kitchen table, the couch, the floor, the bathroom sink, blindfolded and tied to the bedpost. All of this don't make no damn sense. And not once did I use a condom. What was I thinking? I am too old to be this stupid! Now, I'm fucked both literally and figuratively. Devin has me wanting to do more than buy him sneakers, I'ma cook for his ass. Fry him some chicken, some fish, and some collard greens. I'ma ask him does he like grits and eggs, and believe me, I'ma cook that too. I must be under a spell. I have never been with a man that makes me want to buy him groceries. I should've never listened to Jill Scott's new song, because now I feel like I'll do whatever he ask me to. I'ma treat him like he's a sleeveless shirt during a heat wave.

I swear I'm addicted to what his dick did. I need counseling . . . Joan is going to cuss . . . my ass . . . the fuck out! I have to call Tracy.

Devin and I were lying in the bed. I turned over, kissed him on the forehead, and unwrapped the arm that he had thrown over me. Just to make sure this was real, I peeked under the covers. Goddamn, even with it being soft, all ten inches were still intact. This don't make no sense.

When I got in the bathroom, I called Tracy. The 'rent-free live-in' answered the phone. I wanted to hang up because I absolutely could not stand his ass. "Hi," I said dryly, "sorry for calling so early, but is Tracy up?"

"You can't ask me how I'm doin'? Huh, Ms. India? Is it too much for you to say, 'Ju-Ju, how you feelin'?' After all, *you* callin' *my house* at seven o'clock in the goddamn morning!"

Is he drunk? "How are you? Fine," I said, answering my own question. "That's wonderful, now put Tracy on the phone."

"Smart ass! . . . Tracy! High saddity on the phone."

"Hey, girl," Tracy said, taking the phone from Ju-Ju. "You know this niggah here. If you ain't from South Twelfth Street, then you gotta be high saddity. I swear, I can't stand his ass. As soon as I get off the phone with you, I'ma slide him! And that's on my word."

"Tracy," I whispered, cutting her off. "I fucked him."

"Oh hell no you didn't!" She laughed. "You got some of that young dick? Oh, you gon' be turned out! I'ma have to find me a mini-ma'fucker to turn me the hell out. A bitch's pussy is achin' fa sho'. Don't leave out no details. I gotta live vicariously through this piece of dick. Was it long and skinny, or short and fat? Did it have a crook in it? Or was it a souljah, stood straight up, and hit you off with a salute? Hell, is he circumcised?"

"Tracy!"

"Okay, I know that's a bit much," she said apologetically. "Well, just tell me this, did he find the G-spot?"

"Girl," I said, getting hot all over again, "he found three G-spots."

"Hot damn! Oh, it's on, it's on, it's on. Did you give the lil' mofo some head?"

"No . . . not yet."

"Good, don't. This is what you do: fuck the shit out of him this morning. Front, back, and sideways. Then go in the bathroom, get a warm cloth, come back and wash the dick off, this way homes ain't gotta move. And then you suck all the cum out of it. I'm telling you that shit works better than puttin' roots on his ass. I promise you, he'll lose his mind. Ain't no young bitch gon' ever be able to come behind that."

"Tracy, this man got me going so bad that I want to take the oranges in my kitchen and squeeze him some fresh juice."

"Dang, India, it's like that? Oh, you fucked all the way up. Girl, I miss them days. Ju-Ju use to lay it down. Now he stays broke and as far as I'm concerned a broke niggah got a flat-ass dick. Humph, my pussy stays dry when a broke ass is lying in my bed and late notices are on my kitchen table. Something about that just don't turn me on. India, see if homes got a lil' friend. Hell, I'll go to the prom. Ain't no shame in my game. . . ."

I looked in the mirror while Tracy went on and on. *AHHHH!!!! Oh no, this cannot be real.* I have three hickeys on my neck. Three big ones. Tears filled my eyes. *This is some real live teenager shit. I'm thirty-six, with hickeys on my neck. "Tracy, please!"* I yelled so that she would shut up.

"What's wrong with you? You can't be pregnant that fast."

"No! I have three hickeys on my neck! I can't believe this. Hickeys!"

"Chile, please. You acting like your period is late. I say, work it out girl! Do that shit. Hey, India—"

"What?!" I snapped, disgusted that she didn't seem to understand.

"Don't stop get it-get it!"

"Bye, Tracy . . . I'll talk to you on Monday." And I hung up.

"What's up?" Devin said, as I walked back into my bedroom, my robe wrapped around me like a cyclone. "You want me to leave?"

"Leave?" I asked, surprised. "Why would you say that? Why would I want you to leave?"

"Because . . . I know we got caught up last night . . . and I thought since I woke up this morning, greeted by a cold sheet, that maybe you wanted me to bounce."

He was sitting on the edge of the bed, with his boxers and wife-beater on. I sat next to him and crossed my legs. I really wanted to throw them across his lap, but being a horny old freak is what put me in this predicament in the first place.

"I . . . don't know what the hell that was last night," I said, caressing the side of his face, "but I like you. I mean I really like you . . . but I'm also real insecure about this."

"Well, India, I don't know what to tell you. I'm feeling you. I like you. I want to spend time with you. But all I can be is me. I don't have time to prove myself to you. Now," he said, looking me dead in the eyes, "either you wit' it or you ain't. Either you can roll or not. Because just like last night, I was twenty-three then and I'm twenty-three now."

34

"I know, sweetie. I know."

"Well then," he said with a serious look. "Wassup? You wanna chill with me or not?"

"Tell me," I said, lying back on the bed and pulling him on top of me, "if this says *yes* . . ."

Joan has called Devin all day long and in between those times, she's been ringing my phone. Tomorrow is Sunday and I hope she skips her miserable ass to church.

"India," Devin said while taking fresh clothes out of his gym bag, "what do you have planned for the new year? Are you cooking anything?"

I almost swallowed the damn cigarette I was smoking. I wanted to say *Hell no, won't be no black-eyed peas or collard greens,* but then again, I would cook them for him. "Why, you want some collards, honey?"

"No," he laughed, "I want to take you out. Maybe a nice bed-and-breakfast. Sit out on the balcony and watch the new year come in. How does that sound?"

"Like I'ma come back pregnant. That's how it sounds. Now look, let's talk about that later. But for now, tell me something about you that I don't know."

"My middle name"—he smiled—"is Leroy. Devin Leroy Johnson."

"That's some serious Mac Daddy shit."

"Oh, you cracking on me?" He laughed. "And what's your middle name—Johnnie-Mae or Johnnie-Faye. You know how y'all do."

"Y'all?"

"Country mugs." He fell out laughing.

"Country?" I chuckled. "Oh funny, for your information, my middle name is Talani." He sat down in my Queen Anne recliner; I nicely walked over and mushed him in the forehead. As I went to walk away, he grabbed me around the waist and pulled me into his lap. "Don't be a punk." He started tickling me.

"Okay, okay," I laughed, "I give up. I give up."

He stopped tickling me. "India, let's go to the movies."

I placed my head on his shoulder. "And see what?"

"Claudine."

"Claudine?" I lifted my head off his shoulder, and looked at him surprised. "With James Earl Jones and Diahann Carroll?"

"Yeah." He was twirling his fingers through my hair. "James Earl Jones, or better yet Mr. Roop was the man."

"The man? Let's not forget how, in the movie, he owed child support, not to mention he didn't even see his kids."

"He took care of Claudine's army."

"He sure did, which made his shit even worse. Does it make sense that he would take care of Claudine's six kids and not his own?"

"India, you don't know what the man was going through."

I threw my head back, like I was going to faint. "Spare me, please. . . . Anyway, where the hell are we going to see *Claudine* on Thanksgiving weekend in two thousand five?"

"In the Village. It's a small cinema that shows black classics. I've always wanted to go."

"Are you trying to be funny?" I twisted my lips. "Taking me to see some old-ass movie?"

"India, be quiet." He chuckled. "Now get up and let's get dressed."

Before we left for the movies, I seduced him into taking a steamy shower with me.

We took the train to the Village and walked from the subway to the movies. I hadn't had this much fun in a long time. We talked, held hands, and kissed in public. We shared secrets, desires, and even some fears.

After we left the movies and were standing on the corner waiting for a cab, there was guy who tried to slide me his number. Had I been ten years younger, I would've taken the shit, just to get my playgirl on. But this time I didn't. I waved my hand and pointed to Devin. Now, on the real, that shit made a diva feel good. At first, I was feeling a little funny, as if people thought I was Devin's older sister, or worse, his mother. But ole boy, the one that tried to hit on me, squashed all of that.

"I saw ole boy try to slide you his number," Devin said, as he hailed us a cab.

I snapped my fingers. "Ole boy—ole boy—" I wanted to giggle, I was so happy that he actually peeped the shit. Kept him on his toes.

We got in the cab and Devin told the cabby the Uptown address of Amy Ruth's, the restaurant where we were going. Then he looked at me. "India, don't play me. I peeped the whole thing."

"Then why didn't you say something?" I asked.

"I wanted to see what you were going to do."

"And?"

"And you respected your man, that's 'and.' That's what you were supposed to do. You did well."

"I did well? Ha! You are so funny."

"Be quiet," he said, pressing his lips against mine. "And give me a kiss."

Okay, it's Monday and he's gone. Thank God. I haven't fucked this much in a weekend since I was seventeen, my parents went on vacation, and left me home alone. How am I going to face Joan, knowing that I've been dropping hot coochie moves on her baby? Maybe it wouldn't be so bad if I didn't like him . . . so much. But I'm feeling the hell out of him. I keep thinking about him and the smell of his cologne is buried in my nose. When his name rings in my head, I get butterflies. *Do you know the last time I had butterflies?* I am so screwed. . . .

When I got to work and went in the office to sign in, the first person I saw was Joan. Thank God, I wore my orange mock turtleneck and matching leather blazer. At least the turtleneck would hide the hickeys. "Look at you, Ms. India"—Joan smiled—"you're glowing."

"Oh, girl," I said, feeling guilty as hell, "this ole thing. I've had this turtleneck forever, and this denim skirt . . . well, I'll admit the slanted, fringe-bottom hemline does set it all off."

"And those three-inch, square-toed boots you have on are bangin'," Tracy chimed in, winking her eye.

"No," Joan said, looking me up and down, "it's not the clothes, although your outfit is nice. It's something about you. Did you cut your hair? That flip is sharp."

"Ain't it though," Tracy added, standing at her desk with school records in her hand. "Turn around, India. Let us feel the ambiance of what you have on."

In a minute I'ma slap Tracy. She's lucky the principal's door is open; otherwise, I would cold-cop her ass!

"Turn around, India," Joan urged.

I turned around so they could get a quick view and leave me the hell alone. "India," Joan said, walking up close to me, "turn back around."

"Oh goodness, Joan," I huffed, turning around again.

"Now stay still," she said, my back facing her. "Tracy, come here." Joan placed her hand at the nape of my neck and pushed the back of my head forward. "Is this what I think it is?"

"What?" I asked, agitated. "What is it?"

"That ain't nothin', Joan," Tracy said. From the sound of her voice, I could tell she was lying. If she starts stuttering, I know something's up. "It-it-it's just a blemish."

"What is it?" I asked, concerned. "Tell me."

"Just be still," Joan said sternly. Then she laughed. "You have one, two . . . three hickeys on the back of your neck."

I almost passed out. How in the hell did I get three hickeys on the back of my neck? I can't believe this. I was walking around here with six hickeys on me—three in the front and three in the back—telling all my damn business! *And hickeys on the back of my neck?* Hell, I might as well have worn a sign that said, ASK ME HOW TO DO IT DOGGY-STYLE. "All right, that's enough," I said, wiggling away from Joan and Tracy. I turned around and grabbed my purse. Took out my MAC concealer and press powder and handed it to Tracy. "Tracy, cover this up. And hurry before one of these lil' nosy teachers comes in here."

"So," Joan said, as Tracy started covering the hickeys up, "who is he?"

"Would you lower your voice? It's nobody," I said tight-lipped.

"Oh, you're holding out on me?" She frowned.

"Joan," Tracy stressed, putting the finishing touches on the hickeys. "I'm sure she wants to keep some things private."

"Private?" I could tell Joan's feelings were hurt.

"Okay, Joan," I sighed, "I'll tell you. But you can't react in any kind of way. We are at work and this is a school." *Let me see how I can drop some hints about Devin and me.* "Well, Joan, the other day when I came to your house—"

"Mr. Marcus," Tracy interrupted, slightly nudging me in the back, "was in the car and he did it. I told this chile," she said, stepping to the side and pointing to me, "to leave that dirty old man alone. Stop feeding him and letting him in her house. He's like a stray fuckin' cat once you feed him, you can't get rid of him. I told her to let his old ass roam the parking lot."

Mr. Marcus? Is this bitch crazy?

"I know you're lying," Joan said, catching an attitude. "Keep yo' lil' secrets. I don't need to know!" She threw her right shoulder forward and stormed out of the office.

"What the hell is wrong with you?" I turned to Tracy. The office was starting to get full with a few other teachers coming to sign in.

"What's wrong with me!" she snapped, tight-lipped and smiling as one of the teachers walked by. "I know damn well you weren't going to tell her that you were sluttin' it up with her son all weekend, were you?"

"I was going to try."

"Is something wrong?" the vice principal, who'd just walked into the office, asked us. "Ms. Parker, Ms. Greene, is everything okay?"

"Everything's fine. Just fine," Tracy and I said simultaneously.

"I was just telling Ms. Parker," Tracy said, "about my daughter's school play."

"Oooh," the vice principal said, "how nice." She turned and walked out of the office.

"If I were you," Tracy said, with her eyes bulged and her lips tight, "I would keep quiet. Those three hickeys on the back of your neck don't leave much to the imagination, Ms. Hit it from the back! Don't be the cause of you and Joan falling out."

"Bye, Tracy," I snapped, pissed off. "I have to go and pick up my students from the auditorium.

I am so not here today. Every five minutes Devin is running through my mind. My students must think I'm crazy. I've loaded them up with more work than I know they can do all because I don't want to be bothered—I can't take this. I'm going to cut him off. We're done, over with. This is too much of a risk. Along with losing my friend, I can't take the chance of having my heart broken by a twenty-three-year-old. I looked at the clock and it was twelve thirty. Oh good, lunchtime.

"Come on, class. Let's get ready for lunch."

I took my students to the cafeteria and dragged myself to the teachers' room. I was not in the mood to be grilled in the smoke pits of the educated brothel, but I knew it was coming. When I walked in, Joan was drinking a Diet Coke and having a smoke while Tracy was eating a salad. Immediately Joan huffed and rolled her eyes.

"Don't be mad at me," I said to Joan, sitting down to eat my sandwich. "Tracy was the one who said it."

"Yeah, but you have the hickeys." Joan took a drag, "And I want to know from who? And I hope not another woman's husband; you know how I feel about that."

"Naw," Tracy said. "It sure ain't from somebody's husband."

"Well, who is he?" Joan insisted on knowing.

"He's just a guy," I said.

"A guy?" Joan smirked. "Is he a sugar daddy or a tender roni. Tell me."

"A tender roni." Tracy laughed, with spit flying out of her mouth.

I shot her such a look that I was hoping she could tell I wanted to punch her in the face.

"I'm just playing," she said, taking up a forkful of salad. "I don't know who he is."

"India," Joan nagged. "Are you going to tell me or what?"

"Okay, listen. And I have to tell it quick, because the second period lunch teachers will be in here any minute."

"I'm all ears," Joan said.

Tracy's eyes were popped open, as if she didn't know what to expect.

"I met a guy on BlackPlanet.com." I sighed, hanging my head low.

"You did what?" Tracy asked. I couldn't tell whether she was surprised or embarrassed.

I shot her ass the evil eye. "Oh yeah," Tracy said, now playing along. "Black Planet. Uhmm hmm. But I'll tell you this, that shit don't work. I posted Ju-Ju an ad last month and not one person responded."

"Ju-Ju? Why would you place Ju-Ju an ad?" I asked, with a confused look on my face. "What did it say?"

"It said, 'He might not pay no rent, but he got a big dick. Please come get him. Signed, Wanted out by the New Year.' "

"Oh please." Joan frowned, taking a sip of her soda. "I have to admit I've even been a little curious about internet dating myself. I'm just so tired of chasing Devin Senior around that I don't know what to do. The last time I jumped out a bush, I sprained my ankle and it wasn't even him. I'm just about done. Plus D.J.'s grown. And guess what? He stayed out all weekend with some tramp."

"*Tramp?*" I was offended. "Is that the nicest thing you can call the girl?"

"Yes, it is, because she's a ho. Any lil' girl that drops her drawls for a man all weekend is a no-good hussie *tramp*. And she needs to be slapped!"

"And if the girl is a tramp," I snapped, "what does that make him?"

"It makes him a man. Now please tell us about Mr. Black Planet and don't spare any details. I have to hear this. Start by telling us his name and then describe him. This way we can get the visual going." She crossed her legs and smiled. Tracy sat back and shook her head.

"His name . . ."—I hesitated—"was Faraad." *Yeah that's it.* "Faraad."

"How old is he?" Joan asked.

"Uhh . . . twenty-nine."

"Oh hell, a young thang. You go, girl! But one word of advice: be sure you screw him real good before you meet the mama. This way your coochie will have already taken control and nothing the old broad says will make a difference."

"But first you have to slide him the dick test." Tracy laughed. "Before you go and meet the mama. Because if he fails, he's not a keeper."

"The dick test?" I frowned.

"Yes, the dick test," Tracy confirmed. "It goes like this: you wait for him to go to sleep, then you unbuckle his pants or dip your hands in the slit of his boxers, whichever one, and you proceed to hit him off with some head. If the shit stays soft in your mouth for longer than ten seconds, it's a soggy dick. Cut him off."

"Why?" Joan asked.

"Why?" Tracy looked surprised. "That's the sign of a weak dick. Trust me. Put ten years on him and his ass'll be needing Viagra."

"You are crazy!" I fell out laughing. "But you two can slow down, because I don't think I'll be seeing Black Planet anymore."

"Why not?" Joan asked concerned.

"Well if you would let me finish," I said.

"Okay, go ahead." Joan frowned, lighting another cigarette. "First tell us what his ad said."

"It said, 'Hi, I'm a black, twenty-nine-year-old businessman, looking for the perfect one. If any of you ladies fit the bill, hit me up.' Well . . . I hit him up—"

"Where'd you meet . . . ? Wait . . . wait . . ." Joan interrupted. "Did you talk on the phone first?"

"Dang, Joan." I sighed, *I need me a few minutes to get this lie together, and she's rushing me!* "I'll get to that. . . . We started emailing each other and then we spoke on the phone."

"How long?" she pressed.

"Almost a month ago."

"When did you get to see him?"

"On Black Friday."

"That's why I didn't get my damn camera," she complained.

"You want me to tell the story or not?" I snapped.

"Go on."

"Okay, he invited me to come and see him. He said that he was closing early and giving his employees half a day off."

"His employees?" Joan smiled. "I'm impressed."

"Me too," Tracy added. "Damn, his ass was really runnin' shit, huh?"

"Anyway"—I rolled my eyes—"I jumped in my car and drove over to 155 Chancellor Avenue in Irvington, the address of where he worked. Now, truthfully it's been a while since I've been up by Valley Fair, so I really didn't know the area that well anymore. When I got in the vicinity of 152, 153, and so on, I couldn't find 155 anywhere. There was a Wendy's, an ice cream parlor, an African braiding shop, and a liquor store. Still, no 155. I decided to stop in the ice cream parlor and was told that 155 was next door."

"Don't tell me, the African braiding shop?" Joan frowned.

"Oh hell no." Tracy sighed.

"Oh hell yes." I rolled my eyes. "He was braiding his ass off! Doing double-strand twist and the whole shit. I couldn't believe it. And I knew it was him because he had his name designed on the side of his head, looking like a tired-ass K-Solo."

"That's a hot-ghetto-ass-mess!" Tracy was so pissed that I think she forgot this was a lie. "His ass sittin' up there," she continued, "with Ampro gel slapped on the back of his hand. I can hear him now: 'What you want, human or synthetic?' "

"I hope you turned around and went home, India," Joan said.

"Joan," Tracy chimed in, "how could she have gone home and she has hickeys on her neck? You gotta stop being so easy, India. I mean, really."

"Shut up," I snarled at her. I turned back to Joan. "I almost talked myself into leaving, but before I could do that," I said, taking a bite of my sandwich, "I noticed that he was fine."

"How fine?" Joan asked.

"Girl, he was every bit six-one, six-packed down, light mustache, shadow beard, with a tap of Hershey's dark chocolate in his skin."

"Damn," Joan interrupted, "he sounds fine-ass hell. Sort of puts me in the mind of D.J."

"That's exactly what I was thinking." Tracy chuckled.

"Anyway," I continued with the story, "I looked at him and said, 'Jahaad, do you know who I am?' "

"Jahaad?" Joan said, puzzled. "I thought his name was Faraad?"

"Oh yeah." I sighed, trying to keep up with this lie. "Girl, you know I forget at times. . . ." *My nose should be a foot fuckin' long. I don't even remember half of what I've said, and now I'm sitting here with a dumb look on my face because I can't remember if I told them that I stayed in the salon or he came out to the car. Oh, God, please help me out of this lie.* "So we were in his car," I continued.

"The car?" Joan interrupted. "I thought you were in the braiding shop? Isn't that what she said, Tracy?"

"Humph," Tracy grunted. "Don't even start me to lying. Damn if I can remember."

"Ms. Parker, Ms. Parker." A voice came through the intercom. *"Please report to the office."* Thank you Jesus. I wiped my brow. "Excuse me, ladies."

Joan and Tracy are so damn nosy. Why are they following me to the office?

"Ms. Parker," the parent coordinator said, as I walked in the office, "these were just delivered for you."

She handed me a long white box with a red bow wrapped around it, and a small card tucked on the side of the bow. Joan and Tracy were standing so close behind me, I was sure the heat from their breath would melt all the black off me. I turned around. "Could you two step back? Thank you."

They stepped back and I opened the card. It read:

I can't stop thinking about you; thoughts of you are constantly on my mind. When you open the box, just know that track 11 is my dedication to you.

Mac Daddy

Mac Daddy? I thought. *Who is—oh my goodness—Devin? Where did he get Mac Daddy from? He is so silly.* I completely forgot that I teased about his name being some serious Mac Daddy shit. I started blushing and laughing at the same time. I opened the box. Oh my goodness, a dozen long-stemmed red roses! And a Jill Scott CD. I have this CD already. Oh Lord, track number 11, "Whatever," is my favorite song!

"Tracy!" I yelled. "He wants some collard greens!" I held up the CD. "Track number eleven!"

Tracy fell out laughing. "And some chicken wings." She started singing, " 'Do you want some fish and grits? I'll hurry and go get it . . . ' "

"What in the world is wrong with you two?" Joan said, like we were crazy. I looked around and the entire office, including the principal, was staring at us as if we had lost our minds. "Oh, sorry," we said simultaneously. The principal shook his head and walked back into his office. Everyone else resumed doing their jobs. Since I had about ten more minutes left of my lunch, I went upstairs to my classroom. Of course, the two groupies were behind me.

"India," Joan said, as soon as we got into the room, "there's another card attached to the back of that CD."

Before I could flip the CD over to get the card, Joan snatched it off, "Let me see." She ripped it open. "What is this?" She started reading it aloud:

Now that you've laughed at my silliness, there's a more serious dedication in the box for you. Track number six.

Forever, D.

I don't know who reached for the box faster, Tracy or me. I snatched the box into my arms and then I took the card out of Joan's hand. "Stop it!" I growled.

"Who the hell is D?" Joan asked. "I thought Black Planet's name was Jahaad."

"It was Faraad," Tracy corrected her.

"Whatever, but who is D?" Joan asked.

"Don't worry about it." I smiled, taking out the Carl Thomas CD that was tucked along the side of the box. I couldn't think of what track number 6 was and my lunch period was over, so I couldn't listen to it. "Joan, I think we have some children to pick up. And, Tracy"—I pointed toward the door—"Principal Britt will be looking for you in a minute." I knew Joan was talking about me when she and Tracy walked out but I didn't give a damn. I picked up my cell phone before I ran to the cafeteria to get my class, and called Devin.

"'This is Devin,' he said, answering his phone. He was sounding so astute that I could imagine him in a tailor-made Hugo Boss suit and Prada loafers.

"Is this a good time?" I hesitated.

"It's always a good time for you. You get the flowers?"

"And the CDs."

He laughed. "Make sure you listen to them."

"I will."

"I miss you," he said.

"I miss you too."

"I want to see you later," he said.

"You don't have to ask."

"I'll see you around seven." And he hung up.

I really didn't want to let him go, but I knew I needed to get back to work. I held the phone to my chest. *Please God, let him be the one.*

After work, I couldn't get in my car fast enough. I told all the lil' second-grade cock blockers I tutor after school they had to go home. "Ms. Parker has an emergency." What I really wanted to say was, "You ain't gotta go home but you gotta get the hell outta

here. Ms. Parker's waitin' on a dingaling to sing her a lullaby!"
But since they're children, I gave them the G-rated version.

I started my engine up and slid in the Carl Thomas CD *Let's
Talk About It,* hit track number six, "Make It Alright," and I felt
like my whole body lit up. I can't even lie, I felt lifted and I
haven't felt this lifted since I was in college, smoking hydro. I
turned the volume up and listened to the words of the song.
" 'Don't have to look no further . . . / I'm just here to love
ya. . . .' " Oh God, he was really listening to me this weekend.
He heard me when I told him, "I'm tired of being alone . . . and
I don't want my heart broken . . . again. . . . It's about to be a
new year and I want new things. . . ." I thought he would be
turned off, but he's not. *I must be in Heaven.* I looked over at
the box of roses on my front seat, smiled, and started singing at
the top of my lungs. I think cloud nine drove me home.

As soon as I pulled in the parking lot, I saw Mr. Marcus.

"Hey, Indian." He waved. "I was just coming to see you."

"For what, Mr. Marcus?" I said, getting out of my car.

"I was coming to see if we were gonna get this New Year's
thing poppin'."

"What New Year's thing?" I frowned, opening my front
door.

"The smoke machines," he insisted, while following me into
the house. "Remember, we 'spose to set it off for two thousand
and six. Remember, ain't no party like a Marcus Robinson
party? You done forgot that quick?"

"Mr. Marcus"—I dropped my bags on the couch, hung up
my coat, and kicked my boots into the closet—"I never agreed

on any type of smoke machine, Christmas, New Year's Eve, or any other kind of party with you."

He closed the front door and leaned back against it. "Young-blood done left ya?" he asked, smacking his lips. "That's what this is about? He threw you on that island's countertop, didn't he? You wrapped them big legs around him and he did all kinda freaky thangs to you, didn't he?"

How does he know that?

"Oh baby," Mr. Marcus whined, shaking his body down to the floor and coming back up again. *"Don't stop, don't ever-ever-ever stop.* That's what you said to him, didn't you?"

"Mr. Marcus," I snapped, with my hands on my hips. "I know you weren't looking in my damn window!"

"Indian, I don't do them thangs. Sandy Jones was the one lookin'. She told me that she saw it all. She said that one time you were even hanging off the edge of the counter, with one leg on the side of his face and the other one damn near touching the floor. Now that's what I call wide open, Indian."

I cannot believe this shit. I knew I should've shut the blinds! The entire fuckin' town house complex probably saw me gettin' my freak on.

"You'se a freaky-deaky lil' thang. I like that." Mr. Marcus moved my bags out of his way, sat his bald-headed ass on my couch, and crossed his legs. "You got a cigarette, Indian?"

"No!" I snapped.

"Don't lie to an old man, now. I see the cigarettes sticking out your purse right there."

"Take the whole goddamn pack, Mr. Marcus!"

"You got an attitude, Indian?" he said, taking the cigarettes and then reaching back into my purse for the pack of matches.

"*In-di-a!*" I yelled, "*In-di-a! In . . . di . . . a!* Don't call me a fuckin' *Indian* no more!"

"Ain't no need for you to get mad, like I told you before, I'ma grown ass man, dawg," he said, taking a drag. "If you want me to leave, all you gotta tell me is, 'Bust a move, Mr. Marcus. Bust a ma'fuckin' move.' Now, truthfully, you ain't got no reason to be mad. Sandy Jones the one who should be pissed."

"Mr. Marcus, I don't even know Sandy Jones."

"You don't know Sandy?" he asked, perplexed with his eyes squinted tight. "Humph. Well, she sho' 'nough know you. Front, back, and side. That's why she's jacked up now. Called me over there. Lured me with some smothered pork chops, knowing damn well I ain't 'spose to eat pork. And the next thing I know, her old ass is spread-eagle on the countertop! Blew my mind, Indian! Blew my mind."

I couldn't believe this. "What did you do?"

"Hell, I showcased some skills. I put it down, ya heard. This old freak ain't had no action since his wife died. Hell, Sandy had them legs open—and she's a big girl so she had that extra meat smack-dab in the middle of her thighs—I snuggled my ass in between there, my pants and my briefs around my ankles, my socks pulled up to my knees, and her legs thrown over my shoulders. Now, Indian, Big Daddy was taxin' it. Tearin' that ass up like it was a part-time job!"

"Yeah, one you've been laid off from," I mumbled.

"What you say, Indian?"

"Nothing." I was sick to my stomach. I thought I would die, just envisioning his wrinkled ass stroking somebody.

"Well, let me tell you what happened next." He took a pull of his cigarette and blew the smoke from the corner of his mouth. "She got mad."

"Why'd she get mad, Mr. Marcus?"

" 'Cause after five minutes, I was done. I'm sixty-six years old. What the hell I look like? I need my damn energy. She's lucky she even got up on Big Daddy. Well, she put me out and told me not to ever come back. You should've seen her. Now imagine she gonna put me out, and she got more bullet holes in her ass—"

"Bullet holes?"

"Yeah," he said. "She got dents in her ass. I call 'em bullet holes and she got more of 'em than a shootin' range board. She really oughta be glad that I even came near that."

"Okay, I've heard enough. Mr. Marcus you should be ashamed of yourself! An old man like you gettin' ya freak on, and on top of somebody's island where they put their food on!"

"You got nerve Indian—"

"Bust a move, Mr. Marcus, bust a ma'fuckin' move!" I pointed to the door. "Go home."

"Bust a move, huh?" Mr. Marcus said, shocked, while standing up. "Marcus Robinson got to leave?"

"That's what I said." I knew I was hurting his feelings but he had worked my last nerve. I'd find him tomorrow and apologize but as for now I wanted him out. I opened the front door and Devin was standing there with his finger on the bell. He was looking so good that I wanted to place a red bow on his head and save him for Christmas. He had on a pleated and cuffed pair of camel-colored dress pants. The cuff of his pants fell slightly over his Prada loafers. He also had on a thick ecru-colored, braided turtleneck, with a long brown cashmere trench coat. Devin looked so good that I wasn't even mad with Mr. Marcus anymore.

"Hey, baby," he said, giving me a kiss on the lips. Don't ask me why but I had to fight with my legs so they wouldn't gap open.

"You're early," I said, giving him a hug and taking in the smell of his cologne.

"I know. I hustled a little and the train was on time. So I was able to run home, get my truck, and come straight here."

"You should've brought clothes for the night." I winked. "I would've made sure you got to work on time."

"You never know."

"Never know what?" Mr. Marcus interrupted. Damn, I almost forgot he was standing here. "Didn't I tell you to bust a move?"

"Oh, you just gonna do me dirty? Here I've been good to you all these years and this is what you do to me?"

What did he say? "Mr. Marcus, please. Don't try and make it seem like we were a couple."

"So what was I? A booty call?"

"Bust a move," I snapped. "Bust a ma'fuckin' move!"

"It's all good," Mr. Marcus said, walking out the door. "Youngblood," he called to Devin. "That's yo' black Expedition?"

"Yeah," Devin said. "What about it?"

"Make sure don't no lights get knocked out!"

"He's kidding, right?" Devin said, as Mr. Marcus hopped along. "That was a joke?"

"Don't worry about Mr. Marcus," I said, kissing him softly.

"What should I worry about?" he said, responding to my kisses and closing the front door behind him.

"Me?" I leaned over the arm of the couch and pulled him with me. I thought we would've landed on the cushions, but we rolled to the floor. "Damn, baby, don't attack me." He laughed.

"I've been thinking about you all day," I said.

He was lying flat on the floor and I was straddled across his lap. He sat up a little and took his coat off. He lay back down on the floor and I pulled his sweater off him, revealing his glued-tight wife-beater. He pulled me close to his chest as I went to unbuckle his pants. "I want to talk to you," he said, his hands palmed on my behind.

"About what?"

"Do you think it's possible to love someone after just a weekend of being with them?"

Did he say "love"? "Why, Devin?" I asked with a serious face.

"Because that's how I feel."

"Are you for real?"

"I'm as real as it gets." We both sat up, but I was still straddled across him. "I can't stop thinking about you," he said, looking directly in my eyes. "Hell, I even smell your perfume when you're not around. I want to be with you all the time."

"Love, Devin? I don't know if this is love . . . already," I said, shaking my head.

"Damn, India. Why do you have a time frame on love? Just go with it."

"I don't have a time frame. But it's too soon." *I can't believe we're holding this conversation. I mean, I want to be in love and I want him to be the one . . . but I'm not sure if I'll know what to do if I'm not by myself anymore.* "Sweetie, I like you. I know that I miss you, I keep thinking about you. I get butterflies when I'm around you. But love you, after a weekend together? I'm not sure about that. This is the honeymoon stage. What happens a month from now, a year from now, when things change? And what about Joan?"

"I don't want to talk about my mother," he snapped.

"She's a part of this."

"See, that's your problem," he said sternly. "It's too much about other people. My mother has her place and this ain't it . . . at least not at this moment. Now, back to your question about what happens a month from now or a year from now. I can't answer that and neither can you. We could be married and you could be pregnant in a year. Or we could part ways and never see each other again, after a month. But what I know is that right now what I feel is real . . . and I can't imagine it going away." He kissed me on the lips. "As bad as I want to make love to you, I say we don't tonight. Let's talk, nothing else."

"Talk? We can talk in about an hour." *Shit, can't he feel the pulse in my coochie racing? Humph, we can talk after I get a nut. Hell, I have been talking all day.*

"No, we won't talk and you know it. India, I'm feeling the hell out of you. And that's real." He was holding my face in the palms of his hands. "We have the rest of our lives to make love to each other. But I want to get to know you now."

"Well, what do you want to know?" I said, getting off his lap and sitting with my knees hunched up to my chest.

"Tell me," he said, sitting with his back to the couch. "What makes you smile, makes you cry, makes you laugh, and then tell me what you dream about the most. Afterward, we'll go from there. . . ."

"Okay, let's see," I said, sliding over and placing my head on his shoulder. "Where do we begin . . . ?"

I watched him breathe for about an hour last night. He fell asleep with his head in my lap. I gently laid his head on the floor, unbuckled his pants, and hit him off with a 68. Now when he comes here after work, he owes me one—that'll make it a nice and nasty 69. I called Tracy at six o'clock this morning after Devin left here to go to work.

"Tracy," I whispered. Why I was whispering I don't know, because nobody else was here but me.

"What, girly-girl? What happened? You saw me out last night with that bum niggah who lives down the street?"

Damn, Tracy sounds a lil' rough this morning. I could've sworn she asked me about somebody who lives down the street. "What, Tracy?"

She cleared her throat, "Yeah, girl. Rasul Williams." As she said that, her voice went high pitch and started to crack. That's when I knew it wasn't Tracy on the phone. *"Ju-Ju! Get yo' ass off the phone!"* I yelled. *Oh, I can't stand his ass!*

"How you know it was me?" He laughed.

"Anyway," I said, ignoring him, "don't you have to get ready for work? Oh, I forgot, you don't have a job. Now put Tracy on the phone."

"You gon' get enough of calling my house all early in the morning. Tracy, Stuck-up on the phone."

"Hey, girl," Tracy said picking up the line.

"He's crazy, Tracy. I swear he is."

"I know, girl. Believe me, I know. Wassup? You drop it like it's hot to your CDs last night?" She laughed.

"Girl, I think I'm in love."

"In love?" I could tell she was smiling. "Oh shit, did he pass the dick test?"

"He passed it girl. I waited for him to fall asleep and I hit him off lovely. I was counting to ten in my head and by the time I got to three, my cheeks blew up like I had jawbreakers in my mouth!"

"Goddamn! That's dangerous, that mofo'll have you pregnant just by cumming down your throat."

"Tracy, you are nasty!" I was disgusted.

"No I ain't," she snapped. "I'm just keepin' it real. Another thing. Joan called me complaining last night about how D.J. stayed out again. She thinks he's back to sneaking around with the nineteen-year-old hoochie."

"Really?"

"Yeah, why don't you call her house and hang up a few times, this way she'll think it's the nineteen-year-old for real."

"Tracy, that nineteen-year-old is the least of my worries."

"What's your worry?" she asked.

"How can I be falling in love, not only with a twenty-three-year-old, but within a weekend? Am I crazy?"

"Girl, India, just let yourself go."

"I can't, Tracy, I just can't."

"Y'all know," Joan said into a stream of smoke, "D.J.'s been out every night since Black Friday and yesterday made a month." She twisted her lips and crossed her legs.

In the midst of Christmas shopping, Joan, Tracy, and I were having lunch at Papa Razzi, a restaurant inside the Mall at Short Hills. Truth be told, I wanted to slap Joan in the mouth. All she'd been doing was complaining about how Devin was never home anymore and how she couldn't seem to catch up with Devin Senior either. It was on the tip of my tongue to say, *Get the fuck over it, Joan. They're both getting some ass, don't you understand?*

"India," Joan said, taking a drag, "do you think I can get my digital camera back anytime soon? I found this receipt for a suite in the Embassy over in Manhattan and it's got Devin Senior's name on it."

"How do you know it's for him?" Tracy asked, circling her spaghetti around her fork. I kicked her under the table. "I mean, it's a shame that he would do such a thing," she said.

"Ain't it though?" Joan complained. "But not to worry because I'ma pound this ma'fucker in the head this time. The Embassy Suites will never be the same. And I promise you that."

"Joan," I said, in between bites of my salmon, "Christmas is Saturday, take it down. Maybe he has something special planned for the two of you."

"Girl, paleeze." She rolled her eyes. "I know his ass and he's a slick one. Trust me. Now D.J. is another one that's working my nerves. At first, I thought he was sneaking around with the nineteen-year-old hoochie. But I don't think so anymore. I think it's a wrinkled-pussy old bitch he's laid up with. The stank ass."

Did she just call me a wrinkled-pussy old bitch? I looked at Tracy for confirmation and she was gagging on spaghetti. "Joan," I snapped, "why does she have to be a wrinkled-pussy old bitch? Damn, that's a lil' harsh, wouldn't you say?"

"No it's not harsh, she's a wrinkled . . . pussy . . . old . . . bitch, and when I catch her I'ma check her chin."

I don't think so.

"Let me tell you how I know she's old," Joan continued. "D.J.'s going to jazz clubs, all of a sudden he's got silk boxers, fruity bath oils, and shit. The other day I found a Victoria's Secret bag with some lingerie in it and it certainly wasn't for me."

"It wasn't for him, was it?" Tracy snickered.

"Hell no—" slipped out my mouth. Joan looked at me like I

was crazy. "I mean I hope not. He's so endowed—meaning he's so handsome. What I'm trying to say is that I hope he didn't buy the shit for himself."

"No, it wasn't for him," Joan assured us. "It was for some fat-ass heifer. I can't remember the size, but if I wanted to I'm sure I could have used it for a lace comforter set."

Oh no she didn't! Hold me back, God, because in a few minutes I'ma drop-kick this bitch! "Joan, yo' ass is being a bit extra," I said, trying to talk myself into being calm. "Devin is grown and trust me, he's far from being a little boy, so let it go. And just for the record your pussy doesn't wrinkle until you get in your forties."

"Are you trying to insinuate something about me, India? I'm the only one here in my forties?"

"Well, hell, you put the shit out there. Who the fuck thinks of a wrinkled pussy? That's disgusting! And you should hope that your son has better taste than to be screwing some fat-ass, wrinkled-pussy old bitch!" I slammed my fist into the table. *That'll teach her to call me out my name!*

"Well don't you sound awfully sure of yourself? But I know the bitch is old. Devin comes home the next afternoon after being out all night. What lil' young broad can have a lil' boy lay up in her parents' house all night and into the afternoon? Not a one. Then when the weekend comes and he claims he's going out, he's dressed to the nines. Hugo Boss suits, Kenneth Cole, Jack Spade, and shit—that's an old bitch. Don't no young chick want his ass sitting around her like he's dressed for church."

I looked at Joan, gave her the screw face, and said, "Whatever."

"So . . ." Tracy said, giving me a look like I had lost my damn mind, "anything special planned for Christmas?"

"What's the problem, India?" Devin asked, taking it upon himself to slide the straw I was sucking on out of my mouth. We were sitting at a small round table in the corner of Diva's Lounge while the spoken word artist recited a poem. The room was dimly lit and filled with light clouds of smoke. Most of the people were nodding their heads and jamming to the poetry as if it were club music.

The flame flickering from the tea-light candle on the table lit up Devin's face. He leaned forward on both elbows, squinting his eyes. "I'm trying real hard to enjoy your company, but for the past hour you've been buggin' the fuck out. What's up?"

Hmm, where should I start? How exactly do I say "Your mama called me a wrinkled-pussy, fat-ass old bitch. My period is playing hide and fuckin' seek and one more thing, ole girl sitting across the room seems to know you. Which must be why she keeps looking over here, giving me the evil eye. But if she sends one more dart this way, I'ma slide her ass!"

I shot his ass a look and flicked my hand like *Psst ma'fucker please.*

"What's all the hand action?" he asked, backing away. "What are you looking at?" He turned his head and followed the direction of my eyes. Ole girl waved and he turned back around. "Ignore her."

"Are you trying to be funny?" I snapped. "Who the hell is she, first of all, and second of all, *you* ignore her. I'ma gank her ass!"

"Calm down, India. It ain't that deep. She's Monique. I used to date her."

"Don't tell *me* what's deep. That's your ex-girlfriend?!" I was livid. "What is this, teenybopper night? Why do you have me someplace where your nineteen-year-old ex-girlfriend hangs out."

"Teenybopper? Don't play me, India. Furthermore, I never said she was my ex-girlfriend. I said we used to date. I didn't know she was going to be here, and besides, who cares?"

"I care, and I swear, if she looks at me one more time and rolls her eyes, I'ma slap her!"

A sly smile ran across his face. "Is my baby jealous? You're too cute to be jealous of a chicken."

"Don't call her a chicken." I laughed. "She wasn't a chicken when you were bangin' her."

"You don't know whether I was bangin' her or not. Stop assuming. And she was a chicken, that's why I stopped seeing her."

I couldn't help but laugh. "Chill, baby," he said. "Let me tell you about what I have planned for New Year's. I rented us the Presidential Suite at the Embassy in Manhattan."

"The Presidential Suite?" *Damn, either this wrinkled pussy got him whipped or he loves my ass.* I looked at my sweetie and smiled. "I guess your mother didn't know about the presidential part, but she announced to Tracy and me when we were Christmas shopping yesterday that she found a receipt for the Embassy Suites. She thinks it belongs to your father."

"What?" He took a sip of his Ketel One martini. "And I

called myself eliminating hassle by paying for the suite in advance. I'll be sure to tell her the shit is mine." He laughed. "I don't want her jumping out of any bushes again."

I couldn't believe he knew that. "Who told you that?"

"Please, who do you think went and picked her up the last time she jumped out and sprained her ankle?"

I started cracking up. I laughed so hard that I was crying. When I looked up to tell Devin how silly he was, Monique, his ex-girlfriend, was standing over our table and pointing her finger in his face. "You got a problem?" she spat at him.

"Monique, be a lady and go sit down," Devin said to her. "This is not the time or the place."

"Don't be telling me what the fuck to do!" She turned, looked at me from head to foot, and rolled her eyes.

This bitch has officially lost her mind. Should I slam her ass now or drag her outside and do it?

She turned back toward Devin and grabbed him by the collar.

Oh, hell no! I nicely reached my hand across the table, knocked her hand off his collar, leaned back, and gave her ass a Fat Joe look that dared her to say something else. "Have you lost you're goddamn mind?" I asked perplexed. "Trust me; you would want to keep your hands to yourself."

"Don't you worry about it. This is my hand and I can put it anywhere that I want." She turned back to Devin. "So this is the bitch that you left me for? What is she, like twenty-six? Her old ass!"

"Thanks for the compliment, boo-boo"—I leaned forward

and starting speaking slow—"but you . . . better . . . back . . . the fuck up . . . *little girl.*"

"Oh, no you didn't! Who are you talking to?" She seemed to be in shock.

"Monique—" Devin interrupted. "I'm asking you again to please go sit down and leave my wife and me alone."

His wife? My entire face lit up.

"You married this bitch?" she spat.

"I got this, hubby," I said to Devin. I tapped my index finger on the table. "Are you fuckin' crazy?" I said to her. "I will take your lil' young ass and light you the fuck up! Why would you think that showing yo' ass is going to convince him to want you? You look like an idiot and I'm sure if your mother were here she would beat yo' ass for embarrassing yourself. But I tell you what, since you want to get in a man's face and carry on in public, then don't shed one tear when you get yo' ass busted. Grow up! This is real life, sweetie, and see me, I'll drag your lil' ass, put you across my knee, and fuck you up. Now your best bet is to carry yourself back across the room, so you can stop looking ridiculous!"

"For your information," she said, "he ain't never tell me that he didn't want me."

"What?" I frowned. "He's sitting here with me, he just told you I was his wife, and you think there's hope of him wanting you? He just played you."

"Damn, Monique, how many hints do you need?" Devin snapped. "What the hell is wrong with you?"

"Hints?" I snapped. "That's what's wrong with her, you're dropping hints. Tell her ass in plain English."

"I'ma give you one more chance, Devin. Who do you want?" she asked.

"Are you for real?" I couldn't believe this shit. "Devin, you better catch her. Spell it out, before it all goes down."

"I'm not doing that," he snapped. "I haven't talked to this chick in months. We weren't even dating that long. Please."

"Devin," I said, "you of all people know that the length of time doesn't matter. It's what you do *in* that length of time that matters. Now tell her!"

He cut his eyes. "Monique, I don't want you. There's no us, understand? Stop embarrassing yourself. How many times do I have to tell you to leave me the hell alone? Bounce. Beat it. I didn't want to hurt your feelings but you're acting real stupid. Now, go sit down!"

"Comprende?" I said to her.

She stood there for a moment, tapping her foot.

Dear God, please make her move, I really don't want to beat this child down.

"Don't call me no more," she said to him with tearful eyes. "I'm finished with you."

"Girl, please," he said, agitated.

She knocked his drink in his lap as she walked away.

"She's a stupid ass!" he said, taking napkins and wiping his jeans off. "Let's go!"

While Devin was driving back to my house I asked him, "Did you ever come out and tell her that you didn't want her, at least before now?"

"Something like that." He frowned. "I was trying not to hurt her feelings. So I told her it was me, and not her. That I needed some time. After that, she called the house for a little while, but after my mom told her ass off, that was the last I heard from her."

"It's me, not you? I need some time? Are you for real? You are so typical. How the hell is a woman, or a little girl for that matter, supposed to decipher what the fuck that means? Do you know how much hope that leaves someone who's in love with you to hold on to? How about telling them flat out, 'It was nice while it lasted, but we're done. I don't want to be in this relationship anymore. Go and see other people, because I will be. Thank you and goodbye.' How about some shit like that?"

"Damn, you just want me to keep it gully, huh? I was trying to be nice."

"Yeah." I smirked. "And being nice got yo' ass collared and a drink knocked in your lap. See, that's the problem with men. You say crazy-ass-leave-a-broad-in-limbo shit and expect her not to flip when she sees you with another chick. Say what the fuck you have to say when you have to say it. Don't play word games. Because they get your ass into situations like this!" I was pissed. "See, what happened tonight is the very thing that I was talking about happening with this age-difference shit." We made a right into my parking lot. "I'll get out here!" I grabbed my purse and my poncho. "Good night, go home!"

"What the fuck is your problem?" Devin said, slamming the front door.

I left it unlocked on purpose; I was hoping he would follow me.

"You lost your damn mind? Letting some lil' young-ass girl punk you out of your man."

"Punk me out of my man! Don't even try that reverse psychology shit with me."

"I'm not trying reverse psychology with you. I'm telling you what I see. You got mad 'cause she stepped to me. She could've been thirty-three and tried the same shit. Her reaction was about how she felt, not about her age."

"Whatever. I don't have time to be dealing with some little girl."

"What the hell, are you feeling old? Shit, she asked were you twenty-six, she didn't even realize she was giving you a compliment. Fuck her. Keep it moving."

"Don't talk shit to me, you should've done that with your lil' nineteen-year-old groupie!" I kicked my shoes off, but I really wanted to take one and knock him in the head with it.

"India," he said, blocking my path. "This is crazy. What else is up? This is not about some nineteen-year-old broad. Now tell me, what's the problem?"

"Nothing," I said, trying to get around him.

"Stop lying. Spill it."

"Okay, you want to know, you really want to know?" I pointed my finger. "Your mother . . . well . . . she called me a wrinkled-pussy, fat-ass old bitch. And that really hurt my feelings."

I could tell he wanted to laugh. "She called you a what?"

"She didn't know she was calling me that . . . at least I don't think so . . . but she said that whoever you were dating had to be a wrinkled-pussy, fat-ass old bitch. And I took offense."

"Well you're not fat"—he smiled—"you're just enough. And the wrinkled-pussy part, uhmm, get naked, spread-eagle, and let me see it. I'll tell you." He couldn't hold it in any longer and he fell out laughing.

"I'm glad you find that funny, and I hope you laugh at this, but my period is over a week late."

"It's what?"

"Oh, do I detect a hint of laughter in your voice?"

"Did you take a pregnancy test?" he asked seriously.

"No. Not yet. I'ma wait another week and see if my period shows up."

"A week? And if it doesn't?"

"I'ma cry."

"You don't want my baby?"

"Yes, Devin, but not today. We haven't even been together that long."

"Everything has to have a time with you," he snapped. "Why can't you just let some shit go? You know what?" He reached in his back pocket and pulled out his wallet. "Here you go." He threw three hundred dollars at me. The money floated in the air and then landed on the floor.

"What is that for?" I frowned.

"The abortion." He turned toward the door. "I'm out."

I ran to block his path. "Where are you going? I never said I wanted an abortion."

"Well what do you want? I'm tired of this shit and I'll tell you this, if you're pregnant and you have an abortion, you'll be ending this year without me. Tell me, India, did I do something to you?"

"No . . . sweetie . . . it's not you . . . it's me. . . . I just need some time," I said, using his lines.

"Oh, now you're trying to be funny." He chuckled. "This is serious."

"You left yourself open for that. I'm sorry." I grabbed him around the waist and placed my head in the center of his chest. "I'll take the pregnancy test tomorrow, and if I am, we'll talk about it. Okay? Please. I don't want to argue anymore."

I sat down on the couch and pulled him by the hand. "Stand right there," I said, positioning him directly in front of me.

I unbuckled his belt and unzipped his pants, licking the trail of soft black hair from his navel to his dick. I could feel the tension from our argument easing up. He grabbed the back of my hair, pulling it with a firm but not a hurtful grip. I slid his pants down to his ankles and kissed the tip of his dick.

He closed his eyes and bit his bottom lip. "Damn, India. I need you to know that it's all about you, baby."

"I know, Devin. I know it is." I grabbed his ass cheeks with both of my hands and started sucking his dick. I could tell he wanted to explode. I slid my hands in between his ass cheeks and let my fingertips run from the tip of his tailbone to his scrotum. A few minutes later, I felt like my mouth was being baptized.

*   *   *

Now what the hell my panties were doing on top of the lamp shade I don't know. All I know is that my clothes were thrown from one end of my living room to the other. This morning I left Devin sleeping on the floor. As I went to take a shower, I noticed that my period had finally decided to stop playing with me . . . and just when I started thinking that having his baby wouldn't be so bad after all.

After my shower, I came back into the living room and threw my purple chenille comforter over him. I picked his pants up off the floor and his wallet fell out. I knew I was wrong but I peeked in it. The first thing I saw was a phone number with the name Cherise on it. *Who the hell is Cherise?* Immediately I called the bitch's number. Her voice mail came on and Beyoncé's "Dangerously in Love" was playing.

I took his wallet and snuck back in the bathroom. I started rummaging through it to see what else I could find. *I'm so stupid. I should've known that this was too good to be true.* Tears that I couldn't control fell from my eyes. I felt like I was going crazy. I pulled out phone numbers, business cards, and condoms. *We don't even use condoms. Okay, India, you're crazy. Is this what you really want? Take yourself in there and be done with the dumb shit. Don't listen to any excuses; tell him thank you and goodbye. You'll cry now, but not nearly as much as you'll cry later. No drama. No stress.*

I walked out the bathroom and back into the living room. "Monique," I heard him say as I approached the living room. "I'm sorry about last night. Tomorrow I'm off and she'll be at work." As I came closer to him I could see him looking out the window and talking on his cell phone.

When he turned around, we locked eyes. I was trying my best not to cry. "Get your shit!" I yelled. "And get the fuck out!" *Damn, that is not what I meant to say or how I meant to handle this. I'm thirty-six, not nineteen . . . or twenty-three . . . I can end this without cussin' him out.*

I took a deep breath. "I can't do this anymore."

"What is wrong with you?"

"Let's not play pretend!" I yelled. "I heard what you just said to Monique."

"India, that's not what you think it is."

"I don't give a good goddamn what it is."

He looked at me and then he pointed to his wallet in my hand. "You've been looking through my things," he accused.

"Don't even try it!"

"What the hell do you mean, don't try it? You've been looking through my wallet. Why would you do that?"

"Don't try and put it on me," I screamed. "Ask that bitch Monique and Cherise!" I said, throwing the number at him. "Don't ask me shit!"

I could tell in his eyes that he was hurting. But how could he be hurting when he's the one who's been playing me? "Fuck you, Devin!" I threw every piece of paper, every fuckin' phone number, and the condoms he had tucked away at him. "You ain't shit, but some lil' young niggah from the block. I should've known better than to be fuckin' with you! I asked you from the beginning to leave me alone and you wouldn't take no for an answer. Well, now you don't have a choice, 'cause we're done! This shit is the fuck over!"

"India, it's no problem. Because I promise you that you will never have to worry about me again. Fuck me? No. Fuck you! I gave you everything. Some shit you don't even know about. I'm a lil' niggah from the block, huh? Well, it's all good, because one thing's for sure. You won't ever have to worry about this lil' niggah from the block no more!" He slipped on his clothes, picked his wallet off the floor, and slammed the door behind him.

Fuck him. I cried, sitting on the windowsill in my bedroom, looking at the falling snow and the blinking Christmas lights. I haven't been frumpy and puffing on a cigarette in a long time, but hell, life is full of surprises. I had the radio on and 101.9 was jamming Tina Turner's "What's Love Got to Do With It." I jumped up and started slow dancing across the floor, moving my shoulders and feet from side to side, taking long drags off my cigarette and singing at the top of my lungs: " 'What's love got to do, got to do with it? / What's love but a second-hand emotion?' "

Don't look now, but I'm perfecting pathetic.

Last night, in celebration of Christmas Eve, I killed a bottle of Chardonnay all by myself and brought in Christmas drunk as a skunk. The way I feel, I'ma do the same for New Year's. The only difference will be that I'ma go to church on New Year's first, then get drunk.

I should've known this shit was bound to happen. It always does. Somehow, I always convince myself that Mr. Wrong is right on time. I was so crazy thinking that I could kiss this year goodbye and this upcoming New Year would be one of the best in my life. Well, news flash, India, you've . . . just . . . been . . . cranked!

As I mashed my cigarette into the ashtray, the doorbell rang. I walked down the stairs, into the living room, and looked through the peephole. *Oh hell no, it's Mr. Marcus. I don't care that today is Christmas; he will not be getting up in here.* I sat my miserable ass on the couch and put my feet up. I'll open the gifts from my mother and my sister later.

"Indian! Indian!" I heard Mr. Marcus yelling at the top of his lungs, banging on my front door. *I swear I could kick his ass.* "In . . di . . an! I ain't goin' nowhere. Let me in!"

He is fuckin' crazy. I snatched the door open and he smiled. "Merry Christmas, Indian." Then he ducked. "Ho-ho-ho."

"What the hell are you duckin' for, Mr. Marcus?"

"Well, when I went over to Sandy Jones's to wish her a merry Christmas I told her 'Ho-ho-ho' and she took a swing at me. Said she was tired of folks calling her names. So, I figured when it came to you I wouldn't take no chances."

I didn't even respond. I just looked at his ass.

"What? You got an attitude, Indian?" he asked, rearing back.

I took a deep breath. I wanted to slam the door in his face. "I don't have an attitude."

"Well I can't tell." He tipped his head to the side. "I can make all yo' pain go away. If you just let me. You don't need Youngblood, Big Daddy in the house."

He's a basket case. "Mr. Marcus—"

"Wait, wait," he said defensively. "It ain't what you think. Ain't nobody been in your window again."

"What is it then?!"

He handed me a long, slim red box with a white bow on top. "I'm reppin' for the Wise Men and everything. It's my main man, Jesus', birthday, you know." Mr. Marcus laughed, stepping into my living room.

I know this is some shit from the Ninety-Nine Cent Store. I took off the top of the box and my eyes popped open. It was a diamond tennis bracelet. At least three carats. I almost thought the shit was real for a minute until I remembered who it was from.

"Mr. Marcus, I can't accept this." I handed it back. "You really shouldn't be giving out your wife's jewelry."

"My wife?"

"Yes, your wife."

"That wasn't my wife's. I gave all of her stuff to my daughter." He placed the box back in my hand.

"Where'd you get this from then, Mr. Marcus?"

"See, Indian, your problem is that you think everybody is always up to something. Nothing is ever as it seems with you. I gave you this because I love you. I'm in love with you and at one time I wanted to spend the rest of my life with you."

Who the hell is he talking to? Me?

"I didn't want to leave," Mr. Marcus continued, "but I couldn't take . . . uhmm, wait, Indian, give me a minute." He pulled his reading glasses out of his front shirt pocket and slid them on. Each lens looked like the bottom of a Coke bottle. I can't even lie; I was trying hard not to laugh. He reached in his side pocket and took out a note. "Now let me see what this says," he mumbled at first, and then he said, "okay, okay, this is where I left off: 'I couldn't take the way you treated me. You violated my trust. After you read this, Mr. Marcus, hand her the box.' Okay, Indian, here go the box. . . . Oh, I gave it to you already. Well, what did you think of my speech?"

"Who gave you that, Mr. Marcus?"

"Let me see the box, Indian." I handed him the box and he looked at the inside of the top lid. "It's from . . . Monique and Cherise Jewelers. For those who are dangerously in love." Then he smiled. "That's hot, ain't it?"

Immediately when I heard "Monique and Cherise" my heart knocked. "Mr. Marcus, give me that." I looked at the name and address of the jewelers. *Wait, wait, there's a phone number underneath the address. . . .* I ran in the kitchen and grabbed my purse. I still had the number I found in Devin's wallet. I pulled it out and read it. *I can't believe that I'm so stupid. It's the same number.* I started crying. *I'ma mess.*

"Indian, don't cry." He handed me some tissue from the box of Kleenex on my coffee table. "If I didn't love you I wouldn't have given it to you."

"Mr. Marcus, please!"

"Okay, okay. Come on and sit down. Let Marcus Robinson tell you something." We sat down on the couch. I continued to wipe my eyes. "You know I'm a little too old for you. And that Sandy Jones turned me out, so it can't be no more me and you."

I took the tissue away from my eyes and looked at him.

"But listen. Youngblood is a good guy. He ain't the best-lookin' young man, but he seems smart—"

"Mr. Marcus, he's fine."

"Well, if you say so. But that ain't the point. The point is that you have to want the best for yourself and believe that when it comes, it's real. You really hurt Youngblood and he told me that when he gave me this bracelet to give to you."

"He was actually here last night?"

"Yeah, he came through. He drove his dad's car, because he didn't want you to come outside and see his car parked there. Now you do what you want, but sometimes in life, we meet the one for us and we chase 'em away because of our own foolishness. But you ain't got to listen to Mr. Marcus." He got up to leave. "I'm out, Indian. I'm trying to get up on this honey and set everything up for the new year. You're welcome to attend if you'd like."

"Mr. Marcus—"

"All right, Indian, maybe next time. Anyway, you better go on and call Youngblood before he be slamming somebody else on the counter." He winked his eye and shut the door.

I dialed Devin's cell number at least three times before I finally let the call go all the way through. His voice mail came on and I hung up.

I called Tracy. When Ju-Ju answered the line, I tried to hold it in but I couldn't. I started crying. "Stuck-up, that's you?" Ju-Ju said.

"Put Tracy on the phone!"

"Wo, slow yo roll, homes. Merry Christmas. You know what I'm sayin'? I'm Santa up in this ma'fucker. This is my goddamn

North Pole, you just a broke-ass elf who's callin' my crib at eight o'clock on Christmas morning. Besides, you would wanna be talking to me. 'Cause Ju-Ju got the 411."

"On what?" I snapped.

"On Joan."

"What about Joan?"

"She was on her way over there last night to kick . . . yo' ass."

"What?"

"Sho'nough. Ju-Ju ain't gon' lie. She was so mad that she told Tracy as soon as you opened the door, she was gon' put you in a choke hold."

"Tracy told you that?"

"Naw, not really. Joan thought I was Tracy when I answered the phone. I was able to fake her out. You're the only one who ain't never fell for the shit. But don't worry, we got it straight. I told her that he was grown and that overall you was a decent broad. Good job, no kids, you ain't had no man since I could remember, so I couldn't imagine you being a jump-off."

"Excuse you?"

"Hell, I was trying to help you out."

"Don't help me! Now put Tracy on the phone."

"Ungrateful ass! Tracy! Cryin' ass on the phone!"

Tracy picked up the phone. "Merry Christmas, girl! Jasmine got a lil' gift for her Aunty India. When are you coming over?"

"Tracy," I started crying again. "It's over. I was wrong, and now I'ma chain-smoking, horny old maid."

"Calm down, India. Don't cry. I talked Joan out of bustin'

yo' ass, for now. But I need you to know that she thinks you're messing with her husband. I tried to tell her it wasn't so, but Ju-Ju had already fucked it up with the shit he said. She didn't want to hear any more after that."

"What?!"

"Yes, she swears it's you. She said that she found a diamond tennis bracelet last night, and when he left, it left. She refuses to believe that it has anything to do with D.J. She said that she rode all over Newark looking for her husband and something told her to check out your spot, and when she did, Devin Senior's truck was sitting right there in your parking lot."

"It was Devin *Junior*. He drove his father's car over here, when he gave Mr. Marcus the gift."

"Oh well," she said, taking a deep breath. "Better keep an eye on the bushes. You know that heifer is crazy."

"I'ma call her right now and straighten this shit out. I don't want her husband. It's her son."

"And what part of that do you think will make her feel better?"

"I can't believe this. She should know me better than to think I would sleep with her husband. I have to go Tracy." I started crying again. "And by the way, Merry Christmas."

Thank God Christmas is over! I felt like a complete ass yesterday, but now I'm determined to be a big girl about the situation. Hell, I've been without a man before and somehow I've managed to stay alive. I mean really, I won't die just because the big dick picked itself up and left.

I turned on the CD player and placed Aretha Franklin's *Respect* on repeat. It was four o'clock in the evening and in between bouncing my shoulders, chanting "R-E-S-P-E-C-T," chain smoking, eating three slices of chocolate cheesecake, and a tub of Cool Whip, I was determined to get my party on.

So, I was wrong about Devin and maybe the way I treated him was fucked up, but that was life and worse things happen every day. Better to cry now than to cry later. Plus, I'm thinking about never speaking to his mama ever again. Tracy called this morning and told me that Joan uninvited me to her Kwanzaa celebration. "I hate to be the one to break it to you," Tracy said, "but Joan told me that if you step foot in her house, she would take her Kinara and shove the seven principles up yo' ass!" I couldn't believe it. At first my feelings were hurt, but then I figured fuck her too.

Who the hell was I fooling? I was downright miserable. I was trying to convince myself that what happened between Devin and me was for the best; but it didn't feel like my aching heart and horny coochie agreed. I solemnly swore that I was hereby declared an old maid. I buried my face in the mud cloth throw pillow and for three days all I could do was sit on the couch, cry, and eat my miseries away.

It was ten o'clock at night on New Year's Eve and *Eyewitness News* was showing New Year's around the world. I was snacking on Chex mix and reading Patti LaBelle's cookbook, trying to figure out how many cups of water I needed to boil these black-eyed peas. Then I was trying to figure out was it rice and collard greens or just collard greens. I swear I can't take it. It's New Year's Eve and I'm doing the same shit that I swore I would never do again.

Joan is still not speaking to me, but I don't give a damn. Yesterday I called her, wished her a merry Christmas, happy Kwanzaa, and then I lowered the boom: *"Joan, I love you like a play cousin, but if you jump out the bushes on me we will throw. Period. Afterward I'ma still love you. But first I'ma kick yo' ass."*

She hung up on me.

I haven't heard from Devin and I haven't called him since Christmas day. I felt my throat swelling up as I filled the measuring cup with water. I swallowed the lump and wiped some of the tears that escaped down my cheeks. I guess my mother was right; I am alone. But fuck it, I'm still fly. I put the cookbook down, went upstairs, showered, and changed into a midcalf demin skirt, tight red sweater, and the tennis bracelet Devin gave me.

When I came back in my kitchen, I peeked through my miniblinds and saw Mr. Marcus loading smoke machines into his house. If he comes over here with another open invitation to his New Year's shindig, I'ma cuss his ass out.

As I shut the blinds, my doorbell rang. Since I was standing at the sink, getting ready to read my cookbook again, I pressed the talk button on the intercom. "Who is it?"

"Devin."

I dropped the cookbook in the sink. The dishwater splashed in my face as the book sank to the bottom. My heart was beating fast and I didn't know whether to swing the door open and apologize or let him stand outside.

I massaged my temples and decided to open the door. He was leaning against the iron railing in a blue goose-down vest, cream-colored hoody, and baggy blue jeans. He looked me up and down. His eyes smiled as he tucked his bottom lip in. We stared at each other for a minute and then he said, "I've never been one for holding back anything that I have to say and I don't like unsettling goodbyes."

"Devin, I-I . . ."

"India," he said, cutting me off. "You talk too much. Be quiet. This is the last day of the year and I wanted to tell you that for the short amount of time you were in my life, I loved the hell out of you. But you need to get it together."

I was doing everything I could not to cry.

His eyes were glassy. I wanted to tell him that I loved him, but I couldn't. "I just wanted you to know that I didn't play you. I was trying to be good to you, but I realized that something in you didn't allow me to give you the best that I had." He kissed me on the forehead. "It's all good, baby girl. You'll get it together one day."

He walked toward his car. I stood there and watched him pull off. I felt lost as I walked down the stairs and shivered while the snow fell over my head. When I turned around to go back in the house, I heard rambling in the bush. *I know, Lord, that you said there is always a ram in the bush, but uhh, you would give a sistah some forewarning, right?*

I heard it again. I squinted my eyes and peeked over to see

whether it was a stray cat or a squirrel. I was too scared to get close, so I took the shovel on the side of steps, slammed it into the bush, and Joan fell out.

"What the hell!" I was holding my chest and breathing heavy. "Are you goddamn crazy? Joan!"

"India!" Joan yelled, dusting herself off. "I don't know whether to be happy that you're not messing with my husband or to slap you upside the fuckin' head for messing with my baby! I can't believe it! My baby, India? At first, when I thought you were seeing Devin Senior I was prepared to practice some dropkicks on you. But never in a million years did I think this was going on. I can't believe it. You're the wrinkled-pussy old bitch?" She started pacing back and forth.

"I'm not a wrinkled-pussy old bitch! And another thing, Devin's not a baby! He's grown and I love him!" *Did I just admit that?* "And I'm sick and tired of not knowing what to do because you're his mother! I don't want to hurt him; I want to be with him. And I'm *not* sorry about that! Now skip yo' ass outta here! God only knows how happy I am to be kissing this year goodbye! And if you can't get over me loving Devin, then you can go right along with it!"

"Aren't you the least bit embarrassed?" Joan asked, still pacing.

"No!" I said with tears flooding my eyes. "I'm in love with him. I was just too stupid to realize it! And now he's gone."

"I can't believe this. You're really serious?"

"Yes!" I couldn't take standing there anymore, so I stormed up the stairs.

"Then," she yelled, "you should go and be with him."

I spun around. "What did you say?"

"I'm serious." She cleared her throat. "The man told you he loves you. Go to him."

"You mean to tell me you're not mad?" I asked, wiping my eyes.

"Of course I am. I wanna kick yo' ass! But what can I really do? D.J. is grown and God only knows that I can't take another night of his ass sitting around me looking pitiful. So . . . I guess"—she cleared her throat—"if you two love each other, then somehow I'll live with that."

"Joan—" Suddenly I was speechless.

"Gon' get!" she snapped. "Take ya old ass outta here and go find him before I change my mind!"

"I don't know where he is," I said.

"He's at the Embassy, Indian!" Mr. Marcus yelled, standing on his stoop, grinning at Joan and me. What the hell . . . does he have on . . . ? "Mr. Marcus! Why do you have that sheet wrapped around you? Do you have on any clothes? Get in the house!"

"You got an attitude, Indian? I invited you to find out what's underneath the sheet. Besides, I'ma love machine, don't let this belly fool you! I'm the black Zeus, you better recognize! Don't you see these leaves on my head? Now you better get on to the Embassy before some hoochie be delivering room service to Youngblood."

I looked at Joan. "I said get out of here!" She smirked.

I ran in the house, grabbed my red fox jacket, car keys, and purse. Then I ran back out and jumped in my car.

*   *   *

It was eleven o'clock, I was in the Holland Tunnel and stuck in traffic. Who the hell hangs out in Manhattan on New Year's Eve? Is Dick Clark's ball that hot? I started to panic because I didn't want to be stuck in my car bringing the new year in. I needed a cigarette. I rummaged through my purse, pulled out one and lit it. With my nerves on edge it felt like the best damn drag I'd ever had.

Now I needed some music. Jill Scott. I hadn't heard my favorite song in a while. I turned the volume up and right at the point where Jill sang, " 'Do you want some money baby?' " my cell phone rang.

It was Tracy. "Oh, you just gon' leave a bitch hangin' while you go sneak some forbidden dick?"

"Hey, Tracy, girl. Joan knows." I blew out the smoke. "She seems okay with it. For now, anyway. It'll probably sink in tomorrow and she'll be blowing up my phone."

"She came over here and told me what happened."

"For real? What'd she say?"

"You really want to know, India?" Tracy sighed.

"Yeah." I mashed my cigarette into the ashtray. "Tell me."

"Don't get mad, but she told us that she prays her grandchildren don't all have Down syndrome, fucking around with your old ass. 'Cause all of your pregnancies will be high risk."

"That bitch. Did she really say that?"

"Yeah, girl. I wouldn't lie to you. She's sitting in my living room drinking Banana Red Mad Dog with Ju-Ju. Getting drunk and telling lies."

"Getting drunk with Ju-Ju? Where's her husband?"

"On his way over here. I called and told him that he needed to come and get her. I said, 'This don't make no sense. She's jumping out of bushes for yo' ass.' "

I laughed. "Damn, Tracy, this traffic! I can't end up stuck in traffic for New Year's. I swear, I need to see his face."

"You will, girl. You will. But look, I'm getting ready to sneak out of here and go see my new boo."

"What new boo? Are you cheating on Ju-Ju?"

"And you know this." She chuckled. "Boo's name is Rasul Williams. He's lives down the street. Let me tell you, I screwed his ass the other day and he had me screaming so loud it's a wonder I didn't get arrested for violating the noise ordinance."

"Why didn't you tell me about him?"

"I don't know . . . anyway, let me call Jasmine at my mother's and wish them a happy new year and then go tip my ass out of here. Love ya, girl!"

"Love you too, Tracy."

Finally traffic let up. It was eleven thirty and I felt like I would never make it on time. When I came out of the tunnel, it was twenty to twelve. I flew through the streets of Manhattan like a bat out of hell. When I arrived at the hotel, I pulled in front and threw my keys to the valet attendant. "Please park my car!"

"Which room, Ms.?"

"I don't know yet."

I went to the front desk. "Devin Johnson's room, please."

"One minute, ma'am," the clerk said. "I'm sorry, but it says here that Mr. Johnson has checked out."

"Checked out?" I couldn't believe it. *Please tell me I heard wrong.*

"Yes, the computer says the suite is vacant." She looked at me apologetically.

I stood there and stared at her. I didn't know what to say, how to feel, or what to think. The noise from the people partying in the bar drifted into the lobby as they began the New Year's countdown. Before I had a chance to talk myself out of crying, tears were already running down my face and sliding between my lips. I sniffed, wiped my tears, and fluffed my flip. *Fuck it.* By the time the countdown was down to one, I headed into the bar and sat down. Confetti was everywhere, noisemakers were blowing, and the people were yelling, *"Happy New Year!!"*

The bartender looked at me. "Happy New Year, young lady—what's your flavor?"

"I'll take a bottle of chilled champagne and a glass."

"A whole bottle?" the bartender asked.

"Yup."

He sat the bottle in front of me. As he filled my glass, I lit a cigarette and took a drag. "Spending this New Year's alone?" he asked.

"Something like that." I picked up my glass of champagne and stared at it. The frost was sliding over my fingers. I took a sip and mumbled to myself, "This is for the black-eyed peas . . ." I took another sip. "And this is for the collard greens . . ."

"If I tell you something," a sexy male voice whispered into my ear, "I want you to take it the right way, okay?"

"What?" I said, practically holding my breath. Tears were again forming in my eyes. I knew that this was Devin. In an effort not to cry, I closed my eyes as he continued.

"You got a fat ass." He laughed.

"Oh," I said, putting my cigarette out. I swiveled around on the bar stool to face him. "You like me for my ass?"

"Correction," he said looking me in the eyes and kissing my tears away, "I no longer like you. I love you."

I couldn't play this game anymore. I jumped up and hugged him. "I'm so sorry Devin. I love you so much. I'll do whatever, just give me another chance." Shit, all I could think to do was sing to him, and I didn't care who heard me. " 'Do you want some money baby / . . . Do you want some fish and grits?' "

"Baby," he said, rubbing my back. "Okay, baby, stop singing."

"Why?"

"Everybody's looking and you can't sing."

I couldn't help but laugh. When I looked around people were looking and the bartender winked his eye. He gave me a thumbs-up as he flipped a quarter to a man standing near the jukebox. "This one's on me," he said.

The man dropped the quarter in the jukebox and Jill Scott's "Whatever" lit up the place.

I lay my head against Devin's chest. He held me around the waist and we started to slow dance. "I love you," I said to him. "I need you to know that and I can't fight it anymore."

"Hearing that makes this all worth it." He bent his head down and placed his lips against mine. Holding me tight, he said, "Happy New Year."

Every New Year

BRENDA L. THOMAS

Post-Christmas Rush

December 28

I can't believe my argument with Terrell last night. His only reason for accusing me of being ungrateful—an ungrateful bitch is what I'm sure he really wanted to call me—was that I hadn't swooned over his Christmas Eve marriage proposal. I'd accepted the dazzling diamond ring but hadn't worn it since Christmas day. I reasoned that in my profession jewelry wasn't a good thing to flash, especially rings. I'm sure I'll marry him eventually but right now I don't have time to plan a wedding. Wasn't it enough that I'd agreed to take time off from work to celebrate New Year's with him by going on a ten-day cruise?

Right now, though, I was wasting time sitting here under a hair dryer, fanning through an outdated copy of *Suede* magazine. Try as I might, I was unable to make sense out of the

Dominican chatter of my hairstylist. Repeatedly, I glanced out the window onto the street to keep an eye on my car. Fifty-third and Woodland Avenue was not the safest neighborhood in Philadelphia. No, it was worse than that. It was more like a war zone from all the stories I'd heard on the news. I could see why people living here were so depressed. Half the neighborhood was burned out, and outside a grimy Chinese takeout on the opposite corner always stood a crowd of thugs hustling drugs. Nevertheless, I braved this crime-infested neighborhood on the wrong side of City Line Avenue every two weeks because it was the only place where I could go to get my hair bone straight.

Not that I was trying to portray some type of white woman image but the Dominican perm kept me from having to fuss with my hair during my hectic days. And in my profession, everything had to have its place. My hair and clothes were neat, and I did my nails myself because it was important for them to be trimmed and manicured. My hands were my number one instrument on the job.

My patience was short when it came to getting my hair wrapped, or maybe I was just anxious to get the hell out of there. I was praying that the snow that had been falling that morning would stop soon. I bundled up and exited the salon. I know that as soon as I opened the door of my Saab, at least three crackheads would be begging to clean off my windshield for a measly two dollars. I had the money ready to avoid an incident.

An hour later I was on I-95. My office hadn't opened yet so I called the answering service to check for messages. Relaxed, since there were no emergencies, I turned up my radio to listen to my best friend, Cat, a psychologist, hosting her weekly talk show on relationships. I had to wonder if people, especially women, ever tired of hearing themselves complain about commitment phobia men. But Cat made it sound entertaining, handling her callers and their many problems with a dry humor that kept me in stitches.

Exiting I-95 at Cottman Avenue, I cruised down State Road, through the gates of the Crumholt Fuhrman Correctional Facility (CFCF), and up to the guard post. I flashed my identification and the guard nodded good morning. I parked in a visitor parking space and gathered up my bag as I prepared myself for a morning that I knew would make me laugh, at least later in my recollection of it.

After passing through the metal detector and having my bag searched, I sipped on a cup of the extra-strong java the correctional officers had brewed and moved on to the infirmary, where I waited for inmate number 764327 to arrive.

In light of the fact that the infirmary was situated inside a prison, it was better maintained than some of the public health clinics I'd seen.

Ahmed, which I'm sure wasn't the name his parents had given him, was on the far end of handsome mostly because of the battle scars on his face. But his grooming was impeccable. His prison-issued khakis had razor-sharp creases, his jet black hair was smoothed back in neat waves and he always smelled like the scented almond oil that was sold at the hair salon.

"Doctor Cyn. Hey, what's up?" he asked, his hands jammed in his pockets.

"The important question is, how are you feeling?"

"I'm cool. This my last checkup, right?"

"Yes, your regular doctor will be returning next week so you'll be rid of me," I stated as I took a seat on my examining stool.

"Hey, look, I'd rather have you grabbing my balls on any day than that old bastard."

Ignoring his comment, I suggested, "Why don't you change into a gown and let me know when you're ready."

Moments later Ahmed appeared from behind the curtain dressed in a green gown, sitting himself down on the exam table, his exposed skin glistening from more oils, I assumed.

I opened a jar of lubricant.

"Okay, stand up so I can take a look," I said, as I bent him slightly forward, then eased my gloved and lubricated forefinger into his rectum. "Feels smooth as a board. No lumps, Ahmed. Now, if you could turn around, I'd like to show you how to do a self-exam."

"Yeah, whatever you say, doc," he answered, while pulling up his gown from the front.

Ahmed's penis was long and thin. I'm sure it made up in length for what it lacked in width.

Using my right hand, I lifted his penis while I gently rolled his scrotal sac between my thumb and the fingers of my left hand.

"The best time to examine your testicles is right after you shower."

His erection started to rise immediately upon my touch, as I had no doubt it would.

"The scrotal skin is most relaxed at this time and the testicles can be felt more easily. You should do this while you're standing up, and it'll only take you a few minutes," I said, as my gloved hands moved over the surface of his scrotum.

"Oh shit, doc. You see what you done started?"

Ignoring his comment, I added, "You should pay attention to any swelling. It's also important for you to gently feel the scrotal sac to locate and examine each testicle separately."

"Damn, doc. Why don't you stroke on that thing a little bit."

I could tell he wasn't really listening to me because I could hear a slight groan behind his words. Besides my last two exams, I wondered when was the last time inmate number 764327 had been touched by a woman in such an intimate place?

"Doctor Cyn, you sure you got gloves on down there?" he asked, sounding like a man who was about to ejaculate.

I knew what he was referring to, as I'd often heard that the thin texture of my exam gloves tended to make my patients think that they were feeling my skin against their own. That's the way I wanted it to feel, natural. It had always been my goal to ensure that every touch was a little more sensual than clinical.

"I'm all through down here. Everything feels fine, Ahmed. It looks like the surgery was a success."

"Shit, the only thing that could feel better is if you finished me off."

Again I ignored him, pulled off my gloves and tossed them into the metal trash can.

"Doc, let me ask you something?"

"Sure, what is it?"

"When I get outta here, you gonna let me take you on a date as a thank-you?"

"There's no need to thank me. I'm just doing my job."

"Aww, you just saying that 'cause you're engaged to that state trooper Negro?"

"How'd you know that?" I asked, surprised that he knew my personal business.

"C'mon, doc. We know everything in here. Plus the word on the block is that he sent a message through one of the guards that we better not fuck with you."

"Well, I don't know what was said but you should know that Dr. Cynthia Lampley can take care of herself," I answered. I was not surprised that Terrell would do such a thing.

"That's what I thought. So here's the thing. Any man that has to put that kinda word out must be some kinda blade, right?"

"I don't get it."

"You know, a punk-ass Negro unable to hold on to his woman."

Now I felt like I needed to defend Terrell. "My fiancé is not a punk. Your examination is over and I have to go. You take care of yourself."

How embarrassing for me that Terrell would do such a thing. I'd never felt threatened making visits to CFCF. It had been his constant badgering that I needed to let a man handle the inmates that made me take this assignment in the first place. Actually, I was going to miss coming up here and receiving all the attention I pretended to ignore from the inmates and guards alike. And only to myself did I ever admit how stimulating it was to see the quick rise of an incarcerated man's penis. As for Terrell's message, I would definitely be discussing that with him when I got home tonight.

As I waited to be buzzed back into the waiting area so I could exit the facility, the familiar cell block chatter began.

"Doctor Cyn, when you gonna feel on my wood?"

"Yo, doc. Hey, my dick is swollen. Can you help a brothah out with those fat lips."

Rather than be insulted or annoyed at their catcalling, I just smiled to myself.

When I decided to step into the role of prison urologist, I'd been well aware that these men were used to having male doctors.

Ever since high school, when most of my classmates dreaded health education classes, I'd been intrigued with every aspect of the human body, particularly the male body. I knew my interest in male anatomy and physiology was the reason I'd become so successful. My success had come with lots of hard work, long hours and sacrifices, but I loved my job.

In addition to a practice I shared with two other doctors, I also put in hours at Bryn Mawr Hospital. It had become an ongoing joke between my partners about how fast I was able to make a man drop his pants for a penile examination. What they didn't realize was how much enjoyment I received from performing those exams. And even now, after having been a urologist for six years and having seen more penises than a Las Vegas prostitute, the sight of one still turned me on.

CHAPTER 1

All in a Day's Work

Before I walked into the second floor suite of the medical building that housed my office, I knew I had a full schedule that held everything from kidney stones to a reverse vasectomy.

I spoke to the receptionist and medical assistants who were bustling about getting the office ready for the day. There was jazz playing on the intercom and MSNBC on the television. A few patients had already begun to arrive. Mr. Goldstein was one of them. I chuckled to myself. Not only was Mr. Goldstein there a half hour early, but I was certain he'd visited the spa to ensure his body was silky smooth, even having gone so far as having his back hair waxed.

Then there was poor Hezekiah, my seventeen-year-old patient whose mother had decided to have him circumcised. She finally realized that all that foreskin was partly the reason he kept getting infections. The other reason was because he refused to use condoms.

101

My office sat at the end of the hall. I'd decorated its walls with commendations and certificates I'd received from various medical boards. The certificate I was most proud of was the one I received last year when I served as the keynote speaker at the annual American Urological Association's convention in Berlin.

I hung up my coat and sat behind my desk to review my appointment schedule. Staring at me from my bookcase was an array of framed pictures. Of course there was one of Terrell looking very official in his uniform and hat with that silly strap digging into his chin. There were separate pictures of my parents who, even though divorced for almost twenty years, still refused to be in the same room with each other. Neither of them had remarried. Three years ago both had become snowbirds and moved to Coral Gables, Florida. My sister, Dawn, whose family picture was also there, was constantly trying to convince me that our parents were having an affair.

Before I could get too caught up in the sentimentalities of my family, doctors Richard Bright and Milton McKinley appeared in my office doorway.

"How are my partners this morning?" I asked, then took a sip of my third cup of java.

"Light day for me," Richard responded, shifting the glasses perched on the edge of his nose.

Milton chimed in, "I have two surgeries. What about you?"

"Poor Mr. Goldstein is already here with his cologne smelling up the reception area. I have a new patient coming in and I need to make a visit over at the hospital."

Milton didn't waste a moment to get in a dig. "I'm sure

somebody will be happy to have the magic touch of Dr. Lampley."

"It's all in a day's work, my friend."

Always concerned about the bottom line, Richard added, "The office is still kinda slow because of the holidays, but I have no doubt this place will be busy right after New Year's."

"Yep. And while you fellows are busy working, I'll be cruising the Hawaiian Islands."

"Don't tell me you're really going to take your vacation. I still won't believe it until you're actually gone," Milton said. I guessed he was not looking forward to handling my patients.

"Yes. Terrell and I are out of here first thing in the morning."

"When are you going to finally marry that man?" Richard asked.

"If you two will excuse me, I have work to do," I answered. Marrying Terrell right now was the last thing on my mind.

As I prepared for my first patient, I wondered if I really had a good reason not to marry Terrell. He'd always been a trustworthy man, financially savvy, caring and came from a solid family background. His future was secure—he was quite satisfied as a Pennsylvania state trooper, cruising up and down I-476. He'd argued when I'd suggested he take the test to move up the ladder to sergeant or crime scene investigator. But I was determined not to give up easily; if he wanted me to change then I'd have to see some changes in him.

The most obvious issue I had with Terrell was his need to control every decision in our relationship. Most times his manipulation was subtle, like when he'd convinced me that it was my decision to let him move in six months ago. Sometimes it was small, like deciding where to go for dinner or what movie to watch. But the one thing he couldn't control was what I did for a living. We'd argued about that last night, along with my lack of interest in his friends. I'd gone and told him how bored I was of socializing with his coworkers and their wives, who continuously pestered me about when I was going to take some time off from work to settle down and start a family.

I guess what my mother told me and my sister growing up had been true: "Women marry men not for who they are but for who we think they'll become." In my case that meant I was still waiting to see the light come on in Terrell's eyes for something other than the number of arrests he'd made.

My sister had warned me that dating a law enforcement officer could be tough, that they were controlling and insecure. Of course, I never saw signs of that when Terrell and I met and began dating.

Thank goodness the intercom rang because I was about to get caught up in thoughts of the man I had and the one I wanted, whoever that fantasy man might be. It was time for my day at the office to begin.

By 2:00 P.M. I was getting hungry but had one more patient to see before I took a break. Mr. Lawrence Petrose had been experiencing sexual performance problems since he'd begun taking diabetes medication. More specifically, he'd been unable to sustain an erection. He'd only been married for a year and was anxious to have children, but at the rate Mr. Petrose was performing, it didn't seem likely to happen. He'd recently had a prostate exam so I knew there were no problems there and his diabetes medicine wasn't a high dosage. From my initial consultation with him and his wife, I thought they probably needed to slow down and prolong their foreplay. Seemed like they were rushing into sex like they were rushing to have children.

While Mr. Petrose undressed I prepared my magic hands for his examination. From the cabinet I unscrewed my special lavender oil, which I would massage into my hands after slipping on my ultrathin gloves. This way I would be able to ensure he achieved an erection simply through touch and talk. If that didn't work then I'd be convinced that the problem was physical and not mental. Most doctors I knew supplied their patients with a *Playboy* magazine or allowed them to watch porno when they needed them to get an erection or give a sperm sample. But not Dr. Cynthia Lampley. Maybe I was too full of myself, but judging by the reaction of 85 percent of my patients, my exams were successful.

Even before I started my exam, I could see Mr. Petrose would be easy. He was probably, like most men, excited by the fact that another woman would be touching him intimately in front of his wife. Who knows, maybe that alone turned both of them on? Just by checking his vital signs I could see I'd been correct in my assumption. His penis was already beginning to rise.

Acting as if I didn't notice the rise in Mr. Petrose's penis, I did take note of its upward turn. I knew that if this type of penis wasn't handled correctly that sex could be painful. However, I also knew that this penis could make a woman with a tilted uterus, like my own, have an intense orgasm. Mrs. Petrose, who sat in a chair across from us, began to squirm in her seat when she saw her husband's penis begin to trickle with sperm.

Seeing the smiles on both of their faces I excused myself from the room and waited to speak with them once he dressed. But somehow I knew that Mrs. Petrose wouldn't be passing up the opportunity to finish her husband off. Just the thought of what might be going on behind me in the other room made me think of Terrell and how much better our sex life could be if sometimes he'd let me take the lead.

After they were gone I closed my office door and chewed on a turkey sandwich and a crunchy kosher pickle Terrell had packed for me. I checked messages and reminded the secretary to ensure that all my patients had been notified that I'd be on vacation.

When I couldn't reach Terrell on his cell phone I put a call in to my friend Cat, whom I missed brunch with last week because I had to handle one of Richard's postsurgery patients.

"What's up Doctor Dick?"

"Yeah yeah, very funny," I said, sipping through my straw, which was the only way I could drink soda.

"You still at the office? Aren't you leaving for vacation in the morning?"

"If I don't, I won't have a boyfriend," I said, picking at the crumbs from my potato chips.

"Didn't I tell you he bypassed being a boyfriend when he

put that rock on your finger. He's now referred to as a fiancé. C'mon, say it with me. You can't even say the word, can you?"

"Please, don't start with your psychobabble stuff."

"Whoa, hold on now, Doctor Dick. You're the one who claims you love that cowboy."

"After last night, I'm about ready to chop his head off."

"What happened?"

"Nothing really. It's the same old complaints about my job."

"I tried to warn you that he wouldn't be able to handle you touching dicks all day. And you know your butt can't hide how much you enjoy it."

She was right. I knew Terrell tried to look at it like it was just a job, but he claimed that I spoke about work with too much intensity, that he could see the arousal in my eyes. It made him wish I'd chosen a different profession. However, even with all of my fascination of the male penis, I'd never crossed the line and slept with a patient.

"Well, it's too late now. If he starts that shit tonight, then he can cruise for ten days by himself."

"You silly woman. Look, I have to run, I have a counseling session with a lesbian couple in a few minutes. But if I don't talk to you, please promise me you'll try to have a good time. I mean, the worst-case scenario is he gets on your nerves and you push him overboard."

"You're just as crazy as your patients, you know that?"

"Love you too."

CHAPTER 2

Penis Emergency

For some reason tonight I was exhausted and would've preferred just to fall into bed for a few hours. My last patient had been a difficult one. He was considering reversing his vasectomy, and there was nothing more pitiful than a man crying over his penis.

When I arrived home that evening I didn't even bother to discuss what happened at CFCF with Terrell. It wasn't worth the aggravation. Actually, the thought of cruising around the Hawaiian Islands was finally beginning to appeal to me. No hospitals, no examinations and no little, supersize, white, black or shriveled penises. No other penises than the one that I hadn't had in over three weeks because of all the extra hours I'd been putting in at the hospital.

Terrell had brought home Szechuan, and after we ate all I wanted to do was sleep, but I had to finish packing. My freshly permed hair had gotten wet in the snow so rather than fool with it I'd pulled it back in a bun to keep it managable. I guess it didn't matter anyway since, according to Terrell, all we'd do on vacation was lie around the pool on board the ship. While he sat slumped on the couch watching back-to-back episodes of *COPS,* I ran around the town house trying to put together a summer wardrobe. I hadn't even had time to shop for anything new, but Terrell had picked up some things for me. His selections were a little skimpier than I would've chosen myself but what the hell, we were on vacation, something I hadn't done in two years.

While I was in the bathroom pulling out my toiletries and makeup I heard the house phone ringing. I peeked my head into the bedroom to check the caller ID. Terrell must've looked at the box downstairs because I heard his voice bellowing up the steps.

"Don't answer that. You're on vacation."

It was the doctor's answering service we used. "I'm not," I yelled back, yet wondered why they were calling. Maybe they'd forgotten I'd started my vacation, which meant the secretary forgot to tell them.

Next my cell phone rang.

"Cynthia, vacation, remember?"

Now I was really curious. Granted, my vacation had officially started when I left work that evening, but the service seemed desperate to reach me. When the house phone rang again I snatched it up.

"Yes, this is Dr. Lampley. Oh my goodness, no!" I looked at my watch. "How long ago did the EMTs call? Did you try to reach Doctors Milton and Richard? What do you mean? Why can't they?"

My cell phone rang again and this time it was Milton's number. By now Terrell was standing in the bedroom doorway. I put the service on hold and answered the cell. Milton yelled that I needed to meet my patient, Mr. Baniff, at Bryn Mawr Hospital because he wouldn't allow anybody to touch him.

"Okay, tell him I'll be right there," I said, looking at Terrell, who was as angry as a raging bull. I'm sure if I looked close, I'd see smoke coming out of his large nose.

"Cyn, I don't want to hear no shit about you going to the hospital!"

"Listen, I won't be long. Mr. Baniff has been rushed to the emergency room," I said, hoping he wasn't going to continue to block my path.

"That's what you got partners for."

"I know, I know. But, Terrell, please understand. It's an emergency and he won't let them touch him."

"And what if you weren't here? What if we'd already left?"

"But I am here and we haven't left, so kindly move out of my way."

"Cynthia, I'm tired of you running outta the house every time one of them patients has a hard dick. Shit, you're more concerned about their dicks than you are about this one. Why not try letting one of your lazy-ass partners handle it," he said, reminding me that it had been three weeks since we'd had sex.

This wasn't the first time my job had gotten in the way of our plans. I had to leave Terrell's birthday party at Dave &

Busters because I was on call, and then at Christmas I had to leave his family dinner early to handle one of Milton's patients.

"Well, isn't the fact that your dick needs satisfying the reason we're going on this vacation anyway?" I responded.

"C'mon now, Cyn. What the fuck could be so damn serious that you have to rush outta here before we leave on vacation?" he whined. I couldn't believe he was begging me not to go.

"Listen, sweetheart," I began, as I laid my hand on his cheek. "I promise I'll be back in time for us to catch our flight."

When I put my hands on his face I could tell he was softening. Maybe I did have magic hands after all.

"If you're not, I'm going without you. That ship isn't gonna just wait for us, you know," he said from behind me as I made my way down the stairs.

"Worst case, you take my luggage with you to the airport and I'll meet you there, okay?"

"I'm not playing with you Cyn. I'll leave your ass. What's the damn emergency anyway?"

By now we were at the front door and he was helping me put on my coat.

"Well, if you must know, I have a patient who's managed to get himself stuck."

"Stuck how? In traffic?"

I stood on my toes and kissed him on the cheek. "No, the old bastard is stuck inside his mistress. Too much Cialis," I said, walking out the door where I could hear Terrell laughing, knowing that he'd be sharing that information with his coworkers.

Arriving at the hospital, I pulled up to the valet who saw

that I was in a rush and hurried out of his booth to take my keys. I clipped my badge onto the outside of my blouse and passed through the mostly empty emergency room waiting area. One of the advantages of being in a suburban hospital was that people had health insurance and didn't have to use the emergency room as their primary doctor versus those hospitals in the inner city. I saw the head nurse coming toward me.

"Dr. Lampley, you can come right this way," she said, handing me Mr. Baniff's chart.

Stepping into the room and behind the curtain, I had to stop myself from gasping when I saw a highly made up black woman with long blond braids practically in tears straddling my pale-faced patient, Mr. Howard Baniff, backward.

"Hi, Mr. Baniff. It's Dr. Lampley," I said, from the side of the bed.

Mr. Baniff was sweating profusely, and when he looked up at me I could tell he was in pain by the mere redness of his face. "Doc, please, can you help me?"

"How long have you been like this?"

"Too damn long," his mistress offered.

"I'm sorry. I didn't get your name."

"She doesn't have a name," he strained to say.

"So, should we just call her mistress?"

"'Heidi' will do," the young woman answered.

"It's been an hour and a half."

"Did you take more than one Cialis pill?" I asked, remembering what I'd prescribed to him.

"I took one and it took such a long time to work that I didn't think it worked so I took another one."

"You're a liar. Doc, he took two and it was getting so good that his ole ass didn't want it to go down so he took another one. I told him he was gonna hurt himself."

"Shut the hell up, Heidi!"

"Mr. Baniff, I'm going to need you to tell me the truth."

"Damn it. Does it matter how many I took? At this point I just want her off of me."

"Let's take a look."

The nurse had already begun running an IV of fluids. I snapped on my gloves and sat on the stool while the attending intern readjusted the light so I could get as close as possible to see the best way to disentangle them. I wished humans were like dogs so I could've just tossed cold water on them.

"Okay, Mr. Baniff. First I'm going to have the nurse inject you with a shot of Valium and see if that'll relax you enough for your erection to soften."

"How the hell long is that going to take?"

"I'm not sure. That's what we're going to find out."

"Doctor, I can't stay on top of his ole ass all day. I have to get home."

"We'll give you a shot too, Heidi," I said, wondering if that was her real name.

"Also, I'm going to have the orderlies slide you onto a wider table in case we have to take you into surgery."

"Surgery? You're going to cut us apart? What the hell am I

supposed to tell my wife," he cried, referring to the governor's daughter.

"You old bastard. I don't believe this is happening. That's it. I'm never coming the fuck out here again," Heidi screamed at him.

"Both of you, please calm down. You're only making things worse and nobody is getting cut. I know this is terribly uncomfortable for you, but fighting about it is only going to cause more tension, which will make your erection even harder and, of course, more painful for both of you."

While the nurse administered the Valium, I gulped down a cup of coffee because I could feel myself wilting. I began to prep for surgery because I knew that after three doses of Cialis, Mr. Baniff wasn't going to soften that easily.

An hour later Mr. Baniff was still hard inside Heidi so we moved them into surgery. The procedure began by massaging the area with warm water in hopes that he would slip out. But when that didn't work we had the unpleasant task of numbing both of them from the waist down. At that point I began to drain just enough blood from Mr. Baniff's penis for it to soften, and eventually he was able to slide his very wrinkled, red and irritated penis from Heidi's swollen vagina.

I'd paid no attention to the clock during surgery. Once they were both stabilized and had been moved into recovery, I realized it was 6:30 A.M. Quickly, I made my way toward the exit, already knowing that I didn't have enough time to make it to the airport for our 7:41 A.M. flight. Looking down at my pager I could see that Terrell had paged me at least six times. If I'd been a crying woman I would've broken down in tears. I had to think fast on how I could make things right before I spoke to him.

As I walked to my car, the cold air and the snow mixed with rain falling on my head gave me an idea. I sat in the car, grateful to have heated seats, and phoned our travel agent at Distinct Destinations. I explained my dilemma and she put me on hold. I prayed that she could make this work. When she returned, she'd successfully booked me on an 8:33 P.M. flight that evening straight into Los Angeles and then on to Hawaii, which meant I could join Terrell and the cruise ship in the port of Hilo. Next I had to deal with Terrell.

"Terrell, its me. Where are you?"

"I'm at the airport. I told you I would leave without you. Now, where the hell are *you?*"

"I'm just leaving the hospital."

He started to interrupt but I talked over him. "Just listen for a minute. I've spoken with the travel agent. I'm going to fly out later this evening and meet you in Hawaii. She's already arranged to have a driver pick me up at the airport and bring me directly to where the ship is docking. I'll be there in plenty of time to bring in the new year with you. Okay?"

He was silent.

"Please, Terrell. Don't be mad. I know it was stupid of me to come to the hospital and I'm sorry." I cried, hoping it would ease his anger.

"If you don't meet me in Hawaii, then consider this relationship over. This is your last chance, Cynthia."

CHAPTER 3

Cruising

December 29

*O*nce inside the house, I turned on the television to get the weather report. The weatherman was calling for more snow and I was thankful to be flying to warmer climates. I needed to relax, so I walked into the kitchen and grabbed a beer from the fridge. I popped the cap on a bottle of Coors Light, took a seat at the dining room table and propped my feet up on the other chair. No sooner had I taken a swallow of the cold beer than my head began to fall forward, my body suffering from a bad case of sleep deprivation.

The shrill ringing of the phone awakened me but by the time I reacted and went to answer it, the caller had hung up. I looked at the caller ID. It was my mother. I attempted to redial her number but when I looked at myself in the dining room mirror I was disgusted by what I saw. My eyes were puffy, my hair had come loose from its bun and was all over my head, and it didn't help that I had creases from sleeping on the place mat indented in my face. Maybe I had been working too much. I was beginning to look old before my time. I had to do something to bring myself to life, and not just enough to catch my flight. The best idea I could come up with was phoning my hairdresser, praying that she'd squeeze me in just a day after my last appointment.

"Hello, this is Dr. Lampley. May I speak to Blue?"

"Blue's busy doing a head right now."

"Yes, I know she's busy, but it's urgent."

"I'll see. Blue!" the receptionist screamed, more into the phone than away from it.

When Blue came on the line I said, "Blue, I know this is last minute and I would never do this if it wasn't an emergency, but I have to catch a flight this evening and my hair got wet and I look a mess. I'll even pay extra if you fit me in." She promised that she could see me at 3:00 P.M., which would be perfect. Two hours at the salon, two hours to get through the terminal at the airport, easily allowing me to catch my 8:33 P.M. flight to Los Angeles.

Now I needed a ride and didn't have time to fool with unreliable taxis, nor did I want to drive and have to waste time parking. After I showered, I phoned Cat at her office, hoping that maybe she'd have some time in between clients. I didn't get a chance to speak with her but through her secretary she agreed to pick me up at 2:00 P.M. Next I phoned L&S Limo Service, spoke to a dispatcher and scheduled a pickup from the salon to the airport. I was all set.

When Cat arrived I had no idea she'd bought a new car. But I shouldn't have been surprised. Cat didn't have any children, so she and her husband splurged on expensive vacations and luxury cars. This time she was driving a BMW 760. As soon as I sat down in her reclining seat she started her same old drill.

"I don't know why you come to this run-down-ass salon to get your hair done. Aren't you scared around here?" she asked as she whizzed around the snaking curves of Cobbs Creek Parkway.

"It's not that bad. I'm usually here early Tuesday mornings so there's never any problems."

"Yeah, but damn, this shit is so depressing."

Cat, like myself, had never lived in the city. We'd been lucky to have been born and raised in the suburbs, only coming into the city for dinners and professional engagements.

"If I had hair like yours I wouldn't need to go to the salon," I said, as I ruffled her nearly Caucasian-textured hair.

"Yeah, well I'm sure you could find a salon on the Main Line somewhere."

"Cat, give me a break, okay? I'm stressed enough."

When I arrived at the salon it was packed and I couldn't imagine how Blue was going to fit me in. Since I was unscheduled I had to take a number like everyone else. It was like being at the deli counter. When I glanced down at my nails, they too looked ragged. Everything seemed to have fallen apart on me overnight. While I waited, I agreed to allow the Korean woman to give me a manicure and pedicure, hoping her instruments had been sterilized.

Just as my nails were drying, the new shampoo girl signaled it was time for me to get my hair washed. In my paper sandals I tiptoed across the hair-strewn floor. Once I was washed and wrapped with setting lotion, I quickly fell asleep under the dryer. For once it didn't seem like this process was taking too long. I was in need of that forty-five-minute nap under the hair dryer.

Thirty minutes later Blue was still not ready for me. I didn't want to panic so instead I returned my mother's call. She immediately began to complain that my father was flying to Denver to visit my sister and her family when he knew that she'd planned on going the same weekend. Their drama never ended and I couldn't possibly see how my sister thought they were having any type of relationship.

Finally, Blue waved me over to her chair just when a crackhead had come through the door and begun to pester me about purchasing one of his bootleg DVDs. At that point I was on the last bit of nerve I had, which was probably the reason why I snapped at him.

"Please, I do not want to buy any of that bullshit. Now leave me alone."

The salon went silent, which embarrassed me, because not only did I never speak in that tone, but also I rarely talked to anyone.

When the town car arrived the driver came inside to get my bags, and loaded them into his trunk. Finally finished, I paid the cashier, doled out my tips and rushed out the door because now it was 6:00 P.M.

Once I was settled in the car and had told the driver which

terminal I was flying out of, I attempted to call Terrell. I got his voice mail so I left him a message, letting him know my flight's arrival time. I prayed he'd receive it because as much of a pain in the ass that he was, I didn't want to lose that man.

The driver had barely driven two blocks down Woodland Avenue when I heard what sounded like firecrackers going off in front of us. I told myself not to be so naïve, it was December, I was in the ghetto and more than likely they were gunshots.

"Ma'am, I think we have a problem," the driver said as he pulled the car to a screeching halt on the snow-slickened street.

I looked out the tinted window and could see people hiding and ducking behind the parked cars.

"Isn't there another way to go?" I asked, fearing that we'd get caught in the crossfire, especially since the gunfire was coming from both sides of the street.

"Look, lady. I can't very well back up and the next intersection is up ahead so my best advice would be to duck down in the backseat," he said, as he put the car back in drive.

"Well, damn. Step on it and run their dumb asses over if you have to! I have a plane to catch," I demanded.

"I don't think we can . . . ," he began to say, but didn't finish because the car had begun to swerve and then careened off toward a group of people on the sidewalk.

"Driver, what the hell are you doing?" I screamed.

When I saw that he was losing control of the car I leaned toward the front seat. I discovered that he couldn't answer me because he had bright red blood trickling from a small hole in the right side of his head. My driver had been shot.

I lunged my body halfway over the front seat and grabbed hold of the steering wheel, all the while hoping that this man wasn't dead and that I myself wouldn't be killed. But I couldn't control the car because he still had his foot on the gas pedal. Before I could make all that was wrong go right we crashed head-first through the plate-glass window of a Dollar Tree store.

CHAPTER 4

Wake-up Call

The screeching sound of tires woke me up. I barely managed to open my crust-filled eyes and didn't want to when the stark brightness of the lights blinded me. I made an attempt at moving, but that too was painful. When I reached over to feel what was sticking me in my hand I saw that I was connected to an IV drip hanging from a pole at the side of the bed. Bringing my left hand up to my face, I found an oxygen tube stuck in my nose. I pulled it out. When I reached out to touch my head to see why it felt like a vise grip was holding it together I felt gauze and tape so instead I brought my hand down, where it brushed across a bruise on my top lip.

What the hell had happened to me?

I forced myself to open my left eye because the other one was swollen shut. I did my best to take in my surroundings. There was a black-and-white television suspended from the ceiling that showed white static and in the corner was a blue vinyl chair whose plastic seat was splitting. Through a partially opened door I could see a bathroom, and when I glanced back up at the ceiling I noticed that the tiles were spotted with brown water stains. However, it was the concentrated smell of ammonia along with the awful noise of sirens below my window that confirmed I was in a hospital. Wincing in pain, I ran my hands along both sides of the bed until I touched what I was hoping would be the call button. I pushed it once, twice, even held it down, but there was no response.

I must've dozed back off when I heard the sound of someone humming. I opened my one eye again.

"Good evening there. I'm glad to see you've regained consciousness," the woman said as she adjusted the blinds.

"How come nobody came when I rang the bell?" I asked through parched lips.

"I'm sorry, your bell must be broken. Here, let me see," she said, taking the bell from my hand and pushing it. "Yep, it's one of the broken ones."

"What happened? Did you say I was unconscious?"

"Dahling, you were caught in the middle of a street war, you poor thing."

"What are you talking about? I was . . . I was . . ." But I couldn't finish what I was saying because I was confused about what I wanted to say.

"Mmmm, what's that? What did you say?" she asked.

I didn't respond because my thoughts were too muddled to comprehend what she was saying.

"By the way, what's your name, dahling? I know you think I should know it but when the ambulance brought you in here they said all your stuff had been stolen. No pocketbook, nothing, not even your coat. So, why don't you tell me your name so we can call your family."

"It's . . . it's . . . my name is . . ."

She looked at me, waiting for a name. Her eyebrows went up and down every time I tried to say my name.

"Go on, I'm listening, sweetie. Take your time. By the way, they call me Nurse Rita."

"I, uhmm . . ."

"Just tell me so we can call somebody and . . ."

Tears fell from my eyes and it pained the right one because it was so swollen.

"Oh no! Don't cry, dahling. You're going to be okay. Now, what were you trying to say? Take your time and tell me your name," she reassured me, while dabbing at my stinging tears with a tissue.

I stared back at her blankly through my one good eye.

"Don't tell me you don't know your name."

"Of course I know my name. It's . . . I think it's . . ." I was breathing harder now because I was trying to force something that wasn't there and it also felt like my lungs were collapsing.

Nurse Rita rushed over and placed the oxygen tube back in my nostrils.

"Calm down. Now you wait right here. I'll be right back. I need to get the doctor."

Something wasn't right. I'd been involved in a shooting. Had I had a gun? Had I been shot? And why the hell couldn't I remember my name? I told myself that I was dreaming and that if I got out of bed I'd wake up. Holding on to the railings at the side of the bed, I attempted to push myself up on my elbows but the pain in my side wouldn't allow for much movement. I felt across the middle of my body and that too was wrapped in bandages.

Nurse Rita reentered the room, running on her tiptoes. "Dr. Strohmile is on his way. Would you like something to drink?"

"Please."

Nurse Rita scurried back out again almost like she was afraid of me, then returned with a small Dixie cup of water that I quickly swallowed after spilling half of it.

"I need to know what happened. Is there a doctor?" I asked, frustrated that this woman couldn't read my chart and tell me what I needed to know. Could she not read?

"The doctor will be right in. I'm going to wait here with you. I guess I should check your vital signs."

While she dallied about with the reading of my pulse, blood pressure and temperature, I tried hard to recall what had landed me in the hospital. But Nurse Rita's constant humming was grating on my nerves.

"Can you stop that damn noise? I can't think."

"Sure, sure. I'm sorry this is bothering you, dahling," she said, as if I'd hurt her feelings.

Once she stopped I was sure I'd be able to think clearer but it wasn't coming. Maybe the doctor could explain better than this woman.

Just as my patience began to wear even thinner the doctor entered the room. Even with one eye closed I could see he didn't look like any doctor I would've chosen. This man couldn't have attended a credible university. What chief of staff would let him dress like that? His hair was filled with little twisties—my guess was they were the start of those awful dreadlocks—and either I was seeing double, which wouldn't have surprised me, but he had two earrings, one in each ear. This couldn't be a real hospital. Doctors didn't dress like that, especially with the dingy lab coat he was wearing.

"Good evening, I'm Dr. Strohmile," he said, offering to shake my hand.

"Please tell me why I'm in here," I begged, declining his motion.

He glanced down at the chart that Nurse Rita handed him. She began to hum again until I cut my eyes at her.

"It doesn't seem like you have any serious injuries, mostly lots of bruising around your face and your ribs. That's why you're wrapped up around the middle, but nothing is broken. I'm sure we can have you out of here in a day or two. So is it all right if I take a look?"

"Don't touch me until you tell me why the hell I'm in here!" I snapped at him.

"Like Nurse Rita explained, you were caught in the midst of a shooting, something pretty regular in the neighborhood in which you were traveling," he stated, then glanced back down at my chart.

I started making an attempt to get out of bed. "Listen, I'm

getting out of here. I don't know what kind of place this is but I'm not letting you or her touch me."

Dr. Strohmile didn't seem bothered by my outburst. "I don't think you want to leave here just yet."

"And why is that?"

"Well, I believe Nurse Rita told me that you couldn't give her your name?"

"I know my damn name. Anyway, shouldn't it be in the chart?" I asked as I painfully tried to sit up in the bed in an effort to leave.

"Why don't you tell me instead?" he asked.

"You're damn right I will. It's . . . it's . . . ," I started to say, then tears fell down my face and before I knew it I was sobbing uncontrollably. "I don't know why . . . I don't . . . I know my name . . . it's . . ."

Nurse Rita ran over and helped me back into bed. Even though Dr. Strohmile didn't assist her I could see the concern in his deep-set eyes.

"Listen, I understand that this isn't a good situation for you and I'd rather not have to sedate you. Why don't we talk while I take a look at those bruises."

I realized I didn't have a choice so I closed my eyes and lay back on the pillow, hoping that I was about to wake up from this dreadful nightmare.

"Good. Now I'm going to unwrap the bandage on your forehead first. How's that? Then we'll get the one from across your ribs."

"Can I remove this thing from my nose? I think I can

breathe on my own now." He nodded yes in response as Nurse Rita wrapped the tube around the stand.

His voice was firm but gentle and somehow I felt like it was okay. I didn't know this man or this seedy place they called a hospital. But I was helpless, so he could've done whatever he wanted to me, him and that Nurse Rita.

I braced myself for his cold touch and when I began to shiver he pulled up the blanket and covered me. I soon learned there was no need to fear the doctor's touch because he was gentle. His voice and his hands were extremely warm. Plus I didn't want to fight him because I sensed that he was holding back the information I needed to know. So I let him complete his exam.

When his face got closer to mine I could smell the fresh scent of his aftershave. He unwrapped the ace bandage from around my ribs, then placed the stethoscope close to my left breast. When he leaned in to check my heart rate I was sure it was the coldness of the room that made my nipple harden. Nonetheless it was embarrassing. But a hard nipple was the least of my worries. I was in need of the one thing that would release me from this nightmare.

"Dr. Strohmile," I whispered.

"Yes?"

"Do you know my name?"

His response must've made me come unglued because when next I opened my eyes the sun had come up.

CHAPTER 5

Bedside Manner

December 30

I wasn't quite sure what to do now. I knew the call bell didn't work, so I lay there and tried to concentrate hard enough to recollect the shooting that had taken away my name. I saw that they'd removed the IV, so it was no wonder my stomach was growling. I sat up stiffly in bed and listened to the sounds of the hospital. There were toilets flushing, patients crying out and the sound of someone dragging through the hallway. I decided I had to at least get myself out of bed and use the bathroom because my bladder was full. Pulling the covers back, I swung my legs and feet over the side of the bed and sat up. I didn't feel too much pain, mostly just a light dizziness, so I sat there for a moment. Finally, I pushed myself up off the bed and made my way into the bathroom.

The first thing I noticed was that for a hospital, this place was not much on cleanliness. Dust clung to the corners of the walls, the baseboards were speckled with mildew, and the cracked bathroom sink needed to be replaced. All of this made me not want to sit on the toilet. I reached for the paper toilet seat dispenser but it was empty. I wasn't surprised. Instead I used toilet paper to line the seat. When I was finished, I was just about to go back to bed when I heard Dr. Strohmile and Nurse Rita talking in hushed tones, probably because they knew I was behind the unlocked door of the bathroom.

"Doctor, I haven't been able to get anything out of her about who she is but the orderlies did hear her talking in her sleep."

"Anything that would help?"

"When the male nurse came in to check on her last night she began asking him about the length and weight of his penis."

"Really?"

"Also, she was crying that she had to get somewhere by New Year's, wherever that was."

"You're sure she was dreaming? Anything else?"

"Well, she hasn't been particularly nice to the nursing staff but it don't bother me."

"That somehow doesn't surprise me. Even with what little we know, I can see she's a woman who's used to better service than what we can provide. But for right now we're all she has."

"Dr. Strohmile, she may not realize it, but you are the best."

"Nurse Rita, you're after my heart." After a pause, he continued. "I'll spend some time with her and see if I can help her recall anything. I'm doubting that her amnesia is permanent, but we'll see."

"Maybe the little dahling just don't wanna remember her life," Nurse Rita mumbled, and then began humming that annoying tune.

Standing at the sink, I had to laugh at the fact that I'd scared a man by asking him about his penis. What kind of person was I that I would do such a thing? I was sure I'd been dreaming. And maybe Nurse Rita had been right. Maybe my life had been so bad that I'd blocked it out. As I looked out the door at Dr. Strohmile, I could see that both he and Nurse Rita were concerned about me. I wondered what they meant by that comment of what kind of woman I was. I looked in the mirror to see if I could answer that question and all that stared back at me was an unkempt swollen-eyed stranger with eight black stitches along her hairline.

Noticing a comb and brush wrapped in plastic on the shelf above the sink, I unwrapped it and combed through my matted hair. Thankfully, there was also a child-size toothbrush and paste to clean the sour taste from my mouth. Finally, feeling somewhat presentable, I exited the bathroom, telling myself that I would not lose my mind today.

"Good morning," Dr. Strohmile said when I stepped out of the bathroom.

Nurse Rita scampered about the room as if she didn't want to hear me go crazy again.

"Not so good if you don't know who you are."

"I can imagine it's a little frustrating, but I'm hoping we can trigger something to help you with your short-term memory loss."

"And what makes you think it's short term? I haven't seen a specialist yet. Didn't you call it amnesia? And I mean, really, what the hell is this place? Some kind of HMO clinic?"

I could tell he was offended when he lowered his gaze.

"It's Cobbs Creek County Hospital," Nurse Rita answered proudly.

"That figures," I said rather smugly as I looked around at the walls that needed a fresh coat of paint.

Dr. Strohmile didn't respond, just nodded his head as if nothing I said affected him.

"I'd like something to eat," I added even though I didn't feel hungry.

"Sure," he answered, then politely asked Nurse Rita to order me a meal tray.

I looked at his profile as he spoke to her and had to admit that even with his funny-looking hair Dr. Strohmile was somewhat handsome. I sized him up to be about six-one and maybe 220 pounds, kind of thick but not fat. He had a strong jawline, deep-set eyes and a little scar across his nose, which had probably been the result of a broken nose. But what shocked me was when I estimated that his penis was probably short and pudgy. When he turned his attention back to me, I was embarrassed by my analysis.

"If you don't mind, I'd like to talk with you for a moment."

"What's there to talk about? I don't remember anything."

"If that's the way you'd like it, then you can wait until the specialist comes tomorrow or whenever he gets here. But in the meantime I suggest you be nicer to the nursing staff since they're the ones whose daily care you're in."

"What's that supposed to mean? You think they're going to poison me?"

"Not at all. But what I am thinking is that when you are ready to talk to someone, there might not be anyone available who wants to listen. So you have a good day."

By now he was walking out of the room and the last thing I wanted was to be alone.

"Okay, okay. Don't go."

"Is that an okay you want to talk?" he asked, giving me his first smile. It lit up his face, exposing pearly white teeth.

"Yeah, that'll probably be good. I'm just embarrassed that I won't know how to answer anything you ask me."

"Why don't I tell you what we do know?"

Nodding my head in the affirmative, I sat up in bed and slid two plastic-covered pillows behind me.

"Here, let me help. Maybe the bed works," he joked, as he reached down and turned the handle at the foot of the bed.

After I was situated, he pulled a tattered blue chair up close to the bed and said, "Now let's see. We know you don't want to be alone for New Year's," he joked.

"I don't think that's funny. I heard the two of you talking about me."

"Well, with your asking the male nurse about the weight of his penis . . . ," he said, pretending to look at his notes.

"How is any of this supposed to help me remember my name and how I ended up in a damn county hospital?"

"I'm sorry, but sometimes you'd be surprised at what'll jump-start a person's memory."

"What about the accident? Why don't you start with that? Nurse Rita said there was a shooting. Where was it?"

"It says here in the police report that you were found unconscious at the intersection of Fifty-sixth and Woodland Avenues. You'd been thrown through the windshield of a car in which your driver was killed."

"I had a driver?"

"Yes, and we've put a call in to his company, but they didn't have him registered as having a client."

"I hope that doesn't mean I was a prostitute."

"I hardly think so. Besides, the company says sometimes the drivers have private clients that they drive around."

"What makes you so sure?"

"First of all, it's easy to see that even with your bruises you're a well-maintained woman. When I removed the ace bandages from around your ribs your body held none of the telltale signs of a prostitute. I mean, you can look at your own hands and feet and see how well you've been taken care of," he said, holding up my hands so I could see how well manicured they were.

"And what kind of signs are they?"

"Usually, those women have the well-worn bodies that go along with their profession. And believe me, I've seen plenty."

"Maybe I was into something illegal."

"No, not really. It reads here that the shooting was between rival drug dealers and you two were simply caught in between."

"Have the police sent out my picture across the wire? I'm sure somebody is looking for me."

"They didn't want to take your picture until you regained consciousness. Why don't I schedule them to come by tomorrow? How's that?"

I fought to hold back tears. Losing it could mean they would put me in restraints, or worse, lock me in the mental ward of the hospital.

"What is it? Do you remember something?"

"Why would I be asking the male nurse about his penis?"

"There could be a lot of reasons, I'm sure. One is you could've simply woken from a dream where you were making love. The other—"

"Doctor, I don't think so."

"Why is that?"

I looked him up and down with his one leg stretched across the floor and the other propped up on the frame of the bed. Just looking at what I supposed was an Afrocentric doctor with his dingy lab coat made me wonder what his naked body looked like underneath, wonder if his skin was firm and smooth or if he was out of shape. I pulled the covers up over me.

"What is it? Did you remember something?"

I shook my head no.

"Please, you should tell me whatever it was you were thinking right then because it could hold some type of clue."

But how could I? It was too embarrassing. But did my embarrassment really matter, considering I didn't know who I was? Maybe I was the type of woman who wondered about men's penises.

"Well . . . I . . . was . . . maybe I shouldn't say it," I said, turning my head from him. I would've kept it turned but he touched me, guiding my chin back around to face him.

"Go ahead. Tell me," he said, now sitting on the edge of the bed.

"I was wondering what you looked like underneath your clothes and what your penis looked like," I mumbled.

Even though he tried to hide it, he was embarrassed. His mouth fell open just a little as he struggled to respond.

"I knew you would think I was crazy," I said, turning my head away from him.

"No, it's not that. It's just that, well, if you were a prostitute I doubt if you'd be using the word penis."

I scooted down under the covers and turned my back to him.

"Dr. Strohmile, I'm tired. Can you come back later?"

During my afternoon nap my dreams were filled with doctors, police officers, prisoners and, crazy enough, there were dancing penises everywhere making fun of me. Every time I reached out to grab one, it would dance away from me. I woke up during the night sweaty, with the sheets clinging to my skin. The hospital gown had twisted around me and my hair lay plastered to my face. But what was worse was that I was incredibly horny and the person I was longing for was Dr. Strohmile.

I wasn't sure what to do with myself. I prayed for sleep, but when it wouldn't come I found myself searching for that spot that longed to be touched. Keeping my eyes on the door, I slid my hands down under the covers and touched my clitoris with my index finger. My body shivered but it felt good. I then slid my finger down to my vulva and touched the wetness that lay there. Turning onto my back, I used the middle finger of my right hand and rubbed my clitoris at its very tip in a circular motion until I was almost at the point of climax. But I wasn't ready, not yet, because this experience felt way too good. To prolong it, I began to tease myself by switching back and forth from the entry to my vagina to my clitoris and back. I moaned and I allowed myself to think about Dr. Strohmile, the fresh scent of his skin and how I'd like to peel off that lab coat and make love to him. This made me realize that my one finger simply wasn't enough, so I slid in another, and before I knew it I had pushed three of my fingers up inside my vagina.

The more intense it became, the harder I rubbed and the deeper I thrust my fingers inside and cupped my palm around my vagina. I had no recollection if I'd ever been that wet before and if I hadn't, then I'd surely missed out on something wonderful. Hell, considering where I'd wound up, something told me that I'd never even done this, never touched myself, but I couldn't imagine why I hadn't, as good as it felt.

I desired more so I began using my other hand to squeeze my nipples. Then I took my eyes off the door and dared to look at my face in the mirror. If I hadn't been almost at my climax I may have laughed at the twisted expression it held.

Finally, panting like a dog, I stretched my legs farther apart. The scent of my oncoming orgasm filled the air. I was ready for my climax, and even more so I was ready for Dr. Strohmile. I held my breath for a moment, almost not wanting it to happen, and then I thought of him and that tongue of his and how its tip curled down around his bottom lip. I lost control, my hips jutted forward and I called out, "Come, come on, come on outta there, please," I begged, and my body listened. Satisfied, I drifted back to sleep, my fingers drenched in sweet wetness.

I woke up to the sound of Nurse Rita's humming. When I turned over to say good afternoon, I found two very official-looking men—detectives, I assumed—standing in the doorway.

My eyes asked the question to Nurse Rita before I spoke.

"They're here to take your picture to see if anybody recognizes you."

"Nurse Rita, I don't want anybody taking pictures of me looking like this."

One of the detectives spoke up. "Look, miss. We're only trying to help you. This hospital isn't going to keep you here forever."

"Then they'll have to drag me out because I'm not taking a picture for you to spread all over every newspaper in Philadelphia."

Nurse Rita's eyebrows went up. "Listen, can you just let me talk to her for a moment?" The detectives moved into the hall, away from the doorway.

"Dahling, I have some good news. You remembered something, or at least I think you did."

I perked up.

"Yep, you remembered what city you were in."

"When? I mean, I'm in Philadelphia. Right?"

"Yes, but nobody told you that. So all I'm asking is that you let the detectives take your picture and maybe you can put some more pieces back together."

"Not looking like this. Nurse Rita, please get me something to wear. And I need to shower."

"All right, what if we get you all prettied up? Then we take our own picture and give it to them when you're ready."

"Okay," I said, holding on to Nurse Rita's arm.

She left the room and I heard her talking to the detectives. When she returned she said, "So this is what we'll do. I'm going to call my niece and have her come down to curl your hair. How's that?"

"But what am I going to wear? I can't be seen on the eleven o'clock news with this hospital gown on as if I'm some mental patient," I said, not sure that I wasn't.

"I'll take care of that too."

By five o'clock I was ready for my picture. Nurse Rita's niece had an easy time doing my hair because she said it looked as if I had it done on a regular basis. As for what I was wearing, I wasn't really sure.

Later that evening, after a dinner of tasteless food, I actually wanted some company. I asked the nurse on duty if I could go to the television room since the TV in my room wasn't working. When I walked down the hall and saw the types of patients that were in there, I immediately wanted to turn around and go back to my room. There was a prostitute in there for being stabbed by her pimp, a crack addict who was HIV positive and a drug dealer who'd been shot. How had I wound up with these people? Or better yet, was I one of them? Then I remembered that Dr. Strohmile had told me I wasn't. Right now I had to have trust in his opinion.

When I'd had enough of their bickering, I began walking down the hall to my room. I noticed Dr. Strohmile coming toward me, and he wasn't dressed in his lab coat, nor did he have his stethoscope hanging around his neck.

"I see you're all dressed up tonight," he said, referring to my updo hairstyle.

"Thank you," I said, hoping that I looked better than I did this morning because he certainly did. The good doctor was dressed in a pair of jeans, a long-sleeved cashmere sweater that gently hugged his torso and a pair of Gucci loafers. Twisties or not, the good doctor had taste and my guess was so did I.

"Listen, I'm sorry about this morning. I don't know why I would say something like that. But it's just so horrifying not knowing who I am."

"It's okay. I was on my way out and I wanted to come by and check on you. Plus I have an idea."

"I'll listen to anything after being in that TV room for an hour."

"Yes, we do have an interesting mix of patients here."

By now we were back in my room. I sat on the side of my bed and, surprisingly, he sat down beside me, bringing with him that scent that had brought me to climax. He reached into the messenger bag he was carrying and pulled out a handheld tape recorder.

"What's this for?"

"I hear you do a lot of talking in your sleep."

"And what are they," I asked, my eyes looking up at the doorway in the direction of the night nursing staff, "saying I say?"

He started laughing. "You sure you wanna know?"

I nodded my head yes. "Anything will help at this point."

He reached over to the foot of the bed and picked up my chart from its slot. Why hadn't I thought to look at that thing?

"Let's see here. Well, you're still promising someone you'll be there for New Year's and also something about where to put your fingers. It's mostly scrambled."

I covered my mouth to stop laughing. "Stop, stop, that's enough. What the hell kind of person am I?"

"I don't know, but you sure know a lot about a man's body."

"I'm sure I do," I said, looking at Dr. Strohmile as if I wanted to see what I could find out about his.

"Anyway, I was thinking that maybe we could set up the tape recorder and see what we can capture during the night."

"What about the specialist?"

"Unfortunately, he won't be able to make it for a day or two."

"Huh, what kind of hospital . . . ," I began to say but stopped myself.

"I know what you were going to say and you're right. We don't get all the assistance we need here. Sorry to say, but we're last on the list, so it may just come down to me helping you get your memory back."

"Whatever you think will help."

"All right, so once you're asleep the nurse will turn on the recorder and we'll see what we can get."

"Okay, but I have one request."

"What's that?"

"I have to be the first one to listen to the tape."

"Agreed."

He leaned over me and set the recorder on the nightstand. Foolishly, I was almost hoping he would kiss me.

"I think it's time for me to go. I, uhmm, have other patients to see." He stood and walked toward the door.

It was the first time I'd heard the good doctor stumble over his words.

"I'll see you in the morning?" I asked softly.

"Yes. Good night."

"Dr. Strohmile, one more thing?"

"Yes?" He responded, but didn't turn back around.

"What day is it?"

"December thirtieth, and I'm hoping that if we work hard enough we can get you to your destination by New Year's."

The warm bedside manner of the good Dr. Strohmile was making me more comfortable with seeing him and less afraid of not knowing who I was.

CHAPTER 6

Stroke of Midnight

New Year's Eve

I still didn't have a working television but Nurse Rita had placed a clock radio in my room. When I woke up, the voice of the woman discussing relationships sounded familiar, so I figured this must be a station that I listen to regularly. Then I remembered the tape recorder and nearly fell out of the bed reaching for it.

I also remembered that sometime during the night I'd woken up from a nightmare of being caught in a shooting. In the dream there was blood dripping from my face and I could see the window of a Dollar Tree store. There had also been a bedroom, possibly my bedroom, but when I'd opened my eyes it had been unclear as to where I was. Where were my magazines and my scrubs that usually littered the chair in my room? And where was the man whose hat sat on my dresser? But what part of this nightmare was reality and what part was a dream? Confused, I'd drifted back to sleep.

Before I could listen to the tape, Nurse Rita came in with my late breakfast tray. She asked me if I wanted to listen to what was on the tape but I pulled it from her hands. I wanted to be the first one to listen to whatever I'd said overnight because right now I was caught up in who I'd been and who I was right now.

All day I held on to the tape, afraid to listen. The only thing that kept me sane was the sweet humming of Nurse Rita in the hallway. I'd become accustomed to it. The peculiar thing, though, was that I hadn't seen Dr. Strohmile all day. When I'd asked Nurse Rita where he was, she'd said he'd taken the day off to celebrate. That left me feeling more empty than I already was. Where was I supposed to have been on New Year's Eve? I had had somewhere to go, which was probably why I had a driver. But I didn't know what that destination had been or whom it had been with. What if someone was somewhere waiting for me?

Finally, I decided to listen to the tape. But there was nothing there—at least nothing I could make any sense of. A lot of mumbo jumbo about patients and penises.

I hadn't eaten much during the day, and just as I began to fall back off to sleep, I smelled a man enter my room. I turned over, anticipating Dr. Strohmile, and there he was wearing a tux underneath his lab coat.

"I wanted to come check on you to see if you'd made any progress with the tape."

I wanted to tell him that I'd begun to remember some things. But I wasn't sure if that meant he'd leave or he'd stay, and I wanted him to stay so very badly.

"No, nothing. So you can leave and bring in your New Year's with whoever is waiting for you."

"I see you're not in a good mood tonight. That's why I came by. You know, to help you bring in the new year before I go."

"Are you serious? Why would you want to be stuck in this grimy hospital?"

"I'm not going to respond to that, but would you like to go for a ride with me or not?"

How could I resist him? "Do I have a choice?"

"You always have choices. So what'll it be?"

I got up from the bed that had begun to get comfortable over the last few days. I was ready to walk with him when he offered up a wheelchair.

"I don't need that thing."

"Maybe you do, maybe you don't. But two wheels beat two heels on any day."

I sat down in the chair and he pushed me out of the room. I had hoped that maybe he was taking me out of this place but instead he wheeled me into the community room. Some of the old patients and some new ones were watching New Year's Eve festivities on the television.

"I thought you might like some company to bring in the new year."

"I don't want to be in here with these people. I'd rather go back to my room," I said, disappointed.

The other patients looked at me as if I'd cursed them. Maybe I had. I had no reason to be angry at them, but at least they knew who they were, and I had to admit that they seemed more comfortable with who they were than I was, even if they were mostly drug addicts and gunshot victims.

"I'd like to return to my room."

"Certainly, but I need to make a stop."

When we got in front of the elevator, he stopped and pressed the up button.

"Where are you taking me now?" I asked as he pushed me through the open doors.

He didn't bother to answer, just pushed the button for floor nine and waited for the doors to close. When we exited the elevator, it appeared that we were on a deserted floor, but then again most of this hospital seemed deserted. I was about to ask what his intentions were when he wheeled me into the room marked SURGERY. Shock was the first thing that hit me, especially when I saw that he'd set up the room for a romantic dinner, complete with candles and champagne—all the things I had been looking forward to enjoying with someone, if only I could remember who that someone was. Rather than further stress myself over those details, I simply told myself that Dr. Strohmile would have to do.

"Why'd you do all this?"

"I figured you didn't want to bring in the new year alone. Would I be correct?"

"Yes, but all this?"

"Well, I'm a bit of a chef, and if I had waited any longer

these would've gotten cold," he said as he moved to uncover the platter that held two large lobster tails.

He draped my neck with a bib and did the same with his.

"Do I have to stay in this wheelchair?"

"Well judging from the other chairs in this room, I think that one might be the safest."

I surveyed the room and the other chairs that were stacked up against the wall. "Yeah, I think you're right. Can I at least sit closer?"

"Sure," he said, but I could tell he was somewhat nervous. He cut into my lobster and said, "Here, try this."

"Dr. Strohmile, why'd you do all this?"

"Ethically, I'm totally out of line, but there's been something about you that since we met has continued to tug at me even when I'm not in your presence."

"But what about . . ." I stopped myself because I began to remember Blue and the hair salon.

"What about what?"

"I mean, you're dressed, obviously, to go out with someone, and now you're here in this place with me."

"Was I supposed to go out? I'm sorry, I must've forgotten."

We both laughed and then I poured us a glass of champagne. Relaxed, I felt free enough to ask him whatever I wanted. And as I asked him questions about himself, some parts of my memory began returning.

"Can we forget you're a doctor for the night?"

"And why would you want to forget that?"

Rather than answer, I stood up from the wheelchair, leaned

in close to him, and slid my tongue into his mouth. I heard him gasp for air, and then he stood up and pulled me close.

Before I knew it, my hand was on his chest, guiding him toward the operating table. I wanted Dr. Strohmile and I wanted him my way.

"What do you want me to do?"

"Lie down and let me have you," I said.

I unraveled his bow tie and began to undress him. His body was pudgy and full, just right for a well-fed man. But the thing that captured me was when he stepped out of his boxers and I saw that beautiful instrument that was his penis. I remembered that I knew penises, that I'd examined them before, that I had an office where I worked with penises, but right now I wanted to put a stop to those memories.

I began to undress myself from that hospital gown, and rather than stand there naked, I slipped my arms into his dingy lab coat. When he lay down on the table I walked around him, just admiring his body and watching his chest heave up and down in anticipation of my touch. I picked up an instrument that lay on the table and went over his body inch by inch, dipping the long, cold steel rod into my champagne glass, then running the dripping rod up and down the good doctor's chest all the way to his toes, each time making circular motions with the rod. My memory floated back to me. I could hear Cat's voice from the radio, see her face, her new car. To shake it from my thoughts I leaned in to kiss him and he tried hard to pull me down, but instead I brought his hand to my breasts. He massaged them before bringing his fingers up to trace my lips.

"These," he said, "these succulent lips are what I haven't been able to get out of my mind."

"And the good thing is, you're going to have them."

A shiver went through me and that's when it happened. When I knew I was Dr. Cynthia Lampley, urologist, but it was too late because right now I had an exam to finish.

I was going to make love to every inch of this human's anatomy better than I ever had to Terrell or anyone before him.

Oh my God, Terrell. I'd forgotten him too. He was waiting for me at the port in Hawaii, and he was probably panicked that I hadn't arrived. What was worse was that he might have thought that I simply hadn't chosen to come.

Dr. Strohmile's voice interrupted my thoughts. "I've been dying for my nameless woman since I walked into your room."

And nameless is what I wanted to be, if only for a few more moments. Standing at the foot of the table, I bent Dr. Strohmile's knees and positioned his feet in the stirrups that were at the sides of the operating table. When I saw him spread apart, lying open for me, I did what I'd dreamed of doing. I took him in my mouth. When he screamed out, I swallowed, caught my breath and took him in deeper. But he was ready to take control, so he pushed my head away, leaned down, cupped me under my arms with his hands and brought me up to him.

"Ohhhhh, ohhhh Doc . . . tor . . . ," I cried out in passion as his penis filled me.

Somehow my foot must've touched a button on the side of the table because it began to slowly incline to a slanted position. All of this made his penis sink farther up into my vagina, slam-

ming against its walls until both of us screamed out in the ecstasy of the moment, releasing pent-up orgasms from both of us.

It was sometime before sunrise when Dr. Strohmile wheeled
me back to my room and sat at my bedside, watching me until
I fell asleep wishing that if my life hadn't been this good, then,
maybe, there would be no need for my memory to ever return.

CHAPTER 7

New Year's Day

"Cyn, Cyn, it's me, Terrell. Wake up, please, baby."

Confused as usual about where I was, I opened my eyes and saw Terrell standing there. I reached up, crying, and flung my arms around him.

"Terrell, Terrell. Oh my God. I'm so happy to see you," I cried out to him. "You won't believe what I've been through. I was trying to get to you, I swear, but I was in a shooting and I lost my mind. I mean my memory, and then . . ."

When I looked past him I saw my parents standing there holding hands.

"How'd you find me?" I asked, turning toward Terrell.

"When you didn't show up I thought maybe you'd changed your mind about us, the marriage. And then I called your office, I called Cat and when all the pieces didn't fit I flew back home to find you."

"Then they posted your picture in the paper and on the news," said my father. "And that's when your prisoner, Ahmed Bridges, the inmate you were treating at CFCF, called into the precinct identifying who you were, and so here we are."

"Honey, do you know who we are? They said you lost your memory," my mother asked.

"Yes, yes, I remembered everything. I'm sorry I missed spending New Year's with you, Terrell. Last night was . . ." But I stopped myself when I heard that sweet humming.

Standing over at the door was Nurse Rita, smiling at me. Somehow I knew she had been part of the magnificent night I'd had with Dr. Strohmile. Where was he? What if he came now? How would I explain? I had to get out of that hospital before he came on duty. At that point Cat entered the room.

"I told you about going to that salon and now look at you. But wait a minute. You actually look good. Like you've had some rest. As a matter of fact, I've never seen you glowing like this."

"Yes, Cynthia, you do look rested," my father added.

"I don't know how the hell she could've rested in a place like this," Terrell said, looking around the room as if it were going to attack him.

I saw Nurse Rita's shoulders rise up and I knew that at any moment she'd be ready to take him on.

"Actually, they took really good care of me. I don't think I could've ended up anyplace better."

"Well let's get you dressed and out of here. I've brought you some clothes."

Nurse Rita chimed in, "Would you like to see the doctor before you leave?"

"They really have doctors in this place?" Cat joked.

"No, that's okay, Nurse Rita."

Behind Rita I saw the same detectives who'd come by earlier to take my picture.

"Is it okay to ask her a few questions, Terrell?" asked one of the plainclothes detectives who'd now returned.

Terrell turned to me. "You up for that?"

"Sure."

Cat and my parents left the room while the detectives and Terrell questioned me on the accident and to see if I remembered anything about the gunmen. I didn't have many details for them. It all had happened so fast that I didn't have time to take in anyone's looks. According to the detectives, the gunmen were still at large. Unfortunately, the driver was killed. He'd been a husband and father of three.

The detectives left and I dressed so I could leave. As Terrell pushed my wheelchair toward the elevator, I saw Dr. Strohmile in the hallway with a panicked look on his face, talking with Nurse Rita, who was trying to reassure him about something. I wanted to stop and tell him how much last night had meant to me but I was sure I needed to lose that memory.

CHAPTER 8

Back into the Swing, Almost

I stayed home for three days. However, had it been up to Terrell, he would've had me take a month off. But I was feeling good. Actually, I hadn't felt this good in a while. Sometimes I even found myself humming. Terrell and I spent every moment together talking about our future.

As Terrell and I talked he seemed more willing to stop holding on so tight to the reins of our relationship. He blamed his need for control on his job. I, in turn, also promised not to work so much and to set a date for our wedding and a long honeymoon. I did all of this in hopes of erasing the memory of the good Dr. Strohmile. I hadn't told anyone, not even Cat, about what had occurred on that deserted floor of the hospital. How would she ever understand my making the best love ever in a dusty operating room of an inner-city hospital? I wondered what Cat's Thursday morning callers would think of such a thing.

I was pleased that Terrell had scheduled to take the test for chief investigator at the Media precinct. He'd planned on telling me while we were on vacation. The more Terrell talked, the more I believed he was the man for me. He loved me and I could see he was willing to make the necessary changes to secure that I would be in his future.

I also discovered that my sister had been correct. My parents were indeed having an affair, if that made any sense. They claimed they hadn't wanted to confuse us, but we were grown women so I don't know what the real reason was. I was just glad they seemed happy.

My mother always believed in the motto that in life there are no coincidences. If she was correct, why did I get into that dreadful accident and why did I land in Cobbs Creek County Hospital with no memory? More important, why couldn't I stop thinking about the good Dr. Strohmile?

Every day I was tempted to call him and thank him but I wasn't sure what I was thanking him for. I looked at Terrell and measured the two of them and their differences, of which there were many. If Terrell ever found out what happened he'd be devastated.

On my fourth day home, I gathered up enough nerve to make the call. Disguising my voice and calling from a number that couldn't be detected on caller ID, I dialed the number for my friend's radio show.

"Hello, caller."

"Yo, this is Shawna from Southwest Philly and I think I'm having a slight problem."

"Hi, Shawna. You've reached Dr. Cat."

"Yeah, I know," I answered, trying to sound like one of the young girls I'd heard call in.

"So, Shawna, why don't you tell me and my listening audience what you think the problem might be."

"Well, I've met this man—I mean, this brother—and just in a matter of days I think we may have fallen in love."

"That doesn't sound like a problem."

"It is because I'm already engaged to a man who's really nice and he's a good man. But I never thought we were a match because we don't have a lot in common. You know, like careers and stuff."

"Now that does sound like a problem. So what is the status of you and this other man?"

"I'm not sure. I haven't seen him or talked to him since we spent a few days together but I can't stop thinking about him. It's like he touched a part of me that had never been touched before."

"I see, and did you and this man make love?"

"Did we? Yes, and it was fantastic. I mean, the bomb. Like I said, he touched my soul."

"Well, it sounds like you need to see this brother before you walk down the aisle. You also need to make sure you're not just settling for the man you're with just because he's familiar. I mean, who knows? Maybe this brother is your soul mate, and sometimes we never marry that one because it always seems too unbelievable. So before you marry that man and wind up cheating on him with your soul mate, get in touch with him and see how he feels about all this."

"I may do that. I just may."

"Shawna."

"Yes? I mean, yeah."

"Your voice sounds somewhat familiar. Have you called in before?"

"No, but I gotta roll. Thank you."

So that's what I decided to do, follow Cat's suggestion and get the nerve up to see the good doctor. Because if I didn't, I'd never know if Dr. Strohmile was my soul mate.

CHAPTER 9

Checkup

I'd been back to work for a week and had even gone back to the salon in Southwest Philly. No need to be scared now. I left the office one afternoon, and rather than go home I decided to take a ride and found myself sitting in front of Cobbs Creek County Hospital. What was I waiting for? Was I going inside? Terrell would kill me if he knew I was back in this neighborhood but I wanted to see Dr. Strohmile. I had to see him before I got married so I could know whether there was more to us than my stay in the hospital.

Sitting there behind the wheel of my car, I realized that I didn't even know what kind of car he drove. For all I knew he might have already gone home for the day. But then I saw a black Jetta pull up with a redheaded white woman driving and there he was on the passenger side. Dr. Strohmile leaned over, kissed her on the lips, and then disappeared inside the hospital. I sat there feeling like a fool. How could I have thought that this man didn't have a girlfriend. Maybe she was even his wife but he hadn't worn a ring. Where had she been on New Year's? It didn't matter that she was white. Hell, Cat was married to a white man. But this was the man I wanted, the man I thought was my soul mate, so how could he possibly be with someone else? Weren't soul mates supposed to be everything you were always looking for? How could I have been so foolish as to listen to Cat and her stupid callers?

Just as I started up the car, someone tapped on my driver-side window, startling me.

"Looking for someone, dahling?"

"Nurse Rita, oh my gosh!"

I stepped out of the car and flung my arms around her. I was so happy to see her. She'd taken such good care of me and had been so patient with my behavior.

"How you feeling, dahling? Oops, I mean, Dr. Lampley, right?"

I had to laugh because it was so funny to hear her call me doctor. For those few days she'd treated me like a little girl, almost like a daughter.

"Don't call me that. Just call me Cynthia. How are you? I was hoping I'd see you."

"Now really. For some reason I don't quite believe you're sneaking around this neighborhood to see an old lady like myself."

"No, I was, really. Uhmm, I wanted to thank you for everything and I wanted to tell you that if you ever want a change of scenery you have a job with me, with my practice, or wherever you want in the suburbs. How's that sound?"

"That's so nice of you, dahling, but I'm fine right here. Right here where people need me."

"I didn't mean to insult you."

"Oh, forget about me. Now, as for Dr. Strohmile, I guess you'd have to find out on your own where he'd like to be."

"Nurse Rita! I'm engaged and Dr. Strohmile, well, he was just doing his job."

"And a good one at that, huh, dahling?"

"Yes, he was very good. But look, I better be going. I need to get into the office. Thanks again, Nurse Rita."

"And Dr. Strohmile, what should I tell him?"

"No need to bother."

EPILOGUE

*A*fter seeing Dr. Strohmile with his girlfriend I jumped into my work to keep my mind off of him. The following Friday I sped through the day as usual, but right before I left for the weekend, the receptionist buzzed and said I had a new patient. Knowing that we usually scheduled new patients for the mornings, I was just about to buzz her back and tell her he had to see someone else when there was a tap on my office door. When I opened it, standing before me was Dr. Strohmile. My breath, and my ethics, left me when he stepped into my office and kissed me passionately on the mouth.

"Wait, wait," I tried to say while struggling for air.

But he wouldn't let me go. He just kept pressing that wicked tongue of his deeper into my mouth, searching for the satisfaction it had given him on New Year's Eve.

I pulled away. "Dr. Stroh . . . mile, this isn't . . ."

To shut me up he circled my lips with his tongue, then

whispered against them, "Whatever you were trying to say couldn't have been more important than that."

"No, it wasn't. But I'm engaged and you have . . . you have that redheaded white woman."

He laughed at my description of her.

"I mean . . . I don't mean . . ." I tried to speak but I was tongue-tied.

"I don't know what you mean and right now I don't care. All I know is that since that night, since that time we spent at the hospital I can't stop thinking about you. You're for me, Dr. Lampley. I know it, I feel it in my soul."

"But how can that be? We're both in relationships. I'm engaged. What are we gonna do, walk out on these people?"

"What do"—he kissed me—"you want me to do, nameless lady?" he asked while his hands made their way up my skirt.

"What are you doing? We can't have sex here in my office."

"Sure we can. And really, Dr. Lampley, I think you want to make love to me right now. Or maybe you'd like it better in the exam room. You do have some stirrups in there, don't you?"

"Yes but . . ." He didn't let me answer and I didn't want to, so instead I pulled him into my arms and stepped back through the door toward my exam room.

Before I knew it, he'd opened my lab coat and was pulling up my blouse while I fought to unbuckle his belt and unzip his pants. His fat penis popped out, curved, hard, and ready for me.

He pulled at my stockings, popping them from my garter belt, and then slipped off my panties. They fell in a puddle around my left leg.

Just as I was about to move toward the table, he gripped the cheeks of my ass and hoisted me up in the air. I wrapped my legs around his waist and he easily slid up into me.

"Oh, oh, my good doctor, please," I cried out to him as he thrust himself inside me. From somewhere I heard a buzzing. *Not right now. Please, no more patients.* But we both knew I had to answer, so he slid from inside me and leaned against the table, stroking himself with one hand and my lips with the other.

I pushed the button on the wall to respond to the receptionist but nobody was there. Before I could return to my soul mate, I heard knocking on the outside door of my office.

I panicked. I hadn't remembered to lock it so I buttoned my lab coat to hide my slightly torn blouse, smoothed down my hair, stepped into my panties and slid my feet quickly back into my shoes.

Kissing Dr. Strohmile one more time, I said, "Wait, wait right here. Don't go away, please."

Just as I closed the door to my exam room, my office door opened and in stepped Terrell.

"Cyn, you still working in here? I didn't interrupt you with a patient, did I?"

"Uh, no, I mean, yes, but we're not finished. I mean, we are but . . ."

With a puzzled look on his face as to what I was trying to say, Terrell kissed me on the lips, lips that were still tender from Dr. Strohmile's mouth.

"Give me a minute," I said, feeling trapped with Terrell on

one side and Dr. Strohmile behind the other door. Before I could step back into my exam room and make a choice, Dr. Strohmile walked back into my office looking as calm as if nothing had happened.

"Doctor Strohmile, you're leaving?" I asked.

Terrell looked at me, clearly hearing the desperation in my voice.

"It seems so, but I'm hoping to see you again next New Year's."

"Cynthia, what's going on here?" Terrell asked.

Dr. Strohmile half turned toward me but kept his eyes more on Terrell.

"Dr. Strohmile, I don't want to wait until next year."

"Next year for what, Cynthia?" Terrell interrupted.

"But what about him?" Dr. Strohmile asked, nodding his head toward Terrell who was standing there in his uniform looking more threatening than I'd ever seen him.

"Yeah, Cyn. What about me? And like I said, what the fuck is going on?"

I saw Dr. Strohmile trying to hide a hopeful smile as we both looked at the quizzical expression on Terrell's face.

I had to make a decision that would change the course of the rest of my life. Would I marry Terrell, eventually having to give up my practice to become the wife and mother that he would demand that I be or could I muster up the courage it would take to fall into a life that Dr. Strohmile and I hadn't even discussed?

So far I hadn't left much to chance in my life. I'd set my

mind on being a urologist and by tenth grade I'd already selected the university I'd attend. By my junior year of college I'd already applied and been accepted at the medical school of my choice. Even winding up with a practice at Bryn Mawr hospital had been planned.

Yes, I knew how to make plans and even Terrell had been part of the plan when he came along. He was settled, had a secure future and was protective of me, maybe even a little obsessive. But I knew he loved me. The question was, did I love him? I didn't want to marry Terrell just because he fit into my plan. I wanted to feel a fire in my belly like I had with Dr. Strohmile.

At that moment I had no time for plans. It was time that I finally took an uncalculated risk, something I'd never done in my life.

I turned my full attention to Terrell.

"Terrell, I'm sorry but I'm not ready to get married. There are some things I need to explore, and I'm not sure that once I've done that, I'll still want to be with you."

"What the hell are you talking about, Cynthia? I know you're not . . . ," he began to say, then trailed off midsentence. By now I wasn't even looking at him. I was looking over his shoulder at Dr. Strohmile.

"This is the man you want to be with?" Terrell asked.

I nodded in response, then smiled as Dr. Strohmile moved from behind Terrell and came to stand by my side.

Looking at Terrell, he said, "Alexander Strohmile is my name, officer. If you need anything else, you can reach me at Cobbs Creek County Hospital."

Terrell looked at both of us like were crazy before he stormed out of the room. But I wasn't concerned. I felt that fire in my belly begin to burn again. I wanted to hurry and get my good doctor back into the exam room to finish what we'd started.

Dangerously in Love

CRYSTAL LACEY WINSLOW

PROLOGUE

Jovie

New Year's Eve 2005

Protected by the warmth of the heavy goose-down comforter, I found myself feeling safe for the first time in years. As I watched the reddish orange flames bursting from the fireplace, I longed to be a little girl again, taking piggyback rides on my father's back. Love was simple back then. Love didn't hurt.

As the fire died down, so did my feelings of security.

What had I done with my life?

I lay still until I heard the sultry voice of Meshell Ndegeocello belting out the words to "Fool of Me."

That song was a click-on switch to my most intimate feelings. I sang along: " 'You made a fool of me / Tell me why. . . .' "

I felt frightened and weak in the sudden darkness that had consumed the spacious brownstone apartment. I started crying softly, afraid that if I really did let go, I might not be able to stop. Slowly, I stood up and looked in the mirror. I was completely naked.

You're too skinny! a voice inside my head shouted as I covered myself with his T-shirt.

He smells so good. . . . I argued, then I sprayed myself with his cologne.

You're pathetic! that mean voice again cried out.

The New Year's cheers coming from outside sounded eerie. Like the theme music in a horror movie. A movie that I'd write an ending to. My father told me that I had to make the end always justify the means. Up until now I had no clue what that really meant. Or if I'd ever be able to use such a philosophy and apply it to my life. Now I seemed able to appreciate everything in a philosophical way.

I'm so alone. . . .

I felt his presence way before I heard his footsteps. He was home and he wasn't alone. I heard a soft giggle. A woman's giggle . . . flirty and sophisticated.

I hate you, bitch!

The anxiety I felt inside my stomach was mounting, and I knew the only way to release this was to explode. I wanted closure. I *needed* closure. My hands trembled as I wrapped them around my shoulders to comfort me because I knew the inevitable.

Why wasn't there ever anybody there to comfort me?

In my bare feet, I crept to the bedroom closet and hid. There I'd finally get all the answers to my thought-provoking questions. Finally, it'd only be him and me . . . and her. With nowhere to run.

I thought he said he loved me!

London

New Year's Eve 2004
Notting Hill, England

This was the last night of the "Larger Than Life" tour. I was hired to bodyguard a rapper, Bugsy, who'd recently got into an altercation with another rapper. The media covered the story and magnified the whole situation. Now they're both sending death threats by way of no-name, nondescript flunkies. It's unfortunate that they aren't wise enough to learn from their predecessors. But fortunately enough for me, their gripes are what keep me employed. I hate to admit that I wish I was able to stay on the job—the first-class incentives have spoiled me. But he's going into seclusion to spend time with his family. I guess I can handle being without a job for a moment. I'm certain another client will come along soon enough. If not, I'll still be fine. Besides, being a bodyguard is only for paying bills. My life's passions are writing and painting.

Since the last part of Bugsy's tour was in England, I had arranged for my longtime girlfriend, Su, to come over so we could spend New Year's Eve together. It's been a long time-honored tradition in my family that whomever you spend New Year's Eve with is most likely to be the person you'll be with for the rest of the new year. I was anticipating spending the rest of my year with Su. She and I had been dating for two years, and I was madly in love with her. She was sassy, classy, sexy and vivacious. She was everything any man could ever want in a woman.

I recently spent my last eight thousand dollars on her engagement ring, so money has been a little tight for me lately. I'm going to pop the question just as the new year comes in. My brother, Lawrence, would say that's a stupid move. He'd complain about me spending all my money on Su. From the first day they met they've never gotten along. She complains that all my brother does is use me. And he complains that all Su does is use me. If I'm not complaining, then why are they?

Su worries about money and bills more than she should. She's a twenty-five-year-old law student with an insurmountable student loan. I try to help her out financially as much as I can, but it's just never enough. I've also tried to explain that once I sell my screenplay we're going to be financially secure. My agent says he's getting pretty good responses to my work. Once I sell the screenplay, I can pay off all my debts, Su's debts, plus provide a decent lifestyle for us.

I looked at Su, sleeping peacefully. She looked like an exotic doll, with her petite body and massive head of jet black hair. She had a small button nose and pouty lips that drove me crazy. She had purposely laid the sheets so they were barely covering her naked body. Her cocoa-colored skin was glowing, and she had a slight smile on her face. I hoped that smile had come from our making love last night. I kissed her luscious lips and she moved slightly, exposing her perky breasts. I climbed back into bed and began sucking her breasts until I heard her moan. Just as I was about to part her thighs, there was a knock at the door. I ignored it until it became a persistent banging. Shit! I'd have to answer it.

"Don't you move," I said, and kissed her forehead.

I ran to open the door, and just as I suspected, there he was, Bugsy.

"Whaddup?" Bugsy stated.

"Hey, man, is everything all right?" I asked, even though I really didn't care.

"Everything is cool. Why? Your bitch-ass wasn't gonna do shit," he bellowed in his grandiose tone. Sometimes I think about what it would feel like to let my fist smash through his smug face. But it was only a fleeting thought. On any other night I would have checked him. But I wanted tonight to be special. I didn't want any distractions or hostility on the night I was going to propose to Su.

Bugsy stood about five-five, but he had presence. He was wearing the obligatory rapper's gear—a button-up shirt, baggy jeans, Scooby-Doo shoes, a large-faced watch, diamond earring and a low-cut Caesar.

"Don't make me have to get my forty-five," I said jokingly, but I really meant every word. My pride made me challenge him but, truthfully, I was hoping he wasn't fool enough to test me.

"Get your shit. I got one, too," Bugsy warned.

"No, seriously, what can I do for you?"

My eyes hooded over and I bit the inside of my cheek. This brother was pushing all the wrong buttons. "You got a gun," I said in a deceptively calm voice. "But the question is, will you use it?"

Sensing tension, Bugsy began to relax. "You know I'm only fucking with you. I came by to ask if you and Su wanted to join us later. Everyone is going to the clock at Trafalgar Square to watch the fireworks. It's tradition out here. Then we're going to hop on the Concord and head back to New York and bring in the new year twice in one night. You know I do it real big."

Before I could respond, Su came out of the bedroom, clad in a silk robe that just barely covered her sexy rear end. Her boobs peeked out, looking for attention.

"Celebrate the new year twice in one year . . . that would be love-ly," she said, putting on a fake British accent.

Bugsy grinned, then replied. "Dat's what's up. So, y'all hangin' out or not?" he asked, but he wasn't looking at me. He was staring directly at Su, who, if I wasn't mistaken, was licking her lips and arching her back seductively. Was I just being a paranoid, insecure man who didn't trust his beautiful girl-friend?

I intervened. "Nah, man, we can't hang out. I've made other plans. Su, I didn't get a chance to tell you, but I wanted to spend the new year at Westminster watching the fireworks there. I've also made dinner arrangements. I want tonight to be special."

"Bugsy, this bloke wasn't listening to you," she said, disrespecting me.

"Excuse me," I said, as my face tightened and my eyes grew small from anger. "Since when do I have to *listen* to Bugsy?"

"London, we have a chance to full-on do something exciting. I'd rather hang out with Bugsy and get VIP treatment. Since we're here, we may as well do things 'big,' as Bugsy just said."

"Why are you speaking like that?" I asked, referring to her newfound British roots.

"Like what?" she asked, looking perplexed with my question.

"Look, the subject isn't up for debating! I've gone to a lot of trouble to make tonight special for us—"

"Listen, you players don't need to get into any beef over me. The invitation is open for the both of y'all. Holla," Bugsy said, and left.

Once he was gone, I flipped. "Goddamn! You should have just come out here with nothing on."

"What are you talking about?" she said, playing dumb.

"Were you getting ready to perform or something? Maybe give him a lap dance? I know Bugsy got a few hit singles out," I said sarcastically. She just looked at me and rolled her eyes. Before I could probe her further, the telephone rang.

"Hell-o!" I screamed into the receiver.

"What's wrong with my baby brother? That ho got you stressed out?" my brother, Lawrence, remarked.

"Watch your mouth! Listen, this is a bad time. What do you want?"

"I need some cash quickly. Could you wire me three hundred dollars?"

"I don't have it right now. I'm broke," I said.

"I'll give it right back as soon as you get home. I need some money for the new year."

"I just told you that I don't have any currency."

"Listen, I wouldn't call if I weren't in a bind. I'm dead broke. I bet you done spent all your money on that Prada-wearing hoochie!"

"You have one more time to disrespect Su before you see my bad side," I warned. "The most I can spare is about one hundred. Is that good enough?"

"That'll do."

As soon as I hung up Su tore into me.

"I know you're not going to give that no-good, lousy, begging, son of a bitch—"

"I'm a grown man, Su. I do what the fuck I want! Now, I already told you that when you and I get into it to leave my family out of it!"

"What?" she yelled. "Fuck your mother! And fuck your brother, too!"

"Watch your fucking mouth!" I screamed. "You're acting like a groupie *bitch* who's looking to start an argument. I see you. I know what this is about. But do what you do."

"I'll be a groupie, but the only *bitch* in the room is you!" she countered.

"I see how this is going down. That brother got your mind," I stated and lifted my eyebrow up in astonishment. Up until now, Su and I have never spoken to each other so harshly. And I had to admit that as a man I was hurt. But my pride refused to let me show it.

"Oh, so now I've lost my mind?" she said, shaking her head in bewilderment.

"That's what I said!" I replied through gritted teeth.

"So, if I'm a groupie, and you're a bitch," she said, unable to let this go, "who's getting *fucked* tonight?"

"You tell me!" I yelled as my stomach did a few somersaults. I didn't like the way this argument was heading. I had big plans for us tonight.

"Please, London. Don't sit up in my face and act all innocent like I'm out of control. How many women have you slept with while we were together?"

I feared questions like that. True, I hadn't been faithful to Su, but I didn't love her any less. I've been tempted on more than one occasion. I thought quickly and tried to salvage the rest of the evening. "Listen, I think this is going too far. Why are we even arguing? I mean, what's this about?"

"This is about you putting the *b* in broke, the *l* in loser, and the *p* in pathetic. I'm so sick of you always trying to control me.

I don't know what type of woman you thought you had, but my name ain't Subservient Su!"

"I never said it was," I replied, almost in surrender. My submissiveness only fueled her fire.

"A moment ago you had a lot to say. A moment ago I was just a million bitches."

"I apologize. I should have never called you outside of your name," I said, trying to manipulate the situation. I needed her to fold and let me win.

"No, don't apologize because I see the real you. You're unsure of yourself. You're flaky. You come off as this heartless, cocky bastard like you're hot shit but inside you're soft like butter. I guess you've never gotten the memo that states you can't fuck, you got a little dick and your tongue game is lousy! If you were handling your business you wouldn't feel threatened every time I'm in the room with eye candy," she spat.

Her words hurt. "Wow, that was below the belt. All this for a rapper who fucks chicks in the bathroom at restaurants. I guess you're next in line," I said, as the reality of the situation started to sink in. I never knew Su had the effrontery to say what she'd said.

"You mean first. I'm never second to anyone!" she yelled before storming off into the bedroom. I could clearly see her getting dressed to go meet up with Bugsy.

"If you walk out that front door, don't come back!" I threatened.

"I wouldn't have it any other way," she challenged.

Needless to say, I didn't hang around my hotel room waiting

for her *not* to come back. I downed a couple shots of Hennessey from the mini bar in my room and tried not to think about how the love of my life had walked out on me. As far as I was concerned, it was her loss. I hopped on the tube and rode to Notting Hill Gate.

It was a cold, dank night, and all I was wearing was a heavy sweater and a thick scarf to cover my neck. I walked up the cobblestone pathway and stumbled into a small bar that had a live band with an attractive young girl singing Nina Simone tunes. Her voice was mesmerizing. Sad and gloomy, it personified my mood. She had these great eyes that burned holes in my flesh when she focused on me. Loose curls framed her oval-shaped face. Her skin was a French vanilla color with just a sprinkle of cinnamon. She looked good enough to eat—literally.

After the set she came out and sat in the crowd. I took this opportunity to go and make her acquaintance. She looked almost frightened as I approached.

"Hello, my name's London, and I just wanted to say you have the most amazing voice I've ever heard."

"Thank you," she said and avoided eye contact.

"You're an American."

"So are you," she chimed in.

"Yes. And I can't wait to go back to the States."

"Me, too. I'm just here to make some extra money. I go back in two days."

"Great. Do you mind if I buy you a drink?"

"I don't drink."

"Neither do I," I lied. "But we should have at least one drink to celebrate the new year coming in. It's tradition," I said, and then signaled to the waitress. "I'd like two glasses of champagne. . . ."

"That'll be forty pounds," she said.

Thirty minutes later I was smashed and telling this poor stranger all my business.

"We were supposed to get married," I said, slurring my words. "I'll kill him if he lays a hand on my Su."

"You poor thing," she sympathized.

"She's the love of my life, and she walked out on me," I cried.

"That's unfortunate," she said, and gently rubbed my hand. "But I must really get back to my hotel."

"Stay. In five minutes it'll be the new year. You know they say whomever you ring the new year in with is probably the person you'll spend the whole year with."

"Really? I've never heard that before."

"Yeah, it's a fact."

"Well, that wouldn't apply to us, would it? I just met you," she said, but there was a yearning in her voice if I wasn't mistaken.

So I humored her and said, "We've just met. It doesn't mean we couldn't get to know each other better."

My comment must have unnerved her because she squirmed in her seat.

"Five, four, three, two, one . . . Happy New Year!" The whole bar erupted in New Year's cheer. I grabbed the stranger, picked her up in a bear hug, swung her around and then planted a fat, wet kiss on her lips. Inwardly, I wished she was Su. She looked at me with a blank expression, pushed me off of her and ran out of the bar. That was twice in one night that I'd been left by a beautiful woman. And I hadn't even gotten a chance to ask her name.

Jovie

November 2005

How can I explain that it was the *pleasure* that frightened me? I celebrated my twenty-fourth birthday as a virgin. I never planned for my life to unfold in such a dull manner. I always wanted to think outside the box, but my shyness put limitations on my actions. I kept having this recurring dream of lost love. In my dreams my lover was a strong, articulate, sensual man. But at the rate I was going, I'd never meet him. When I was approached by the opposite sex, I pushed them away. Sadly, I didn't think there was one man on this earth that could ever meet my high expectations. So rather than deal with disappointment, I played it safe by guarding my heart.

Today started off just like any other day. After I showered, I washed my hands with Dove antibacterial soap, using a scrub brush to scour my hands, arms and elbows until I was almost bleeding. I put on my uniform, ironed crisply with starch, and walked to my part-time job at Sally's Diner. Sally's is a small, legendary black-owned diner up in Harlem.

"Three hundred eight, three hundred nine . . ." I counted each step to work. Every day the count was the same. There were six hundred fifty-three steps from my apartment to my job.

When I arrived, I got right to work. The owner didn't tolerate laziness. He'd fine you one dollar if he saw you slacking off. On this particular day, I was pulling a double shift because I needed extra money. The new year was approaching and I decided that for my resolution I wanted my own apartment. My identical twin sister, Jada, with whom I shared an apartment, got pregnant eight years ago. She'd had a difficult pregnancy and couldn't work for a while so I had to foot the bills. I basically went through my savings. Her pregnancy was traumatic for both of us. We *both* had morning sickness and I felt *every* labor pain. Some scientists say it is common in some identical twins to feel the exact same emotion at the same time. Whether it was fear, lust, happiness, sadness—Jada and I both experienced it. Jada delivered a healthy six-pound baby girl named Joy.

The diner smelled of pork grease and pickles. The aroma sometimes made me nauseous. I couldn't understand how this diner had become so famous. It had the filthiest hygiene standards I've ever encountered, and I wouldn't dare drink a glass of water from there.

"Hi, Jovie," my coworker Allison said as I put on my hairnet.

"What country did the biscuit originate from?" I said in response.

"Goodbye, Jovie," she said, and walked off.

"France," I said underneath my breath, and began working.

My first shift was uneventful and slow. But as the night shift began, I started to get harassed by male patrons who wanted more than what was on the menu. Men are such predators.

"May I take your order?" I asked two male customers.

"I'd like the fried steak, eggs and your telephone number," one boldly stated. I didn't bother to give him eye contact. He continued, "You have the most beautiful lips."

"My lips aren't for sale," I said, while politely moving his hand away from my behind.

"What about the hips and thighs," he retorted.

I didn't respond.

As I walked to get their orders, I could tell they were watching my behind. I took the swish out of my hips so as not to tease them.

It was 10:30 P.M., and we were going to be closing in thirty minutes when a new customer came and sat in my section. He stood approximately six-foot-four with broad, muscular shoulders, small waist, and tree trunk legs and arms. He had hazelnut-colored skin, full lips and a broad nose. He was wearing a vintage blazer, dark blue jeans and a wool cap pulled low. You could tell that he worked out at the gym from the way his biceps bulged through his jacket. His deep, baritone voice gave him character and presence when he ordered and he looked directly in my eyes. For some strange reason, I didn't look away. And the moment felt like déjà vu.

"I'd like the turkey cheeseburger deluxe, extra mayo, and a large iced tea," he said, then smiled. But you could tell he was just being polite, that he wasn't actually smiling at me.

"Does that complete your order?"

"Yes, thank you."

I waited momentarily for a flirtatious remark but nothing happened.

The customer finished his meal, and I placed his $6.85 check on the table. He never bothered to look at it. He just pulled out twenty dollars and said, "Keep the change."

With that he was gone.

For the next week the handsome stranger came into the diner, sat at my table and placed the exact same order. He would always drop twenty dollars on his tab and tell me to keep the change. There was an air of mystery and intrigue surrounding him. On the eighth day, I did something out of character. I said, "What's your name?"

He looked shocked that I'd asked. He was reading the *New York Times* theater section. He stared at me for a long, uncomfortable moment. Embarrassed, I went to walk away, but he grabbed me by my wrist to stop me. He stood up, pulled me in close and whispered, "London. My name's London Phillips."

My heart started to palpitate faster at his touch. There was such a tremendous transfer of energy that I lost my breath. I knew I'd remembered him from somewhere. He was the handsome stranger with the sad eyes who had kissed me as the new year came in last year in England.

"Ah . . . nice name," I stammered.

He smiled bashfully, read my name tag and then said, "Thanks, Jovie."

For the next couple of days I waited for the stranger to return. But he didn't. Maybe I should have told him that we'd met previously in England. But what would that have proved?

London

November 2005

After the breakup between me and Su, I haven't been able to commit to another relationship. Every morning I get up and look inside the dresser drawer and peek at the engagement ring I bought her. I can't get myself to return it. I often wonder how the situation would have turned out if I had been more firm and stopped her. If I had said all the things I wanted to say. Maybe expressed how much in love with her I was and how her actions were truly hurting me. Perhaps instead of challenging her I should have pleaded with her not to go. Often I think about contacting her to rekindle what we had but my stubborn pride won't let me.

That New Year's Eve, it's rumored, she hooked up with

Bugsy. He kept her around for a few weeks then dumped her once his wife found out about her. I've heard that she's since finished law school and is working for a top law firm in lower Manhattan. One part of me would have loved to be at her graduation ceremony. I felt I deserved to be a part of that accomplishment in her life. The other part of me will always resent her for doing what she did best, which was fuck . . . someone other than me. But I'm not a sore loser. I can't knock her hustle. She saw an opportunity and went for it. In the process she gambled and lost a good man.

Despite my love life being in shambles, things are going really well for me in my career. I have a new client that I've been hired to watch. Her name's Jessica and she's an elite, pop star diva. My fee has gone up tremendously, and she pays on time. It's less of a headache than dealing with these wannabe hardcore rappers. They are just illusionists and I'm a bit too old to catch a bullet for someone who instigates violence just to sell a record.

I'm still waiting for my agent to sell my screenplay. I've since written two more that I think are as good as or even better than my first. I've had a lot of time on my hands since I'm not in a relationship. I mean, I have women friends who serve their purpose, but that's it. I'm not looking for anything serious. Besides, I have enough hobbies to keep the average person more than occupied. Between writing screenplays and painting, I hardly have time to do much of anything else.

Tomorrow I have a big day planned. I have to pick up Jessica and take her over to CBS, where she'll sing live on their morning show. Then I'll shoot her over to MTV, where she'll do a live interview and promote her new album. Last, I'll drop her off at the airport; she's flying home to spend her birthday with her mother. But I have today off to do whatever I like.

I thought about going into the diner to see the pretty Jovie, who was unmistakably flirting, but I decided against it. I see something in her eyes that I can't satisfy. There's a yearning in her eyes and sadness, as if she wants to open up but is afraid. Women like her are in Category One. Meaning they deserve more than what I could offer at this time in my life. It's funny because before Su broke my heart, I'd seek out Category One women. Quality women who didn't jump into bed with the next hot rapper. Someone with morals and ethics. Career-minded women. I thought I found that in Su. . . . How wrong was I? Now, I love flighty women. Take-to-bed-on-the-first-night-type women. No kissing, just fucking-type women. That's the type of man I've become.

Since this new client, I've been able to move into a trendy brownstone apartment up in Harlem on 127th Street. I have exposed brick walls, an antique fireplace, cherrywood floors, eighteen-foot ceilings and large storm windows. I'm renting now with the option to buy.

After I jogged around the park, I headed to the gym on 125th Street to work out for a few hours. I had to keep my body buff and in shape. Women love that shit. After my work-out, I noticed the strangest thing. Walking down the street was Jovie, the waitress from the diner, who appeared to be talking to herself. She was so caught up in her conversation she hadn't re-alized she was about to bump straight into me. Quickly, I moved out of her way and then tapped her on her shoulder.

"Oh, gosh!" she screamed and looked at me most peculiarly.

"I'm sorry I frightened you," I said. When she didn't respond and looked at me with a blank expression, I continued, "I'm London. From last week at the diner."

"Oh, yes. London, how are you?"

"I'm doing well, thank you."

"Good. Good."

"Are you okay? You seem a little preoccupied with something."

"I'm fine."

"Were you just talking to yourself?" I couldn't resist asking. She turned bright pink, which confirmed what I already knew.

"Well, my father said it's okay to talk to yourself. You're only crazy if you answer yourself back," she joked. I liked the fact that she could make fun of herself.

"Your father must be a brilliant man." I laughed. "So, where are you headed?"

"I'm on my way to work," she said.

Her oval-shaped eyes were inviting. I looked down at her sexy hips and small waist and lied. "I was just heading over there as well. Do you mind if I walk with you?"

She hesitated for a moment. "Sure . . . sure. That would be fine."

As we walked I took the opportunity to get to know her a little better. She had the softest voice, I had to almost strain to hear her. And her cherubic face gave her an angel-like quality, as if she were untarnished by the cruel world.

"So, what do you do?" I asked. "Besides working at Sally's?"

"I just finished my Bachelor of Arts degree. I'm a singer."

"Really? You don't look the type."

"I don't look like the highly intellectual type? I'm insulted," she joked.

I laughed. "I didn't mean it like that. You don't look like the type of person who'd be able to sing in a room full of people. You seem awfully shy."

"Does my shyness exude?"

"Yes, it does."

"Truthfully, I can *only* sing in a room full of strangers."

"So, let's hear it."

"What?"

"Your voice. Sing for me. I'm a stranger."

"You're not a stranger. I'm your waitress."

"That you are." I smiled. "And I like it. I like you."

I don't know what made me be so forward. But as we walked, I suddenly wanted to sleep with her. I wanted to feel her thighs wrapped tightly around my waist. I usually know within the first five minutes if I'd like a taste of the peach cobbler.

"Did you know that banging your head against a wall for approximately one hour burns a hundred fifty calories?" she said.

"Did I hear you correctly?" I asked.

"Well, did you know that?" she pursued.

"No. No I didn't."

"Just a little bit of trivia for you."

"Okay. . . ."

Once we got to Sally's, Jovie immediately walked in the back to clock in for work. I sat patiently in her area and waited for her to come and take my order. Once I ordered, I watched how she handled herself with the other patrons. I had to control myself a few times from coming to her assistance when men were a little too assertive in trying to get her attention. But she handled them easily. I couldn't help but imagine Su in the same circumstance. Su loved to be adored. She loved attention. She would have grinned, batted her eyes and quite possibly given a few brothers her number. Thinking about her made me lose my appetite, so I didn't even want the turkey cheeseburger I had ordered.

I summoned Jovie and she came over with a smile.

"You're leaving already? You haven't even touched your food. Is everything all right?"

"It was great. I guess I'm just not hungry." I sulked.

"Would you like me to make this to go?"

"Please don't bother," I said as I laid down twenty dollars. When I looked up we made eye contact. "Do you think I could get your number to take you out sometime? I would hate to have to start stalking you by coming here every day?"

She blushed.

"I'm really not dating at the moment," she said softly.

"Then this wouldn't be a date. Just two new friends getting to know each other better. No pressure."

"I really don't know if I could," she said, putting up a front.

"You can. In fact, you *will* get a piece of paper and write your telephone number down so I can call you."

"I don't—"

"Your number," I said with a smile. I loved being assertive with subservient women.

Hesitantly, she looked around, then scrawled her telephone number on the back of my check and scurried off. I wondered briefly if I'd even use her telephone number or why I'd even bothered to ask.

Jovie

I ran home after work to tell Jada about my encounter with the mysterious stranger, but she wasn't there. She'd probably taken Joy out for the day. The apartment was a mess. Our small leather sofa was littered with clothing and toys and the area rug had a cranberry juice stain. I went into the kitchen and there were dishes piled up to the ceiling. As usual, she'd left the lights and television on. Jada thinks I'm her personal maid. But rather than complain, I relish the tasks. I'd have this place spotless in a few hours, only to repeat it all over again once Jada returned home.

After I disinfected the apartment, I went and disinfected myself in the shower. Next, I decided to rearrange my CD and DVD collection in chronological order, a change from the current alphabetical order. As I languished over this task, I didn't hear my telephone ringing until my answering machine picked up.

"Jovie, this is Dr. Welch. You've missed your appointment this week. Please call the office to reschedule."

I decided not to answer that call when the telephone rang again.

"Jovie, I was hoping—" a man's voice said. I immediately picked up.

"Hello?"

"Hello, Jovie?"

"Yes."

"This is London. How are you?"

"I'm doing well, thank you."

"Has anyone ever told you that you have a baby voice over the phone?"

I chuckled. "Numerous times."

"It's driving me crazy," he admitted.

I was a little uneasy with London. He was so sure of himself. He made me feel like he had the right answer for everything.

"Ummm, how's your day going?" I said, changing the subject.

"Better now that I'm talking with you. Listen, what are you doing tonight?"

"I don't have anything planned."

"Now you do. Give me your address and I'll swing by around eight and take you on an *informal* date. As friends . . ."

"Well . . . I . . . don't . . ."

"Yes, you do know. I know that you want to get to know me better. I can see it in your eyes. You're just not good at expressing yourself."

I felt a hot flash go through my body from his cocky attitude. Nevertheless, I gave him my address, realizing I had less than four hours to get ready for my date. Was this a date?

London

I thought I'd resigned myself to a life of noncommittal relationships after Su and I split up. So I don't have a clue as to what possesses me to pursue this girl when I know I'm not looking for anything serious. I can only deduce that I'm craving pain. There is something about Jovie that makes me nostalgic for love.

For some strange reason, I want to impress Jovie tonight. Do something really nice that I know she'll appreciate. Don't get it twisted, if I thought I could take her to BBQ's I would have. But my conscience was telling me to step it up.

I looked outside my window and saw my brother, Lawrence, coming up the street to visit me unannounced. Usually, I'd be glad to see him, but not today. My brother has a draining personality and I have to be mentally prepared for him. And since I wanted to concentrate all my energy on seeing Jovie tonight, I was a little agitated when he rang the doorbell.

Reluctantly, I went to open the door and put on a false smile. "What's up bro?"

"Hey man, I decided to stop by and see if you wanted to go to the gym tonight."

"I already went this morning."

"Aw, man. Why didn't you call me? You know I hate working out alone."

"Quit whining and be a man," I joked.

Immediately, my brother threw a fake left punch and I ducked, weaving around and tossing a right uppercut to his jaw. He jerked his head back as if I had landed a solid one on his chin and he gave me a succession of body shots. We play-boxed for a few minutes before collapsing on the sofa, totally winded.

"Well, I guess this was my workout for the day," Lawrence joked.

"Looking at that gut of yours, I hope you'll reconsider." I went to the refrigerator to get a couple of cold Heinekens. I tossed Lawrence a brew.

As we sat there drinking, I decided to tell him about my date tonight.

"I met this new girl, and I'm taking her out someplace special."

"Why are you telling me?" he said uninterested.

"I don't know. Just because," I reasoned.

"Where are you taking her?"

"Don't know yet. I want it to be someplace with ambiance. You know . . . special."

"Special as in 'I want to hit it later.' Or special as in 'She's a nice girl.'"

"The latter."

"There's no such thing. I may be your older brother, but I'm not phased by women. They're all whores in 'nice girl' clothing.

Su is a prime example of that. That ho-bitch was nothing but a groupie with education."

"Will you knock it off already?" I said, annoyed. "I don't need a lesson on women. I can handle mines. Su fucked up— I'm not fucked up over Su. And I won't make the same mistake twice."

"I know the truth hurts, but if you go into a relationship thinking she's a nice girl, you're already setting yourself up to get hurt. I love you, bro, but I don't have the energy to help you put the pieces back together if this girl breaks your heart."

"You're moving way too fast. We're only having dinner. No one is breaking anyone's heart. If a heart gets broken, then it'll be hers. Because it damn well isn't going to be mine," I boasted.

By the time my brother left, I was drained. I showered quickly and then couldn't decide on what to wear. It was a clear night, but the temperature was frigid. Finally, I decided to wear a pair of dark blue Diesel jeans, hard-bottom shoes, a pullover wool sweater and my three-quarter mink jacket to jazz it up a bit.

I'd decided to take her to Ida Mae's, a nice restaurant in lower Manhattan. From there I didn't have a clue where we'd end up. Hopefully, my place.

Jovie

Why are you doing this?

I don't know, but any minute he's on his way.

So, tell him to leave!

Correct, I'll just say, "Sorry but I can't make it tonight."

No, that won't be any good. You have to completely end it. Tell him you never want to see him again!

He'll think I'm crazy.

Are you?

Of course, I'm not crazy. Crazy is as crazy does.

I laughed hysterically as I paced around the living room. I'd just meticulously arranged the candles on the mantel and I wasn't quite pleased with the job. I decided to rearrange them.

Yea, though I walk through the valley of the shadow of death, I will fear no evil: for thou art with me. Thy rod and thy staff—

Shut up!

You startled me. I thought—

A knock at the front door interrupted me. I ran to the door, hesitated for a moment and then opened it slowly. There stood London, looking absolutely breathtaking.

"Hey, beautiful," he said with a smile.

"Hi, please come in."

He entered and took a quick glance around my small apartment.

"It's so organized in here I'm almost afraid to have a seat. I don't want to move anything out of place," he said.

"Don't be silly. Please sit down. I'll be with you in a moment."

"Do you live alone?"

"Why do you ask that?

"Because I heard you talking to someone when I arrived."

"Oh, that . . . I was on the telephone. But I do live here with my twin sister, Jada, and her daughter, Joy."

"You have a twin?"

"Yes."

"Are you identical or fraternal?"

"We're identical."

"When I was younger I always wanted a twin so I could play mind games on girls. You know, kid stuff. Did you and your sister ever play games with men?"

"I beg your pardon? I don't quite know what kind of games we could play."

"Oh come on . . . you mean to tell me you guys never played games with the guys you were dating? Maybe you'd sleep with a guy then have your sister sleep with him for fun."

I crinkled up my nose and thought that maybe I'd made a mistake in agreeing to go out with London. "Not only is that vulgar, but it's childish," I admonished.

"Perhaps. But I wasn't talking about yesterday. I was thinking more along the lines of when you two were a little younger."

"No!" I yelled, and he looked at me in the most peculiar fashion.

"Hey, Jovie, I'm sorry if I offended you. I guess women really don't think like men. I didn't mean for this to start off on the wrong foot."

"Your comment was a little offensive."

"I understand. I was just being facetious. Will you let me make this up to you?"

"What do you suggest?"

"I'll show you the best time you've had in a long time. I promise you that," he said confidently.

I relaxed, smiled, and said, "You better."

London

Jovie seems a bit conservative and timid, yet there's a fire simmering in her veins, waiting to be ignited by some inappropriate remark or gesture. I'm starting to wonder if her demure, fragile persona was just an act. Still, I was curious enough to continue to pursue her. Once we got to the restaurant, she seemed to have loosened up a bit.

"Do you drink?" I asked.

"No."

"Neither do I," I lied. "I don't drink, smoke or do drugs. What about you . . . do you smoke?"

"No, but my sister does."

"And I thought you said you two were identical," I joked.

"We are." She laughed, and I realized she had the most beautiful smile and perfect teeth. "My sister is everything I'm not. She's sophisticated, smart and a risk taker."

"Tell me about you," I asked.

"What do you want to know?"

"Your likes. Dislikes. How you were as a little girl. Things like that."

"I don't have any history," she explained.

"What? That's ridiculous. Everyone has a history."

"Well, maybe. I just don't remember mine."

"I'll let you get away with that for tonight, seeing how shy you are."

"Did you know that flutterby was the original name for the butterfly?"

I smiled. This one was definitely cut from a different cloth. She was amusing.

"I must admit that I have never come across that tidbit of information."

"How unfortunate for you." She smiled.

"No, how fortunate for me to have met you," I teased. I could see her get uneasy and shift in her seat.

"Will you excuse me? I need to go to the restroom to wash up."

"We've only been here thirty minutes, and you've washed up twice already. Are you seeing someone in the men's room? Because if that's it, tell that brother I don't plan on giving up your company without a fight!"

She smiled politely and walked to the restroom anyway. I

watched as her hips seductively swayed from side to side. As if she could tell I was watching, she took the swish from her hips and walked straight. For most, her actions wouldn't have turned them on. For me, it did just that. I wanted her even more.

When she came back, she started in with a few questions.

"So, now that you know all about me, tell me something about you, London. What do you do?"

"I know nothing about you." I smiled. "But I'll answer your question anyway. I'm a bodyguard for Jessica, the pop star."

"Wow! That must be interesting."

"It pays the bills. But my real passion is writing. For years I've been writing screenplays and having my agent shop them around for buyers. I can almost feel that I'm getting close to closing a deal with a major production company."

"Awesome," she said, encouraging me to continue.

"Yeah, my goal is to make quality films starring African-American actors doing more than just being the villain or co-median."

"You must be so proud of yourself."

"Well yes and no. Yes, I'm proud that I haven't quit. And no, because I haven't made it yet."

"But you will."

"How can you be so sure?" I challenged.

"Because you have determination."

I don't know if it was the way she encouraged me, her sexy mouth or her mesmerizing eyes, but suddenly I had this strong urge to paint her.

"When we're done here, I'd like you to come back to my place. I'd like to paint you."

"Paint me? As in a portrait?" she asked.

"Yes. I'm very good. And when I'm done, just to prove I'm a stand-up kind of guy, I'll give you your painting."

"I'm too shy," she said, resisting.

"I'll make you feel comfortable. I promise. And if you're not comfortable, just say the word and we'll stop."

Reluctantly, Jovie agreed and after dinner we headed back over to my place. I noticed that inside my car she was counting each traffic light. Nothing loud or piercingly obvious but I noticed nevertheless.

When we entered my place, I took her coat and went around lighting candles and starting the fireplace. I then put on *The Very Best of John Coltrane.* I felt good about how the evening was progressing.

I walked over to Jovie, who was practically hugging the sofa. I guessed she was nervous.

"Here, relax," I soothed, and began to massage her tense shoulders. She resisted for a moment, but soon my strong massage soothed her and she submitted to my touch. After about twenty minutes, I walked her over to the fireplace and we sat on the floor. I wanted so desperately to kiss her, but I was afraid that I'd push her away. I didn't want this to be about sex. I wanted it to be about art. I really wanted to paint her curves. . . .

"Are you relaxed?" I asked.

"A little. Are we going to begin?"

"Soon," I said, and ran into my bedroom to get a canvas and my paints. When I came back into the living room, in my most nonassertive voice I said, "I'd like to do a nude painting of you. Nothing vulgar or intrusive."

"Pardon me?" She gasped and clutched her neck.

"I'd like to paint you . . . naked. As I said earlier, you can keep the painting once I'm done," I replied.

"I don't even know you, and you want me to take off all my clothing?"

"This isn't what you think. I'm an artist, Jovie. You're an artist. It's all about the craft," I said and meant it.

"London, I'm sorry but I can't. This is not what I do."

"Jovie, you can trust me. I'll turn around and you can tell me when you're ready. Please do this one thing for me. I know you can do it because all your life you've always wanted to do something spontaneous. Like your sister, Jada," I said persuasively.

She hesitated for a moment, but I could feel her wrestling with the idea in her head.

"Please turn around," she whispered, and I did as I was told. Soon, I heard her clothing hit the floor. And it truly wasn't a sexual thing at that instant. But I had no idea what it would become or what the night would have in store.

Jovie

As I stood there peeling off each piece of clothing inside the apartment of a guy I had just met, I couldn't describe the overwhelming feeling of freedom I was experiencing. I felt like an exhibitionist. I felt anonymous. Was it easier to reveal yourself to a perfect stranger than someone you've grown accustomed to? All my life I've been sweet Jovie. A do-gooder with a heart of gold. Now I was teetering on a wild, daring edge. A side that I've only known vicariously through my sister's escapades.

Once I was completely naked, I covered my sacred parts as best as I could with my hands.

"Are you done?" he asked.

"Yes," I said, my voice barely a whisper.

He turned around slowly so as not to startle me. When his eyes rested on my naked body, I felt tingly inside.

"Here, have a seat right in front of the fireplace. The lighting is perfect," he said, and gently touched my arm to usher me into position. I trembled as his masculine hands guided my movements.

Once he was behind his easel, I felt a little more relaxed because our positions identified what this was really about. I sat and waited impatiently, eager to take a peek at his creation. As his eyes moved from me to his canvas, I wondered if I'd be pleased with the outcome. Was he truly an artist honing his craft or was he a seducer using a clever trick to get a young woman into his bed?

To keep my mind distracted from my nakedness, I began talking. "Did you know that some scientists believe it's possible for identical twins to feel the exact same emotion at the same time?"

"Uh-huh," he responded, distracted.

"When my sister was in labor I felt every labor pain," I pursued.

"That's nice . . . ," he replied, unaware of what I'd just said.

Once he was done, after what seemed like hours, he turned the canvas around and I gasped.

"That's . . . not . . . me . . . ," I stammered.

"Of course that is." He grinned. "This is how I see you."

"She's gorgeous."

"And what are you?"

I looked away and suddenly realized I was still naked.

"I better put my clothes back on."

"What's the rush?" he said, and before I could object he was next to me on the floor. He gently began to kiss me. His tongue was sensual as he explored the inside of my mouth. His large hands discovered my breasts and I moaned in pleasure. His kisses were making me too weak to resist his advances and the wine I drank at the restaurant had me feeling light-headed. I was lost in the moment.

"Come with me," he breathed.

With each step I felt more trepidation. I counted my steps to London's bedroom. There were thirty-eight steps from the living room to his bed.

He stood in front of me and I stared directly into his broad chest. He took his hand and lifted my chin up, and kissed my eyes, my cheeks, and then my lips. He sucked my tongue as he murmured soft words. Before I knew it, he was undressed, his long, thick penis challenging me to get to know it better.

He picked me up, placed me on his king-size bed and gently laid me down. To my delight, his bed was covered in crisp white linen. Tenderly, he placed each of my toes in his mouth and sucked until I felt a prickly feeling run down the back of my neck and down my spine.

Why haven't I stopped him yet?

As his tongue playfully flickered up and down on my nipples they grew harder than cement. Gradually, he moved up, and his warm tongue explored my earlobes. As he nibbled, I sighed from pleasure. I wanted him.

Why am I doing this?

London began tasting my whole body with his tongue. Finally, he parted my legs and moved in between my thighs. He playfully sucked, nibbled and then took his two fingers to separate my nether lips. He then began to suck my clitoris, murmuring, "You taste so good. . . ."

My legs involuntarily shuddered and I screamed out. He paused to reach over and grab an electric massager out of his nightstand. He turned on both the vibrator and heat functions.

"Hold still," he breathed as he began to massage my clitoris. The heat stimulated me and my legs involuntarily began to shake. Hot waves came cascading through my body and my pelvis began thrusting. I was making love to the massager and London was watching intently.

"It feels good?"

"Oh, yes," I crooned. He turned the machine up another notch. It vibrated faster and hotter.

"How does that feel?"

"It feels so go-o-o-o-d," I whispered.

"I can't hear you," he said as he moved the massager in circular motions. "Do you want me to stop?"

"Please, don't stop . . . ," I pleaded.

Sweat poured off of my body as it became an inferno. Strong waves overcame me and I screamed while I climaxed. Hot juices came seeping from inside me and onto his sheets.

I could tell this excited London. He moved up my body and steadied himself to enter me. I held my breath and squeezed my eyes tight in anticipation of what I was about to receive. As London applied pressure, it took a moment before he was able to penetrate my walls. He pushed hard and sank deep into my cave.

"Ah-h-h-h-h," I moaned as a sharp pain shot through my body. Tiny teardrops escaped my eyes as he applied steady pressure. He moved up and down skillfully as I lay there in shock.

"Move," he whispered.

"What?"

"Move. Make love to me back. Move your hips," he suggested.

I followed his lead and thrust my hips back and forth to complement his rhythm. We moved in sync and I wrapped my legs around his waist tightly. Then London grabbed both my legs and positioned my heels to my butt and placed my arms underneath his armpits so I was in the frog's position. This was unbearably painful but I refused to stop. This position allowed London to go deeper inside me. He dug his hands in my loose curls and pulled tightly as he began to thrust harder. Tiny tears began to escape my eyes and drip onto his hands.

"Let's switch positions," I said breathlessly.

He pulled out of me and turned me over. I winced from the pain in my legs. I was lying flat on my stomach. Waiting.

"Jovie, what are you doing?" he asked. "Why are you lying there like that? Get in position. Get on all fours."

Quickly, I did as I was told and jumped in that position. I'm glad he couldn't see my embarrassment. He gently entered me from the back as he grabbed hold of my hips for support. He pumped in and out rapidly and I held on to the headboard for support. His large balls slapped my ass as if to chastise me.

"I'm . . . going . . . to . . . cum," he blurted out as he pumped in and out rapidly. Hot juices burst into my vagina and I felt a tingly sensation as we both climaxed. We both collapsed on his bed, breathing heavily and sweating profusely.

So, this is it?

I immediately felt empty. We lay there in silence and the moment felt awkward. Embarrassed, I tried to jump up to shower away my indiscretions, but London pulled me back down to the bed.

"Where are you going?" he asked.

"To clean up," I whispered.

"I'd prefer you stay here with me for a moment," he said, and pulled me in really close. As I lay in his arms, large tears escaped my eyes and dropped on his chest. Before long, he realized I was crying.

"Jovie, what's wrong, baby-girl? Why are you crying?"

"I don't want to talk about it."

"I thought this was what you wanted."

"I did."

"Then what? Did I hurt you?"

"That's not it," I sobbed.

"Do you think I'm judging you? Because I'm not."

"You may not be judging me. But I'm judging me. I've waited twenty-four years to make love, and I do it with a stranger. How pathetic is that?"

London jumped up in surprise and looked me directly in my eyes. "You were a virgin?" he asked incredulously.

"Uh-huh," I said, and shook my head.

"But how? Why? I mean, why me? I don't even know you. I mean . . . not like that. I'm flattered . . . I'm just confused."

"Look, I can't understand this, either. This is hardly how I pictured my first time. And you're hardly the vision I've been seeking for years."

"But you should have told me. I would have been easier on you. Was I too rough?"

"Truthfully, you were perfect," I said, and closed my eyes and wondered if I'd ever see London again.

"You were great, too," he said, but his voice told another story.

He embraced me and wouldn't let me go. After a while we both drifted off into a peaceful sleep. Somewhere in the middle of the night, I showered away most of my shame. Softly I crept out of London's brownstone, leaving a short poem for him.

London

Last night Jovie and I made love, and it scared the shit out of me. When she told me she was a virgin, I nearly lost it. Had I known that, I would never have slept with her. I'm at a place in my life where sex is casual and entertaining. I love not having any strings attached. Sleeping with someone who gives you their virginity—there's sure to be problems. And why me? As irresistible as I claim to be, I realized that I didn't exactly sweep her off her feet in twenty-four hours. Did I?

Now when I think about her actions and movements, I can assess that it was her first time. She was a little stiff and unsure. The more I thought about last night, the more intrigued I became with her. Why didn't she wait to be with someone who would have appreciated her? Don't women want their first time to be special? Romantic?

This morning I'd woken up with intentions never to call Jovie again. Then I smelled her scent on my sheets . . .

After I'd showered, I'd gotten over her again—until I went in the kitchen and found a poem scribbled on a piece of paper.

I let you in for a moment and we made a love song
Our bodies gently hummed rhythms and melodies
As the intense feelings lingered on
A sharp, B minor, C flat . . .
I'll let you have your way with me
But only if you'd like that

This girl was tugging at my heart, and it was unsettling. After taking hours to come up with the right approach to calling Jovie, I remembered that she'd left her portrait. I wrapped it up in a beautiful burgundy crushed-velvet covering and tied it with a black beaded ribbon and headed over to her place. I was hoping that I wasn't being intrusive by dropping by uninvited.

It was a bit late when I arrived, and I was sure she'd be home from work. I could hear loud music blaring from the apartment, so I had to bang hard to be heard.

"Who is it," an aggressive voice yelled.

"It's London."

"Who?"

"London."

The door swung open and there stood Jovie with a blank expression. She had on a pair of skintight Seven jeans, a pair of high-heeled Prada boots and a black turtleneck T-shirt that read: MELODRAMATIC BRAT, which complemented her small upper-body frame.

"What do you want?" she asked. She looked somewhat different. Wild.

"I came to apologize for last night and to bring over your painting."

"You must be looking for Jovie," she said.

"You're not Jovie," I said.

She put her hands on her hips, "You've got to be joking. Come in."

It was then that I realized this must be Jada, Jovie's twin sister. She pranced around the apartment like a panther. There was confidence in her steps as she led me to the living room. Jovie was correct when she had said they were identical. The only difference was their attitudes.

"So what's going on with you and my little sister?"

"Little sister?"

"She's two minutes younger than I am. So, again, what's the deal with you and Jovie? She came in all flustered, and now you're here bearing gifts and talking apologies."

"It's really a situation Jovie and I need to deal with."

"Listen, if you think I'm going to sit back and watch my sister get her heart broken by some predator—"

"You don't know me!" I yelled.

"And I don't want to know you. But if you don't want to get on my bad side, you'd better back off my sister!" she yelled back. We were in her apartment having a shouting match. This girl really thought she could tell *me* what to do. I'm a grown-ass man. And her sister is grown as well.

"Look, I don't take kindly to threats but I understand where you're coming from. You don't have anything to fear. I'm a good catch and one day I'll make the right woman happy. If your sister plays her cards right, she just may be the one," I reasoned.

"The one? All that means is that she'll be first in line to get her heart broken."

"You've got me mixed up. I'm not that dude," I said convincingly, forgetting about all the women I'd hurt in my past.

"I don't know if you've noticed, but Jovie isn't like your average girl."

"Of course I've noticed. I've noticed that she's someone special. Not average. And I like her."

"She's vulnerable. Did you know she's a virgin?" she spat, and her words made me feel guilty.

"That's her personal business, and I don't think you need to be broadcasting that around."

"Well, the last asshole she was dating dumped her because he couldn't wait. Are you going to do that to her? Because if you are, you should just leave right now and never come back."

"I'd never do that."

"That's what they all say. I'm begging you to leave my sister alone."

The more Jada pleaded with me to leave Jovie alone, the more it made me want to pursue her.

"Look, where's Jovie? I need to speak to her," I said, quite annoyed.

"She's not here!"

"Obviously!"

I left Jovie's painting and decided to head back home. I'd meet up with Jovie tomorrow. Hopefully, she'd be working at the diner. I understood her sister's concerns and why she was so protective of her. But Jovie was an adult. Her sister needed to recognize that.

Jovie

"What's your fantasy?" London asked. He'd called me moments ago to apologize for the other night.

"I . . . I . . . never thought about it. I don't have one," I lied.

"Of course you have. Everyone has. How did you imagine your first time? I'm a visionary person. Describe it for me."

"You're not interested in that."

"Then why am I asking?"

"Well, I . . . um . . . wanted my first time to be in Aspen. We'd just come in from skiing and snow would have just begun to fall. He'd light a fire, and we'd drink hot chocolate and toast marshmallows by an open fireplace. Then he'd lay me down on an exotic rug and make love to me until the sun came up the next day. I'd feel safe . . . loved. We'd fall asleep in each other's arms and in the morning he'd still be there."

"That's it? That's your fantasy? There's nothing complicated about that."

"That depends on who the guy in the picture is."

"Are you disappointed that the guy was me?" he asked.

"I have no regrets."

"But are you disappointed that the guy was me?" he pursued.

"Shocked, not disappointed. I'm shocked, that's all," I explained.

"Fair enough answer. Listen, be ready tonight, same time." Click.

London arrived on time with a beautiful arrangement of long-stemmed yellow roses.

"These are for you," he said as he handed the bundle to me. "Yellow is for friendship."

I grinned. "They're beautiful."

"Are you all right? You seem a little down," he observed.

"I'm just a little tired, that's all."

"Well, I was hoping that we could start over. Put on the brakes and slow it down."

"I'd love that," I agreed.

"Me too."

"Did you know that the first home TV set was displayed in 1928 and the screen size was three by four inches?"

He chuckled. "What does that have to do with anything?"

"It's just an interesting piece of information that not many people know about."

"Well, let me thank you for enlightening me."

"Are you humoring me, Mr. Phillips?" I asked.

"Only if you want me to."

London drove us to 57th Street in his black Nissan Maxima. There he got out and blindfolded me.

"What are you doing?" I asked. As the silk scarf lay across

my eyes and shut out the light, my adrenaline started pumping. The excitement was suffocating me, and I felt light-headed.

"I'm getting to know you better. I should have done this sooner."

Holding my hand, London led me a few yards away from the car. He helped me to what felt like a carriage and assisted me up into the seat. I could hear a horse kicking its feet.

"Where are we going?" I asked.

"To Aspen," he replied, and took off my blindfold.

We both sat back in the carriage and snuggled up underneath the blanket. I felt safe. The horse did a slow trot around Central Park, and London and I had an intimate conversation.

"Jovie, why me? I keep asking myself that question over and over. If you'd waited so long, why not hold out for marriage, or at least the right guy? What was it that you saw in me that allowed you to give away something so precious to someone you just met?"

"It seems odd but I can't explain it. I think I spent so much time guarding my heart and saving myself for the right person that maybe I realized the right person is who you make him to be. If I have a hundred years to ponder, I'll never be able to explain my actions. But I swear to you I don't have any regrets."

"I'm glad you don't have any regrets. But I would like to know what you are looking for. I've just come out of a long-term relationship where I was hurt. I'm not looking for anything serious. Just maybe a great friendship, and I don't know if you can handle that."

"Someone hurt you?"

"Yes, she did."

I tried to listen intently to London, but the rhythm of each trot from the horse distracted me. Cluck, cluck, cluck. . . . I counted each step. Refocusing my attention on London, I said, "Isn't it usually the other way around?"

"No one is exempt from having their heart broken."

"I'll never break your heart," I promised. He looked at me, then kissed the inside of my palm.

"You are so sweet, Jovie. I'm going to start calling you my future."

I didn't respond.

After the romantic carriage ride, we went back to London's apartment. At his front door, again he blindfolded me and my heart raced from anticipation. Once we were inside his living room, he took the blindfold off. He'd set up my winter wonderland in Aspen. He had the fireplace going and the reddish-orange flames looked so inviting. He also had marshmallows, hot chocolate, and a snowflake shaker.

"Shake it," he boasted. "That'll give you your snowfall."

I squealed with delight.

We sat down on the blanket in front of the fireplace and toasted marshmallows and drank hot chocolate. We talked until the sun came up, just getting to know each other. To my surprise London was a perfect gentleman. He never laid a hand on me. And when we awoke in the morning, London was still there holding me in his arms.

London

For the first time in a long time, it wasn't about sex for me. I genuinely wanted to get to know the quirky Jovie. She made me smile, and I wholeheartedly had respect for her. She had begun to fill my void and mend my broken heart. We started spending all of our spare time together, not to mention countless hours on the telephone with her sexy voice seducing me.

It's only been a few weeks, but I feel like I've known her longer. Tonight was the first night that she allowed me to spend the night over at her house. We both agreed not to make love again until she was ready. So far, she hasn't given me the green light. I'm so horny I almost jerked off in the shower. Then I realized that I was taking this whole relationship a tad bit far. There's no reason I can't call one of my jump-offs over and smash her out quickly. What Jovie doesn't know can't hurt her. Then I thought about my baby's soft skin and dreamy smile and realized I'd have to wait. The next time she and I make love, I do want it to be special.

I woke up this morning in Jovie's bed, but she wasn't there. Instead, she'd left a short poem.

I watch you while you're sleeping and breathe in your scent

I rush to fall asleep in your arms and race to wake back
*   up in them*
I appreciate your strong embrace and savor your sweet
*   taste*
You've awakened me . . . I feel alive

I must admit I'm not a big fan of poetry, but everything Jovie does excites me. I jumped out of bed and hopped into the shower. The steam was so thick, I couldn't see my hands. Moments later, Jovie came in from behind and started lathering my back. I jumped because she startled me. She was completely naked except for a pair of four-inch black high heels. Her perky breasts, small waist and round hips had me mesmerized. She looked like an angel.

"What are you doing?" I asked in astonishment. She didn't say a word. She began to aggressively massage my balls in a circular motion that drove me crazy.

"I thought we'd wait," I protested, but she reached up and slid her tongue inside my mouth. We began kissing passionately. My body was yearning desperately to enter her again. She arched her back as I leaned over and sucked her breasts until her nipples were erect. My tongue flicked rapidly as she held on to the shower door for support. Then I hoisted her up by her hips and wrapped her shapely legs around my waist and entered her as gently as my dick allowed. To my amazement she took all my dick and rode me aggressively. Her pussy was so wet I could hear it talking to me, telling me to go hard.

"Is it good?" I crooned. She said nothing, but I could tell she was enjoying it from her facial expressions.

She rode me expertly until I put her down, turned her around and entered her from behind. She leaned over and held on to the shower walls for support. The hot water from the shower was pouring down our backs and I pulled Jovie under further and wet her hair. She looked so sexy submerged in water, I lost my mind.

We made love three times from the shower to her bed. The last time I came so hard that I was physically drained and exhausted. When I thought it couldn't get any better, Jovie, my *sweet* Jovie, went down and engulfed my penis with her mouth. She licked up and down my shaft and sucked my dick like it was her favorite lollipop. I screamed—"Jovie!"—as I came in her mouth. My hot juices flowed with such a force I felt a tingling from my head to my toes.

We lay in bed for a long moment, just breathing. It was eerily quite. *Jovie is certainly a keeper,* I thought. I hit the jackpot without even searching. She just fell into my arms. God was definitely looking out for a brother.

"London," she said sweetly.

"Yes, baby-girl."

"Jovie will never forgive you for fucking her sister."

My heart sank. "What?"

"Don't act as if you didn't have a clue."

"Jada?"

"The one and only," she gloated.

"What the fuck is wrong with you?"

"No, what the fuck is wrong with you? You knew I wasn't Jovie. You knew that innocent, boring, inexperienced Jovie wasn't making love to you that good. But you chose to pretend."

"Jada, what's wrong with you?! Why are you trying to ruin it for your sister? I care about her, and I want to make it work. Please don't tell her about this," I begged, to no avail.

"That's exactly what I'm going to do!"

"You come in here and spread your legs like peanut butter and want me to take responsibility for your actions!"

"*Our* actions!"

"You're crazy."

"My work here is done," she said. She stood up still naked, arched her back and put her hands on her sexy hips. I was drawn to her immediately. I was recharged like the Energizer bunny. I jumped up and dug my fingers into her hair. I pulled her neck back and kissed her roughly. We fell back onto the bed, Jovie's bed, and had fast, frenzied, passionate sex. She reminded me of Su. Wild *and* sexy in bed. . . .

Hours later, I ran home to shower off Jada's juices. I felt so guilty and low. The first time—shame on Jada. The second time—shame on me. How can I even look Jovie in the eye after what happened with me and her sister? And where was Jovie anyway? She never did come home.

Jovie

After work today, I had to rush to the Lime Light Café for rehearsal. It's a trendy jazz and blues bar. The owner is going to let me do a set, three songs a night, for the holiday season to make extra money. Hopefully, I'll get discovered. A lot of famous people come down to the café. The owner used to be a singer on Motown Records in the 1960s.

I warmed up with a cappella sets of notes until my voice was strong. I then cued the house band to let them know that I was ready. They were a tremendously talented mix of men who collectively had fifty years of music experience among them. They also knew how grateful I was for this opportunity.

"Let's start with 'Good Morning Heartache.' Billie Holiday in A minor."

As I belted out the words, I saw a shadowy figure slide to the back of the café. He lingered there, his eyes penetrating mines as I sang.

" 'I've got those Monday blues,' " I belted out. " 'Straight through Sunday blues . . .' "

After my set, the elusive stranger clapped enthusiastically. That's when I realized it was London. I ran to him immediately.

"What are you doing here?" I squealed.

"I wanted to come see my baby-girl."

"Why didn't you tell me?"

"Because you wouldn't have let me come."

"You're right about that," I agreed. "So, now that you've heard me, what do you think?"

"I think you have the most beautiful, compassionate, soulful voice I've ever heard. I am so very proud of you."

"You've never heard a voice like mine before?" I asked.

"Never. Your voice is much too unique."

"Not even in England?"

"England?" he repeated, and within moments his face lit up. "That was you!"

I giggled. "Yup. The one and only."

"Whatever happened that night? I'm surprised we didn't hook up then," he said, trying to put the pieces back together.

"You were much too drunk that night."

"Yeah. I think I scared you off. Didn't I? That's right . . . I kissed you just as the new year came in."

"I almost caught a panic attack."

"I was right!" he boasted. "Didn't I say that whomever you spend New Year's Eve with is most likely the person you'll spend the year with. Look at how fate intervened and brought you back into my life."

"So this is fate?"

"I told you that you were my future."

"Thanks, London," I said, and kissed him. It felt wonderful to be in a relationship with someone who cared about me. I didn't realize I was missing companionship until now. I felt so complete.

"Are you almost done here?" he asked, avoiding eye contact. I got a sense that something was troubling him.

"Yes, I just need to see the owner quickly, and then I'm done. London, are you all right? You seem a little down. As if something is bothering you or on your mind."

"No, no. I'm fine. We need to celebrate tonight."

"Whoa, a celebration! I can't wait. I'll get my coat and I'm ready."

London

At first I couldn't look Jovie in her beautiful eyes. The guilt was killing me. One part of me wanted to share my future with Jovie—that's why I'm taking her out to share in my celebration. The other part of me keeps reliving the wild sex I had with her twin sister, Jada. What's a man to do when he has the best of both worlds at his fingertips?

I took Jovie to the Chin Chin Café, a pricy Chinese restaurant on Third Avenue in Manhattan. I loved how appreciative she was at every little thing I did for her. Things that most women took for granted. She loved that I held doors open for her, helped her with her coat, pulled out her seat. Things that a chivalrous man should do. She even thanked me for the dinners and thanked me again when I cooked her dinner. She was always leaving me a cute note or poem when I would least expect it, either under my pillow, in my suit jacket pocket, my wallet. She was very creative, and almost overnight, I'd fallen for her.

We haven't made love again, so I know what this relationship is and is not about.

When the waiter came around, I ordered the best champagne the house had in stock.

"But you don't drink," Jovie admonished.

"Neither do you. But for tonight, I'd like to make a toast to celebrate."

Once we ordered and the waiter poured our champagne, I leaned over and proposed a toast, "To the sale of my first screenplay and many, many more . . ."

"Oh, London! You've done it! I knew you would!" she cheered. "I'm so proud of you!"

She came around to my side of the table and planted a fat, wet kiss on my cheek and then whispered in my ear, "You are the most talented, amazing, strong-minded man I've ever met."

After dinner I took Jovie to a local billiards hall to play some pool. I wanted to show off my skills.

"Do you play?" I asked.

"Not since I was a little girl. Jada and I would play bumper pool at the local youth center. I'm sure this can't be much more difficult."

"It is, but I'll be easy on you."

"Don't do me any favors," she sassily replied, and I saw a glimpse of Jada's personality. For a moment I wondered if they were playing the exact game I asked Jovie about weeks ago. The one where they'd switch places for a date.

"You wanna put a little wager on that? Don't hurt yourself.

You know I just increased my bank account a few digits," I bragged.

"If I win you'll have to promise to spend Christmas with me," she said, and lowered her eyes.

"That's not a real bet. I was going to do that anyway. Let's make it hard. If you win we'll spend Christmas *and* New Year's Eve together. And if I win, you're going to have to forgive me for at least one mistake I may have made or may make."

"What are you talking about? What do I need to forgive you for?" She seemed to be panicking.

"Nothing yet. But you never know. And you know how women are. I may forget your birthday or something. With this, I have security." I smiled.

"All right, then it's a bet. I take my bets seriously," she warned.

"And so do I!" I agreed.

"What year were Bonnie and Clyde murdered?" she asked.

"Uh, here we go. I'd have to say 1960."

"Wrong!" she said as she smashed the white ball into the triangle-shaped setup. "1934."

As the game got intense, I knew immediately I had been hustled. Jovie slammed each ball in each pocket she called. She skillfully emptied the table, leaving only my odd balls swaying.

"Double or nothing?" I asked.

"You ain't said nothing but a word!"

I played my heart out but was no match for my talented Jovie. She whipped on me mercilessly and I enjoyed every minute of it. I was hoping to win, so I'd be able to use my exemption. But she probably wouldn't have honored it anyway, considering what I wanted her to forgive. And her winning wasn't so bad. Spending Christmas *and* New Year's Eve with her should be great. I'm actually looking forward to it.

Jovie

"One thousand one, one thousand two . . ." I counted the drops of water leaking from the faucet in my bathroom to calm my nerves. If I hadn't, there was no telling what I would have done to myself by now. I'd been in the bathroom for six hours. I was waiting for London to call but he hadn't. Why do men never call when they say they will? Could he be seeing someone else? I never should have forced the holiday on him. Jada said men hate that.

I realized I couldn't stay in there another moment. I needed to go to London's apartment and see if he was seeing someone else. I needed to know. I got dressed quickly and headed over to his place. I'd make it there just before he should be arriving from work. I put on a pair of Nike air trainers, blue jeans, a GAP sweatshirt and trench coat because I could see that it was about to rain.

I arrived at London's brownstone in fifteen minutes and rang the doorbell to make sure he wasn't there. No answer. Then I waited across the street and just watched. Two hours later I was still waiting. As the heavy rain fell on my weakening shoulders and my eyes were blinded from the downpour, I saw a familiar figure standing under a large, stylish umbrella having a chat with a beautiful woman. My pace was hesitant as I walked across the street and startled my unsuspecting boyfriend.

"London?" I whispered.

"Je-sus, Jovie, you startled me. What are you doing here?" I didn't answer him. I couldn't. The woman got the message.

"Okay, London, thanks for letting me share your umbrella. I'll talk to you soon," she said.

"Give Michael my best," London replied, and then turned to me.

"What was that about?" he accused.

"I thought . . . ," I stammered.

"How long have you been out here? You're soaked. Come on, let's go in," he said, and ushered me into his place. "Look, in the future if I'm not here, I keep a spare key underneath my rug. Feel free to come inside and wait for me."

Once inside, he stripped me naked and gave me some warm pajamas to put on and put me in his bed. Then he made me a cup of hot tea with honey and lemon. I was still shivering when London crawled in the bed and gently brushed my hair and massaged my temples.

"You can trust me, Jovie. I won't hurt you," he said soothingly. "There is no one else."

I just shook my head and snuggled up closer to his chest. He smelled so good. I felt foolish for not being more trustful and I wanted to make it up to him. When I gently ran my hand over his six-pack stomach, I knew I wanted to take this farther. We started kissing playfully at first. Then the kisses became more passionate and softer.

"I want you to make love to me," I murmured as I reached for his boxers. But he pushed my hand away.

"Come here," he said, and pulled me in closer to snuggle underneath his strong arm. "I don't want it to be this way with you. I really want to wait and make it special. I have something in mind . . . just let me be a man, so I can truly please you the way you deserve."

"But I'm ready now," I pleaded.

"Soon . . . soon enough we'll be together."

London

Christmas Eve 2005

I'm feeling really good about how my life is progressing. Tomorrow I'm spending the day with Jovie, my new lady, and I'm elated. So far her sister hasn't gone through with her threat to tell Jovie that we had sex. I guess she realizes Jovie could easily accept that on my part it was a mistake. But what about Jada? How did she just slip and fall on my dick?

I'd gone out earlier in the week and purchased Jovie a designer pocketbook from Coach. I usually see a lot of men buying these bags for their ladies at the holidays. Su wouldn't have been caught dead with a Coach pocketbook. Not that Jovie deserves less than Su did, but with Jovie I know she likes me for who I am. Not for the guy I'm about to become.

"Hey, Jovie," I called her at home. "How's it going, babygirl?"

"Wonderful. I can't wait to see you tomorrow. I'm going to bake you gingerbread cookies," she squealed.

"Baby, I don't eat gingerbread cookies." I laughed.

"Neither do I. But I wanted to show you that I can bake."

"Jovie, when we get married, I'm going to hire a cook so you won't have to," I joked, only she took it seriously.

"What did you say?"

"What?"

"You just mentioned marriage."

"It was a joke, Jovie. That's all, so don't go putting any crazy ideas in your head. I'm not popping the question on Christmas." I laughed.

"You better not because I would be turning you down on Christmas!" she retorted.

"You wouldn't dare . . ."

"Wanna bet?"

"I've had enough of your bets." I chuckled. "Listen, I'm going out in a couple of hours with my brother and a few of my friends to a local bar to watch them get drunk and talk smack. What time are you coming over tomorrow?"

"Around noon," she said, and blew a kiss through the

phone. "Have fun tonight." She was so adorable. She does the simplest thing like blow a kiss through the phone, and I get absolutely weak in my knees.

It was still early when I got off the phone with Jovie. Since I had a few hours before I had to meet my brother, I decided to take a nap. I was sleeping peacefully when I heard a firm knock at my door. I assumed it was Lawrence and ran and opened the door. Only it wasn't my brother. It was Jada. I could tell it was her and not Jovie from the scowl in her eyes.

How the hell does she know where I live? I thought.

"What do you want, Jada? And I know it's you from the broom you just climbed off," I said, blocking her from entering my apartment. As she stood there I couldn't help but smell her mesmerizing perfume. It was driving me crazy. She had this wild look in her eyes. That, coupled with the fact that she'd casually let her coat open to reveal Cosabella lingerie, and I knew I'd wake up tomorrow with regrets.

"You don't have to invite me in."

"Good, because that's out of the question."

"Get your coat," she commanded.

"What?"

"Go and get your coat. I'm taking you someplace tonight you'll never forget. It's your Christmas present."

"I'm not going to entertain this." But I hesitated.

"Yes you will. Now, I don't have all day. In fact, I only have about two minutes before my patience runs out."

Just as I was told, I grabbed my coat and followed Jada outside to the street. Briefly, I wondered if she were trying to set me up so Jovie could catch us. But we weren't doing anything, yet. I was just about to share a cab with her twin sister, I reasoned.

Once in the cab, Jada started whispering.

"What's your most intimate, unfulfilled fantasy?"

"I've already had sex in a taxicab, Jada," I said matter-of-factly.

"My, my, aren't you presumptuous." She glared. "Fucking in a taxicab was hardly what I had in mind."

"Well, please don't let me drag it out of you."

Ignoring my sarcasm, she continued, "I've just paid for us to participate in a swinging session over at this loft on Sixty-first Street at Third Avenue. It's quite exclusive."

"What's a swinging session?" I had to ask.

"You and I are posing as a newly married couple. We will meet another newly married couple and have sex. Probably the best sex you'll ever experience."

"You're taking me to have an orgy?"

"Not some low-class, acid-tripping, banging session. These people are clean and professional. The woman is a lawyer and her husband is the president of a Fortune Five Hundred company. You are a screenwriter and I'm a pediatrician. We've been married under a year—"

"Why are you so sure that I'll be down with this?"

"Intrigue breaks down all barriers," she reasoned.

"Why are you doing this?"

"I do it because I like to fuck. And so do you."

"Why are you trying to break up Jovie and me?"

"This isn't about Jovie. It's about you. I like fucking you. If I wanted to break up you and Jovie, I would have done it already. You know how weak she is. Shove her too roughly, and she'll fall apart like a jigsaw puzzle."

"Don't talk about Jovie like that. She's stronger than you think," I stated.

Ignoring my words, she began to talk about the session again. "They're going to want to know if we do full swoop. That means switch partners, and I'm down if you are."

"I'm not sleeping with a man, Jada."

She burst into laughter. "Not him . . . unless you really want to. I'm talking about her. If she's attractive, if you like the way she kisses, you can have her."

I always thought swinging was a myth. Professional and celebrity-types, married individuals loaning out their partners to perfect strangers to heighten their sexual experiences. I had to admit I was intrigued with the possibilities.

I glanced over at Jada, looking scrumptious in her lingerie. I leaned down inside the cab, pulled her panties to one side and began to taste her. She didn't resist. I sucked on her clitoris until she moaned softly. But I wanted more of a reaction from her. So I aggressively began to nibble, suck, and bite on her clit. Then I stuck my index finger in her pussy and twirled it around. Hot juices seeped out onto my finger, and I got excited. My ego wanted to please Jada. I positioned my finger inside her pussy to hit her G-spot while simultaneously licking her clit. This sent Jada into a frenzy. She moaned and groaned loudly but the cab-driver didn't say a word. I wasn't even embarrassed. The best part of eating her pussy was when she grabbed the back of my head, smashed my face even deeper into her pussy and started grinding her sexy hips.

"That's the way I like it," I murmured. "Fuck me."

Soon she climaxed while banging on the cab's window. Slowly, I came up for air just as we pulled up to our destination.

"Next time get a fucking hotel," the disgruntled cabdriver spat. I tipped him a hundred dollars.

We arrived at the loft just past 8:00 P.M. and were led in by the host. He was a flighty individual with shifty eyes. He immediately made me feel uneasy. I looked around at my surroundings and noticed that there were eight closed-room doors. Jada presented the host with two tickets, and he then led us to door number 2. Inside there was a young couple sitting down in front of a fireplace enjoying cocktails. The room was spacious and had a large, king-size bed with four high posts. The bed had large throw pillows and a thick crushed-velvet comforter.

The woman had on a mask with peacock feathers. She had a great body, cocoa-colored skin and a massive amount of jet black hair. Her husband was light skinned, stood six-one with a chiseled, athletic body, a square jawbone and a head full of curly hair. There was something familiar about this lady, only I couldn't quite put my finger on it. Jada took control as soon as she entered the room.

"This is my husband, London. My name's Jada."

"It's a pleasure meeting you two. My name's Gregory and this is my lovely wife, Su."

As soon as he said this, Su took off her mask and my heart sank.

As we sat around drinking champagne to loosen up, I couldn't take my eyes off of Su. She looked even better than when we were together. She never let on that we were once in love or even knew each other. One part of me wanted her so badly, while the other part didn't know if I could stomach entering her again.

After the small talk and preliminaries were over, it was time to get down to business. Gregory, who couldn't take his eyes off Jada, asked, "So, we were hoping that you two did a full swoop."

Jada looked to me for a clue. When she saw me gazing at Su, she knew the answer.

"Yes. We can begin together and then swoop. But I don't do anal," Jada stated.

"I do," Su replied, and I nearly fell off my chair. "Do you participate in that . . . London? That's your name, correct?"

"Yes. I mean, yes. That's my name."

"Well, will you indulge anally?"

"I'm down for whatever," I boasted like a frightened little boy. I always knew that Su was sexually challenging. And up until tonight, I thought that Jada was Su's match. But Su was out of control. She never would have been content in a relationship with me. I realized at the moment that the best thing she could have done for me was to leave. Knowing that, I didn't mind letting her sample the great dick she'd left behind.

I started off kissing Jada while Su and Gregory watched. My

tongue aggressively explored the inside of her mouth, earlobes and neck. She arched her back, encouraging me to continue. I could feel Su's eyes staring at me intently, which made my dick harder than a row of quarters. If I wasn't careful, I would explode prematurely. I knew I had to pace myself if I wanted this to be an experience to remember. As I unhooked Jada's bra and exposed her small breasts, I thought briefly about the first time I laid eyes on Jovie's breasts.

Sweet Jovie . . .

I sucked, nibbled and gently bit down on Jada's nipples until they looked like two copper nickels. She moaned her pleasure and began to rip my shirt open. As each button flew off, I joined in by ripping off her thong panties. She squealed with delight. Her squeal made me think of Jovie.

Sweet Jovie . . . trusting me . . . loving me . . . believing in me . . .

I entered Jada forcefully. As I aggressively pumped in and out *she* dug her nails into my back and pulled them down in a sinister yet sexy gesture. Then a familiar touch entered the picture. Su had come from behind and started nibbling on my ear the way she knew I liked it. Immediately I changed positions and let Jada ride on top while I motioned for Su to come and sit on my face. As Su opened her pussy walls wide, I stuck my tongue far inside her cave. As her sexy hips rocked back and forth, I reached up and massaged her breasts. She felt so soft and familiar that for a fleeting moment, I longed for the past.

Jada's hips were grinding on my dick like a pro. She went up slowly, released her pussy and then contracted as she came down. Then she switched it up and began twirling her hips in a circular motion in a wild and frenzied rhythm. The only sound in the room was the moans and groans of Jada. As Jada exploded on my dick and her warm juices slid down my shaft, Gregory didn't hesitate to flip her over and mount her quickly. Su quickly came and we began to fuck in the missionary position. As I entered her, I thought all my emotions would come flowing back. But they didn't. She felt like what she was. A one-night stand with an old fling. Nothing more. Nothing less.

We flipped from the missionary position and Su rode on top. While on top she spread her legs, did a split and popped her pussy rapidly on my dick. This drove me crazy. She'd certainly learned a move or two since we were together and she was determined to show me each one of them. We were flipping all over the bed and there were times when I didn't know if I could keep up with Su's pace.

"Enter me from the back," she whispered. I hesitated only for a moment. I turned her over and forcefully rammed my dick in her anus. She screamed in pain mixed with pleasure. I pumped in and out while forcefully entangling my hands in her hair and pulling.

"How does it feel?" I said breathlessly. Su was silent until I rammed my dick even harder.

"Oh, yes," she crooned. "Keep it right there."

Over my shoulder I could hear moans and groans coming from Jada and Gregory. I decided not to glance over to see how they were doing. I just concentrated on Su and my pleasure.

Sweat was pouring off my body and dripping from my eyebrows onto Su's back.

"I'm getting ready to cum . . . ," I screamed as hot juices came gushing out. My body started shaking involuntarily and we both collapsed onto the bed, only to begin again ten minutes later.

I awoke on Christmas wrapped between the legs of Su and Jada. It was one-thirty in the afternoon, and I'd missed Jovie. I raced home and arrived after two o'clock, but Jovie had already left. I raced to her apartment, but she didn't answer the door. I went back home feeling pathetic. How could I let Jovie down like this? I tried to shower last night off me, but I wasn't having any luck. I realized that Jada was and always would be bad news. I needed someone to talk to, so I dialed my brother's number. He picked up on the third ring.

"Hello," he said.

"What's up?"

"Shit. Hey, Merry Christmas."

"Man, I'm stressed out. I don't care nothing about this white man's holiday!"

"One guess. Your new girlfriend," he said.

"Yeah. But it's not what you think. She's hasn't hurt me—it's the other way around."

"What'd you do, man?"

"Last night, I sucked her twin sister's pussy out in a cab."

"What the fuck is wrong with you? Why are you running 'round going down on these nasty broads? May Jesus take my life if I ever eat a chick's pussy!"

He was lying.

"Man, you better get in the loop. That's what's up. But bigger than that, did you hear me say I'm fucking my girl's sister?"

"Yeah. So how's the sex?"

"Lawrence, stop playing. I need your advice. I feel so guilty."

"Man, you can't undo what's already done. What do you want me to say? You're old enough to know better. Especially if you have feelings for this girl."

Somewhere around 5:00 P.M., I got a knock at the door. To my delight it was Jovie. I swung the door open and embraced her in a bear hug. She squealed.

"I came by earlier, but you weren't here." She pouted.

"I'm so sorry, baby-girl. Will you please forgive me?"

"This time, but the next time I won't be so kind," she joked. As I led her into my living room, she felt like everything I'd been looking for. She felt pure and untainted. Like fresh air after a smog-filled day. Those two hoes from last night almost made me lose my baby. As we sat and talked, I must have kissed her face a hundred times. Then I went in my bedroom and came out with her gift. I had Bloomingdale's wrap it nicely. Carefully, she took off the bow and then the paper. As she opened the gift and saw the bag, her face lit up like the stadium lights at the Super Bowl.

"London, thank you! It's beautiful. I've never owned such an expensive bag. You shouldn't have," she squealed.

"It's my pleasure," I said, and gave her a fat, juicy kiss on her sexy lips.

"Now, your turn," she said, and handed me a large box.

With the eagerness of a child on his tenth Christmas, I ripped open my gift, and it took my breath. Inside was an antique easel for me to paint canvases on. She had it engraved: *"From the first night I sang to you, I fell in love with London in England. Cheers to not having regrets! Love Jovie."*

"Jovie, this must have cost a fortune."

"I had saved two thousand dollars so I could move into my own apartment. But once I saw that easel, I knew you had to have it. It's a collector's item."

Now I've never been accused of being a bitch-ass brother, but I swear to God, I wanted to shed a few tears at how genuinely sweet this girl was. I don't know what made me do this, but I ran into my bedroom and grabbed the engagement ring I'd bought last year for Su. I couldn't even contain myself. I ran back in the living room and fell onto one knee and blurted out, "Jovie, marry me! Let's do it. Will you marry me?"

Her face transitioned into a million expressions before settling on utter joy.

"Yes! Oh, yes!" She grinned as I put the ring on her finger.

"I mean, we will have a long engagement," I reasoned as reality sank in. "To get to know each other better. But you're the one, kid. I think I could spend the rest of my life with you."

"Out of the hundred and two people on the *Mayflower*, how many men and boys were named John?"

"You've got to be kidding me," I laughed.

"Fifteen. Fifteen were named John," she laughed, and hugged me.

I imagined waking up every morning with Jovie. And that thought put a smile on my face.

Jovie

I know that I'm imperfect. So it is a great surprise that London has just proposed to spend the rest of our lives together. For some reason, I knew he was the one. After work tonight, London is coming to listen to me do a set at the café. I'm so nervous, yet excited at the thought that he cares enough to share my world. I'm opening up with "God Bless the Child" by Billie Holiday, followed by "At Last" by Etta James. At the end I'm going to sing him a number that I wrote for him. I hope he'll appreciate it.

To keep from going crazy, I walked from Sally's on 125th Street in the frigid winter weather to 34th Street. I counted each crack in the sidewalk. There were 2,378 cracks in the sidewalk. This exercise calmed any anxieties.

I ran inside Macy's to pick me up a special dress to wear tonight. I looked around for hours before settling on a basic black form-fitting dress. With that in hand, I decided to walk back uptown.

This isn't going to last.

Of course it will. It'll last just as long as I want it to.

You'll ruin this just like you've done your past relationships.

That's nonsense. I didn't do anything but love them.

Your type of love is smothering.
I'm different with London—

An overweight, short white man interrupted me by shout-ing, "Hey, lady, who are you talking to?" Then he let out a hearty laugh, holding his big fat belly.

I immediately shut up.

I had five minutes before I was to go onstage when I peeked out and saw London arrive. He looked so handsome. I could tell he'd just gotten a neat haircut.

I walked onto the stage with palms sweating. My voice was as smooth as butter as I sang my first tune.

" 'God bless the child that's got his own . . .' " The crowd cheered as I did my Billie Holiday rendition. When I belted out, " 'At last . . .' " the crowd erupted in applause. The energy from the crowd lifted me ten feet. I looked around at all the pa-trons, but the most important face was that of London. He looked so proud as our eyes connected. He winked, and I nod-ded my head.

When it was time for my last number, I said to the crowd, "This is a new number for me. In fact, I just wrote it the other day for a very special person. It's called 'More Love.' "

I looked directly at London.

" 'I was so afraid to let you in . . . didn't want to be your lover although we knew we wouldn't remain friends . . .' " I belted out the words I had written for London. " 'You showed me more love in a brief moment than many people feel in a life-time. You showed me more love and I love you. And I'm so proud to call you all mine,' " I sang.

" 'I've waited, waited, so long for you and just when I stopped praying, you came through to show me more love . . .' "

The crowd went crazy. And so did London. He hopped up on his feet and gave me a standing ovation. The crowd soon followed. I stood onstage completely fulfilled.

London

I think I fell in love all over again the moment Jovie belted out her love song to me. I listened intently to the words and was surprised at how much closer I felt to her afterward.

"You were wonderful," I told her.

"Really?" she asked hesitantly.

"Of course. And don't let anyone ever tell you otherwise."

"I won't," she promised.

"Are you hungry?"

"Are we going out to grab a bite to eat?" she asked.

"I was hoping you'd let me cook for you tonight. I've already gone shopping and it won't take long."

"You're going to cook for me?"

"If you'd like."

"I'd love it," she squealed, and kissed me on my cheek.

We got back to my place, and I started a fire. I had a small fold-up table and chair set that I pulled into the living room right by the fire. Then I gave Jovie the beautiful flower arrangement I'd bought for her earlier. And of course, she loved it.

I ran in the kitchen and quickly whipped up shrimp scampi with linguini and a crisp Caesar salad. After dinner, I brought out ripe strawberries and a bottle of chilled Moët, and poured Jovie and me a glass.

"I feel wonderful tonight. I'm in heaven," she said, and kissed the side of my face.

"Tell me your pleasures," I invited.

"You."

I smiled. "Besides me, tell me what gives you pleasure."

She thought for a moment, and then said, "Singing gives me pleasure."

"What hurts you?"

"When people judge me before getting to know me. I hate that."

"What do you mean?"

"People sometimes think I'm strange and then treat me accordingly. I'm no different from anyone else."

"You're a little quirky, Jovie. But that's what I love about you."

"That's the first time you've said that."

"That you're quirky or that I love you?"

"The latter."

"Oh."

"Is that it? Is that all you can say?"

"I can say more but I'd rather show you."

"Show me that you love me?" She smiled.

"Yeah, something like that. Now stop changing the subject. What are your fears? Do you have any?"

"What's this? Twenty questions?"

"I'm trying to get to know you. Last time I tried, you told me you didn't have any history. I let you off the hook. This time I won't. What are your fears?"

She thought for a moment, looked me directly in my eyes, and stated, "I fear that I'll wake up one morning and not know who I am. I'll be somebody else lying in bed next to a complete stranger. That's my biggest fear." And she began to cry.

I had no idea what she meant.

"I don't have any history . . ." Those were her words.

I embraced Jovie and let her cry her beautiful eyes out. She seemed so lost and alone, and I felt helpless that I couldn't help her. We crawled into bed and I held on to her tightly. I wanted her to know that she had me. And that when she awoke in the morning, I'd be right there. And I felt certain she'd remember me.

Jovie

I awoke the next morning not remembering much of last night. But today I decided not to let fear win. London had to go to work, and so did I.

"Wake up, sleepyhead," he said as he playfully threw a pillow at me.

"I'm up. I'm up," I moaned.

"Come on, let's take a shower," he said.

"Go ahead. You first."

"No, let's take a shower together," he said, and pulled the covers off of me.

"I can't take a shower *with* you."

"Jovie, you're a grown woman. You can do anything you please."

"Well, that doesn't please me."

"Jovie, get your shy behind out of bed and come get in this hot, steamy shower with me. I promise that's as far as it'll go."

Reluctantly, I crawled out of bed and followed London's lead into his bathroom, where he had the shower already running.

"Be still," he said as he started to undress me. Layer by layer, my clothes fell to the bathroom floor, and he never lost eye contact with me. He held my stare and the feeling was incredible. Once we were in the shower he stood me in front of him and began to gently wash my back and arms. Slowly, he brought the washcloth around and began to wash my stomach, then my breasts. I shuddered.

"Be easy," he soothed. "Nothing will happen that you don't want to."

As the washcloth traveled up and down my legs, in between my thighs, up to the nape of my neck and back down to the small of my back, I felt intoxicated. Soon, I grabbed a washcloth and returned the favor. As we lathered each other's bodies, our intimacy was enhanced tenfold.

"I want you . . . ," I said breathlessly.

He looked me directly in my eyes but didn't say anything. I had no idea what was going through his mind or what had gotten into mine. But I knew at that moment what I wanted. When I leaned over and kissed his hesitant lips, his wall of resistance crumbled. He lifted me out of the shower and carried me to his king-size bed and gently laid me down.

"Are you sure you want this?" he asked. I was too weak to answer. I just shook my head and pulled him on top of me.

Our lips met and ignited a fire that had been simmering in me for a long time. I thoroughly enjoyed how soft his lips were and how skillful his tongue was. He sucked on my neck until I was sure he'd left a passion mark, then he moved down to my breasts. Gently, he cupped each breast and began to nibble and suck until I was moaning my pleasure. No part of my body went neglected. He kissed the insides of my ankles, the backs of my thighs, the palms of my hands. He truly took his time with me until he knew I was ready.

He steadied himself on top of me and entered me as gently as his thick penis would allow. I winced from the pain but only momentarily. Soon strong waves of pleasure flowed through my body as we made love. He held me so tightly I could hear his heart beating.

"I want you to cum with me . . . ," he said breathlessly as he brought me to my climax. I wrapped my legs tightly around his back as strong waves flooded through my body. I jerked involuntarily.

"I love you," I said without thinking. Then I realized that I liked the way that sounded and that it was the truth. So, I said it again, "I love you, London."

"I love you, too," he said, and kissed the side of my face. "Are you all right? I didn't hurt you, did I?"

"You didn't hurt me," I assured him. "It couldn't have been any better than this."

London and I had to rush out of his apartment quickly because we were both running late for work.

"What time will you call me tonight?" I asked as we ran out the door.

"I should be home around seven. I'll give you a call shortly thereafter. Enjoy your day."

"I will."

"Do you need anything? Any money for the day?" he asked.

"London, I keep telling you, you're all I need."

"That you have . . . that you have."

I finished work around 5:00 P.M. and couldn't get London off of my mind. I decided to do something special for him since he was always doing wonderful things for me. I had done really well in tips, so I ran to his favorite restaurant, Ida Mae's, and ordered us some soul food to go. Then I stopped at The Body Shop and purchased massage oil. After dinner I'd give London a nice body massage to alleviate any stress from his day.

I got to London's brownstone around 7:30 P.M., but he wasn't home yet. I thought about using his spare key, but I felt it a bit intrusive. I called his cellular phone but he had it turned off. He usually did this when he was with Jessica at the studio or if she was doing radio or television. I wanted to leave a message telling him that I was coming over, but I thought it would be a pleasant surprise.

There was a small diner across from London's apartment where I decided to sit and wait. I sat in the window booth that had a perfect view of his apartment entrance. I ordered a cup of hot chocolate, thinking he wouldn't take much longer. And I was right. Shortly after sitting down, I noticed London getting out of a yellow taxicab. He wasn't alone. She was beautiful. Her beauty was breathtaking and sophisticated. She had a massive amount of wavy hair, cocoa-colored skin, and a long, elegant mink coat. They were cuddling as they fell out the cab. He was looking at her dreamily, and it crushed me. I wanted to run over, scream and shout obscenities, but my legs wouldn't let me. I stood frozen in place for almost an hour before the waitress got annoyed that I hadn't ordered anything more. I went to the telephone and called London. "Hello," he said.

"London." My voice was barely a whisper.

"What's up?"

"Nothing. I . . . um . . . was thinking that I could come over tonight and cook for you. Maybe rent a movie."

"Where are you?"

"Not too far away."

"Well, tonight really isn't a good time for me. I'm working on another screenplay and don't want to be disturbed. I'll have to take a rain check. How about tomorrow?"

"Tomorrow?"

"Yeah, we'll have dinner and a movie."

"But, I was really hoping—"

"Baby-girl, I'm really busy at the moment."

"I understand. Tomorrow would be fine."

"Great! Think about me tonight when you sleep," he said, and hung up.

London

Jovie sounded a little strange just now when I spoke to her. I hope she isn't having any regrets about what happened this morning because it's just the opposite for me. I rather fancy how delicate she is. How soft her kisses are—never aggressive. She's so pure, and even though at times I'm not sure if I did the right thing by giving her the ring, I have every intention of making this work.

"Who was that?"

"That was my future," I snapped at Su.

"Good for you," she said, disinterested.

So I continued, "That's my fiancée."

"So you have a wife and a fiancée? You've been a busy boy since our last encounter."

"The lady you met wasn't my wife."

"I already knew that."

"Really? How?"

"You forget we were once in a relationship. You would never

allow your wife to be touched by another man. You don't have that free spirit. I bet your fiancée is some church mouse who can't fuck you properly."

"Watch it, Su. Watch your mouth."

"Truth hurt?"

"I don't know why you're here or how I fell in love with you in the first place," I said. I was really talking to myself. Thinking out loud.

"Because with me you had the best of both worlds. I was a lady in public and a whore behind closed doors. Isn't that what all men want?"

"What do you want out of life?"

"An occasional fuck."

"That's it? You just want to fuck?"

"Precisely. My life is complicated enough. I don't need a complicated sex life."

"Don't you have any fears, running around fucking on your husband?"

She laughed a hideous cackle, then said, "I'm twenty-six years old, and I can count the number of orgasms I've experienced. I remember each time, and they were few and far apart. It's like people write about great sex, you hear about great sex, but you get into a relationship and there's no great sex. People write about great relationships, I hear about great relationships, but I just can't seem to maintain a great relationship. My biggest *fear* is to go through life unfulfilled."

"Is that why you left me? I didn't fulfill your needs?"

"Yes. I got tired of settling for less with you." Her words

stung for a moment. Then I realized who I was dealing with and realized who I had.

Su and I had sex for old time's sake and I couldn't have cared less if she experienced an orgasm or not. There wasn't any fore-play. No dim lights or romantic candles. I didn't even put on a fire. Just five hours of straight fucking. I kicked her out some-where around 4:00 A.M. I needed to get some rest. I had a full day ahead of me. Plus I wanted to spend time with Jovie. Maybe buy her a nice guilt gift . . .

Jovie

After London lied to me, I couldn't summon the courage to go upstairs and confront him with her. I stood outside in the De-cember blistering cold temperatures waiting for her to leave. To bide my time, I counted each yellow cab that passed in the eight-hour time frame. I counted 543 cabs that drove down London's block. When his guest left, she and I looked eye to eye and she almost said something to me, as if we'd met before. I rushed past her and banged on the door. He was still awake.

"Who is it?"

"Jovie!"

Silence. Then he pulled open the door and smiled. He was wearing a pair of boxers and had a toothbrush in his hand.

"Don't tell me you were in the neighborhood," he joked,

and pulled me inside. "Je-sus, Jovie! You're frozen. Your cheeks feel like icicles."

My eyes welled up with tears.

"Who is she?"

"Who is who?" he asked.

"Mink coat . . . cocoa-colored skin . . . need I go on? Who is she?"

"She's nobody. She's a memory . . . just someone from my past that won't be interfering in our lives again."

"Did you sleep with her?"

"Jovie, this isn't necessary."

"Did you make love to her after you'd just made love to me?" I questioned.

"Don't do this," he replied.

"Answer me!" I cried.

"Please calm down. I know how this looks, but it's not like that. She just came over to help me with some ideas for my new screenplay," he reasoned.

I was already in the room, and I spotted several condoms disposed of in his wastebasket and messy sheets. My heart sank, and then I lost it.

"What is this!" I screamed hysterically and picked up the used condoms and tossed them in his face. "How could you put this ring on my finger, and then make love to that whore!"

"I just told you nothing happened," he said, but was unable to look me in my eyes.

"Do you think I'm a fool?" I yelled, and slapped his face

with all my strength. When I went to slap him again he grabbed my hand. I yanked it away.

"Jovie, listen, it's not what you think."

"Then what is it!" I bellowed. "Answer me!"

"I . . . can't . . . I don't know what to say or how to say it."

"You said you'd never hurt me like this," I said, and collapsed on the floor and began to cry. London bent down next to me and cradled my head.

"I'm so sorry. Please forgive me," he pleaded.

"How can you let that bitch jeopardize what we have? Didn't this ring mean anything to you?" I said as I reached up and dug my fingernails deep into the dark chocolate skin of his arms. Long welts appeared immediately.

"It was her ring first!" he shouted back, and from the look on his face he realized he'd said something he didn't want to.

"What? Did I hear you correctly? Is she the one who hurt you back in England? Is she the love of your life?"

"She was," he replied.

"And you think that less of me that you'd give me a second-hand ring?"

"It's not like that."

I took off the ring and threw it in his face. "Then how is it? How is it?" I kept screaming but he wouldn't answer me. He just kept staring at me with pity in his eyes. A look that I despised. I spit in his face.

"You're pathetic, not me!" I roared, and felt an uncontrollable rage come over me. I lost it and ran into his bathroom and locked the door. There I trashed everything in sight. I smashed bottles of cologne and hair products. Ripped down his shower curtains and finally smashed my wrists against his mirror. I screamed out in pain as my wrists burst open and blood came gurgling out like from a crack in the Hoover dam. Blood spurted out as I watched in horror. As I slipped into unconsciousness I wondered if I'd know who I was when I awoke. Or if I wanted to awake . . .

You were supposed to come with me . . . in the pool . . . you never followed . . . now's your chance to make it right. . . .

London

Jovie throwing a temper tantrum at four in the morning and slashing her wrists had unnerved me. I was basically a quiet man who didn't like conflict. Her actions were quite alarming. When she screamed out in pain I had to kick the door down to gain entry. There I found her collapsed on the bathroom floor saturated in her own blood. I had EMS rush her to the nearest hospital, where they were able to stop the bleeding. She's in stable condition, and she should be able to go home soon.

I left a message at her house notifying Jada as to what had happened. I can just hear Jada's mouth now. In fact, it would be a pleasure not to hear from Jada at all.

The hospital released Jovie in my care, and I grabbed a cab and took her home. As we sat in the cab, she mumbled incoherently to herself. It was as if she were carrying on a full conversation between herself and another person. This was bizarre, but I wrote it off as the effects of the medication given to her in the hospital.

After I got Jovie home and tucked her in bed, I raced out of there. I was no longer tired, so I decided to go to the gym to let off some steam. I worked out until my muscles burned, then showered and ran home and fell into a peaceful sleep. When I awoke, I started to clean up the huge mess Jovie made in the bathroom. There was blood and glass everywhere. I hated to admit that this was my fault, and it all could have been avoided if I had just been a man. What I hated to admit most is that when Jovie took off the engagement ring and flung it at me, I was relieved. At twenty-eight, I'm too young to be thinking about settling down. I'm enjoying my life. And although I care about Jovie, no matter how hard I've tried, I can't be monogamous in relationships. I love sex. I love women. But I also love being in love with that one special person. I don't think I'm any different from any other man on this earth but there is a small part of me that wished I was different. That I could truly commit when I'm in a relationship. I'm partly to blame for Su leaving me. She knew that I'd been unfaithful on more than one occasion and I'm sure she resented me for it. It's not that I'm a bad person. I'm a good dude who gets tempted. The pounding at the door interrupted my thoughts.

"*Who is it?*" I screamed.

No answer. I looked through the peephole and flung the door open. It had to be her. I was disgusted just looking at her.

"What do you want, Jada?"

She pushed past me. She was all bundled up in a ski jacket, hat, and gloves. She looked a little different. Worn.

"What are you trying to pull, you son of a bitch?!"

"Don't disrespect my mother," I warned.

"What happened to Jovie!"

"Why don't you ask Jovie?"

"I'm asking you!"

"Look, Jovie and I are going through some things at the moment, but we will work them out."

"You can't! London, you need to leave my sister alone! Tell her it's over."

"We've already decided not to go on with the engagement, but there is no way I'm giving her up totally. I can't do it."

"You can or I'll make you," she warned.

"And how do you expect to do that? Your sister loves me. And I'm one step away from falling in love with her."

"But you don't love her. If you don't leave her, you'll be the death of us!"

"What do you have to do with this?"

"Jovie told you how we are in tune to each other's emotions. The pain. The hurt. Happiness. Sexual feelings. Everything. I felt my wrist slice open while I was in bed sleeping peacefully with my daughter, Joy."

"Listen, I don't believe you. And if I did, I still wouldn't care. I'm not leaving Jovie."

"I'm pregnant."

"And why should I care?"

"Because you're the father."

"Stop it, Jada! You've gone too far now. I want you out of here," I said, and grabbed her by her wrist. She yelled out in pain, and immediately I released my grip.

"Didn't I tell you, you sick, twisted piece of shit, I felt what went on in here last night. I'm only doing this to save my sister. If I tell Jovie that we've been sleeping together and that I'm carrying your baby, how do you think she'll feel? She just started to trust men again. She'll shut down. No one will be able to pull her out of her shell."

"Why would you want to see her hurt?"

"Because I can't stand to see her with you. You're not good enough for Jovie."

"So what happens when the baby arrives? I would want to be in my child's life. Jovie will have to find out eventually."

"I'm pregnant. That's it. I have one child and don't plan on having another one. Break it off with my sister, and I'll abort the fetus."

"Je-sus! Jada, are you crazy? You can't just kill my baby!"

"Save the theatrics for your screenplays. The deal is you break it off with Jovie today, and I promise to take our secret to my grave. Do we have a deal?"

I thought about the prospect of Jovie finding out that her sister and I were having an affair behind her back and realized that would certainly crush her. Then I realized that I'd never be happy with Jovie as long as Jada was in the picture, which was inevitable. These two sisters were draining me. I realized I had to lose Jovie to save Jovie. And that's exactly what I planned to do.

I had contemplated for hours on how I would end this or even if I could when my telephone rang.

"Hello."

"London." It was Jovie and I could tell she'd been crying.

"Yes."

"London, I'm sorry about today."

"It's okay, baby-girl. How are you feeling?"

"I'm feeling much better, thank you. London, I need to come over so we can talk."

"Jovie, that's not a good idea. You need your rest."

"Why not? Do you have someone there?" she accused, and I felt the tension in my shoulders return.

"I'm alone, Jovie."

"London, I want to come back and get my ring. I acted irrationally and I want to make it up to you."

"Jovie, I think what happened was for the best. It's really not working out between you and me. I think we need our space."

"No . . . no . . . we don't. I don't. What I need is you . . . and my ring back on my finger," she said. She sounded as if she were hyperventilating.

"Jovie, are you all right?"

"Goddamn it! I'm not all right, you fucking son of a bitch!" she exploded.

"Watch your mouth," I yelled back.

"London, you better not ignore me, or I will make you very sorry!" she threatened.

"What's gotten into you?"

"I love you. I love you, London," she said, and she sounded

like sweet Jovie. I decided I needed to get off this emotional roller coaster.

"Jovie, I think it's best we don't see each other anymore. I hate for it to end like this. And for what it's worth, I really care about you."

"You can't just end it."

"It's for the best."

"How long is 'four score and seven years ago—' "

"Stop it!" I exploded. I had had enough of her antics.

"Eighty-seven years," she screamed, ignoring my aggravation.

"You need help, Jovie."

"Will you help me?" she pleaded.

"I am. It just doesn't seem like it at this moment. But I'm helping you by removing myself from your life."

"You're going to miss me when I'm gone," she stated. Almost as if she'd make sure of that.

"Just worry about your feelings," I retorted, and hung up the line.

Jovie

He said he loved me.

Did he say that or did you say it?

I'm certain he said that. Or did we say it together? Perhaps, I could have said it first, but I'm sure he agreed at some point.

You sound a little confused.

Don't patronize me. I'm forgetful, sometimes, but never confused.

You know there's someone else, don't you.

Of course I know! I caught them together, didn't I?

Don't be upset with me. Your anger should be directed toward your cheating, ex-fiancé.

Did he really break it off with me?

He thinks you're pathetic.

Did he say that?

He just as well should have. Now he's going to give the ring to its rightful owner. You know he's giving her back the ring.

When?

Didn't he tell you he was supposed to give it to her last New Year's Eve?

Yes.

Then that's what he plans to do. He'll make up for lost time and give it to her tomorrow night.

But he promised to spend New Year's Eve with me.

Somehow that doesn't look promising.

What am I to do?

I think you know what you have to do.

The telephone ringing startled me. I let my machine pick up.

"Hello, this is Jovie, please leave a message."

"Jovie, this is Dr. Welch. Jovie, I'm concerned. You've missed several appointments. We need to talk. Please call the office as soon as possible to schedule an appointment."

"Dr. Welch, I can't see you right now. I'm in the middle of a crisis," I said to myself as I looked at the telephone. Then I laughed. Why was all of this so very funny?

London

New Year's Eve 2005

I was on location with Jessica, the pop star, in lower Manhattan while she shopped for a few items for her New Year's Eve party. She was having a masquerade at her duplex on Park Avenue. The Gucci store on Fifth Avenue had to shut down to all other patrons while she strolled the aisles. In less than an hour, she'd already gone through what was equivalent to six months' pay for me. After she'd finished spending an obscene amount of money, I had just enough time to drop her off, run home and shower, and return to her duplex in time for the festivities.

I entered Jessica's New Year's Eve party listening to the deafening music of the live band she hired. Her duplex apartment was packed to capacity. By nine o'clock everyone was intoxicated. Jessica immediately scoped me out and came rushing over. I handed her a bottle of champagne I'd picked up.

"Dom Perignon. You have good taste. But you shouldn't have."

"It's just a gesture," I retorted. I was still in a sour mood.

"Give your overcoat to my butler, and let's dance," she yelled. She threw her arms in the air, twirled around like a prima ballerina and headed to the dance floor. The band was playing The Black Eyed Peas's "Let's Get It Started."

I met up with Jessica on the dance floor and showed her a few of my moves. She tried to keep up, but she was no match for a brother from Harlem. As she caught every third beat, I watched as her titties jiggled up and down. Then I grabbed her by her waist, pulled her in close to my dick and started to grind on her. I could tell she was excited.

"Let's get out of here," she said.

"What's the rush? I just got here and I'd like to enjoy the party. Isn't that the actor from *Rush Hour*?"

"Yes."

"Great. Introduce me," I urged.

"Go introduce yourself," she retorted and walked away.

"I guess I have no choice," I replied to no one.

After meeting the actor and telling him all about my screenplays, I networked with a few other celebrities. I was enjoying myself until I remembered how I had spent last New Year's Eve, alone in a hotel room crying my eyes out. That memory prompted me to have a drink. As I picked up a glass of champagne, a beautiful, dark chocolate sister came over to greet me. I recognized her immediately. She was *Playboy*'s Miss November centerfold.

"Drinking alone?" she purred.

"Not anymore," I said and winked. Before we could go further, Jessica appeared and practically pulled me from Miss November's clutches.

"I'm ready to go," she replied again, and then pouted.

"Go where?"

"I want to go to your place and screw your brains out," she said, but instead of turning me on, she turned me off. I wanted to say, I don't screw—I fuck. Instead, I said, "Sorry, but I have other plans." I was meeting Su at my apartment for bring-in-the-new-year sex.

Jovie

I stood almost holding my breath inside London's closet. Watching. I watched as his lips touched her. How he gently caressed her skin. The words of adoration he spoke.

You were supposed to come with me in the pool.

I was afraid.

You never followed . . . but now's your chance to make it right. Do you want to make it right?

I can't.

You can . . . I need you. I want us to be together forever. I need you. . . .

London

Maybe it was the alcohol or the fact that I had one of the world's sexiest women in my arms, but I didn't have a care in the world. Never mind that I'd just broken off an engagement with a woman I cared about. Or that I'd been sleeping with her sister, who might or might not be pregnant by me. All that mattered was I was about to have mind-blowing sex on New Year's Eve.

I went to my dresser drawer and pulled out the ring I had purchased for her last year.

"What's that?" she asked.

"I was supposed to propose to you last year this time. But you walked out of my life."

She was silent. I could tell she was thinking about the possibilities.

"We never would have made it," she said after a moment.

I smiled. "I know. This ring symbolizes happiness. The woman that will wear this ring will embody everything you're not."

"Quit being philosophical so we can do what I came here to do," she snapped. I just laughed because I knew, if only for a fleeting moment, she wished we could have made it.

I charged Su and threw her on my bed. I ripped open her shirt, and we groped each other hungrily. Her pussy resisted as I tried to enter her, so I went down and tasted her clitoris. I worked her up nicely. When I stuck my finger inside her pussy, warm juices seeped out, and I knew she was ready. I entered her, feverishly ready to beat it up nicely.

"Let me wear the ring while you fuck me," she breathed. Quickly, I placed the ring on her finger as I pumped in and out.

"Ask me . . . ask me to marry you," she commanded.

"Will . . . you . . . marry . . . me?" I breathed.

"Yes! Oh, yes," she crooned.

"Is it good?"

"Oh, yes . . . it's so-o-o-o-o good. I want to cum as the ball drops," Su shrieked.

"I'm getting ready to cum," I moaned.

In the background you could hear *Dick Clark's Rockin' Eve.* It was tradition. As we fucked, I couldn't help but listen to the television.

"I want to cum as the ball drops," she begged again.

I rammed my dick inside her pussy to shut her up. She screamed in pleasure.

I could hear Dick Clark counting down the seconds to the new year. Even though my back was to the television, I could still envision the ball dropping.

"Five . . ."

"I'm getting ready to cum," she moaned.

"Four . . ."

"Oh, Daddy, your dick is the best."

"Three . . ."

"It's so good. . . ."

"Two . . ."

"Ahhhhhhh!!!!!!!!!!!!"

"One . . ."

Pow. Pow. Pow. Pow. Pow.

"Happy New Year!"

Silence.

EPILOGUE

London

The doctors say my chances of ever walking again are slim. I tell them that God has a plan for all of us. Sometimes when we are speeding around on a path to nowhere and somehow life slams on the brakes, the best thing we can do is be still. Quiet. In that instance we will find ourselves.

I've been in this hospital for two weeks. It's truly a miracle that I'm alive. I took two bullets in my back, one shattered my spine and the other lodged in a buttock. Su wasn't so lucky. She was shot once in the face and was pronounced dead on arrival at the hospital.

Even though it was Jovie who paralyzed me, murdered Su, and then killed herself, I take full responsibility for her actions. I did to her exactly what was done to me. Su played with my heart, and I played with Jovie's. She must have found out that I was sleeping with her sister, Jada. That must have pushed her over the edge.

On New Year's Eve she was hiding in my closet with my licensed revolver. She must have found it in my nightstand. I guess something inside of her snapped when she watched me make love to Su. I should have recognized the clues, but I was so self-absorbed with meeting my needs, relevant things went overlooked.

At the hospital, I was expecting a visit from my brother when an elderly man appeared. He had salt-and-pepper hair, a black mustache and stood around five-nine. He had a small girl with him. The girl had caramel-colored skin, a small button nose, pink lips and a head full of curly hair.

"Are you London Phillips?" he asked in a thick Southern drawl.

"Who are you?"

"My name is Isaiah Love. I'm the father of Jovie," he said, and put his head down in shame.

"Please, please come in," I stammered.

"I wanted to come sooner, but the nurses said you weren't well enough for visitors. Only immediate family."

"I'm glad you're here," I said as my eyes welled up with tears. "Despite what the papers are saying about Jovie, I don't blame her for this. I blame me. I was horrible to your daughter, sir."

"Now, don't go blaming yourself. That's why I'm here. I don't want you to feel any guilt for what happened at your place."

"You don't understand, and I'm surprised I'm the one to tell you this," I said as my voice quivered. "Sir, I had been sleeping with both your daughters, Jovie and Jada. I think Jada must have told Jovie—"

"London, there is no way you could have been seeing Jovie and Jada at the same time. Jada died eighteen years ago. She was only six years old when she drowned. I told her and Jovie not to go near the pool, but Jada didn't listen. At such a young age, Jada was a defiant, rebellious child. Jovie was the complete opposite. The neighbors said Jada screamed for help, but Jovie just stood there. Jovie was too much in shock to run and get help for her sister. I think she lived with that guilt up until the day she killed herself. You know she drowned herself in your tub."

"Yes . . . yes. I read that in the paper. I didn't know there was any significance."

"Jovie always said she'd hear her sister's voice calling her, telling her to come and join her."

"Th-There's no-no way," I stuttered.

"But it is. For years Jovie had her mother convinced that Jada would come back in spirit and talk to her. Jovie just wouldn't let Jada rest in peace. First Jovie started having conversations with Jada. Jovie kept telling us that Jada wanted her to drown herself so they could be together. We took Jovie to a million psychiatrists before she reached the age of ten. She'd fool the shrinks, and they'd return her back home and within days she'd start all over again. Finally, when she was in her early teens, the doctors diagnosed her with dissociative identity disorder. A fancy name for multiple personality disorder. They realized that Jovie would involuntarily take on Jada's identity. Jovie was an eccentric child who was diagnosed with obsessive-compulsive disorder at the age of five. When she turned eight, they detected schizophrenia. That coupled with dissociative identity disorder drove my wife to an early grave."

"So, you're telling me that the Jovie and Jada I knew were one person?"

"Yes, son, you're correct."

"Your daughter needed help, Mr. Love," I accused, suddenly wanting to place the blame on him.

"And that's exactly what she was getting. For years she saw Dr. Welch and things seemed to get better. We didn't hear about Jada until one day Jovie ended up pregnant. She went through her whole pregnancy insisting that it was Jada's child. Once she gave birth, she gave custody of Joy to me."

All Jovie's words came flooding back.

I fear that I'll wake up one morning and not know who I am. I'll be somebody else lying in bed next to a complete stranger. That's my biggest fear."

"This is Jovie's daughter?"

"Yes. She's the new joy in my life," he said, and smiled at his granddaughter. Then he got serious again. "When I found out she was seeing someone, I should have intervened. But I truly thought that everything was under control."

"I had no idea they were the same person. They seemed so different," I said in disbelief, my voice barely a whisper. I didn't even notice that tears were streaming down my cheeks.

"Jovie told me you're a writer," he stated.

"Yes."

"Maybe you can write about this experience. Maybe something good will come out of it."

"Maybe . . ."

I looked at the precious little girl and wondered how much of her mother she had in her. Was she similar to sweet Jovie? Or as wild and rebellious as Jada? As they left she waved and said, "My grandpapa told me that even in love there is hate. And even through devastation and death there can be hope and joy." She squealed in delight.

Her words were symbolic. "Goodbye, Jovie . . . sweet Jovie . . . ," I whispered, and closed my eyes as I felt a sudden chill go down my paralyzed spine. I thought about what Jovie had said. She said I'd miss her when she was gone. And she was right. I do.

My Boo

DAAIMAH S. POOLE

CHAPTER 1

Another night on the club scene. It was eleven o'clock, and I was out with my roommate, Bianca. We were all early at a Philly club called Azure, trying to make our rounds. If one party wasn't doing it, then it was on to the next. It was always the same ole same. Men trying to pick up women, and women trying to get picked up. Tonight I was one of those women, looking for someone to say hi to me. I had cracked a smile at a few guys, but I wasn't about to approach anyone. I still believe a man should approach a woman. Plus, I've got a boyfriend, but my man is three states away. I wish I could be with him right now, but since I can't I'm waiting for a good-looking brother to look my way and invite me to breakfast. Then, who knows?

I had on my quarter-length black mink jacket, faded blue jeans, black pumps, and bag. Bianca was standing right next to me, looking like summer and winter at the same time. She had on a short white fox fur coat with white rhinestone-studded sandals to show off her fresh pedicure. Underneath she wore a white wife-beater and a pair of my jeans. I had to remember to get my jeans back at the end of the night.

At five foot six, Bianca and I are the same height. I have about ten pounds on her, and we both have the same honey complexion. We're both twenty-three and people always mistake us for sisters. But that's where the similarities end. I have always made my own money. I've been doing hair since I was eleven. Bianca, on the other hand, is always getting money from her parents.

We have been sharing my apartment for the past seven months. Before that, she was living with some dude. Her mom kicked her out for allegedly sleeping with her aunt's boyfriend. Bianca said she didn't do it. I believe she did. She's always had a thing for older men, even when we were young. Older men and other women's men.

Back in the day we used to sit on her porch and daydream. It was always about turning eighteen and being grown. We were going to be hairdressers and clothing designers. She was my right-hand girl back then. Today, I'm on the verge of kicking Bianca's ass out of my apartment. Bianca keeps too much traffic in and out of my place, always bringing home men she just met.

But back to the club. I followed Bianca to the bathroom. "Hold my bag, Gina. I got to go bad," she said as she handed me her bag and rushed into the stall. There was tissue everywhere on the floor, empty glasses with stir sticks, water on the floor, flooded sinks, and girls trying to beautify themselves in the mirror. Bianca came out the stall and washed her hands. She then lit a cigarette and began to smoke.

Blowing smoke out of her mouth, she said, "Gina, this place sucks. Did you see the way these guys are dressed? Their shoes are cheap. Their pants are too tight. I see, like, five guys with their shirts all tucked in, like they were about to go to church. And these cheap-ass bitches." I laughed nervously, looking around the bathroom to see who was listening. Bitches were looking at us like "Who the fuck she calling cheap?" I pushed her drunk ass out of the bathroom before we had a problem. I couldn't tell if she was feeling her drink or just being rude as usual. Bianca's always talking shit, and can't fight worth a damn. I looked down at my cell phone to see the time. It was just after eleven thirty and I was so tired. I had been up since like five in the morning. I got caught up in the hype of Black Friday sales. The lines were crazy and people were pushing, but it was well worth it. I was one of those crazies at the mall before it opened. The good thing is I got a jump start on my holiday shopping, but now I'm paying for it. I knew she was going to be upset, but I was about to break the news to Bianca that I was leaving and going home.

"Uhmm, Bianca, I go to work in the morning," I said, as I positioned my bag on my shoulder.

Bianca turned around and said, "No, you can't leave. Stay just a little longer. Please, girl, I need to meet somebody."

"I'm out of here," I said, as I began to walk away.

"Okay, hold up. Let's go one more place," she said.

"Where else is there to go?" I asked.

"I want to go someplace where there are some thugs," Bianca said.

"Thugs?" I repeated as I looked over at Bianca.

"Yeah, thugs! I need somebody that knows about the street. Them soft-ass dudes in here don't even know what shoes to wear!"

We left Azure and went to a bar near 52nd and Market. I really didn't want to be there. As we walked from the car to the raggedy bar, I asked, "Who could possibly be in here?"

"It be some jawns in here. Don't let the outside fool you."

"In this dirty place?" I yelled over the bass heavy music coming from the speaker by the entrance. We were about half a block from the bar.

"You know how dudes like to stay in their element and don't like to get dressed." Almost immediately, guys started walking up behind us.

"You see those guys?" Bianca asked.

I nodded yes.

"I think they want to steal our coats. Just keep walking. I think one of them got a gun. I just saw him reach for something in his jacket." Bianca began to walk real fast in the direction of the bar.

"You sure?" I turned around to look at the guy starting to walk faster. He had on denim jeans, brown shoes, and a gray trench coat. I jumped when he tapped my shoulder, and Bianca screamed.

"Damn, honey! What's wrong with you?"

"Nothing," I replied.

"Sorry if I scared y'all. I wanted to give y'all my card. I design clothes. Y'all sharp in those furs!" he said snapping his fingers.

"Thank you," I said, as I took his card. Not only was he not a stick-up kid, he was gay. Bianca was so stupid. I took his card and turned my back to him. He got the message and walked away. Talking about a thug. As soon as Bianca saw a thug, she was ready to run.

Turning to Bianca, I said, "I don't think you really want a thug."

"I wasn't scared."

"Yes you were. You were talking about, 'He's going to stick us up.' You ain't even from the hood."

We walked into the bar, where there were a bunch of old heads sitting and drinking. Aretha Franklin was playing on the jukebox.

"I can't believe you brought me to this hole in the wall. I'm about to get out of here. I have clients in the morning," I said. I pulled my bag over my shoulders, ready to leave. On cue, a light-skinned man walked over to where we were. I noticed he had pretty eyes, and full, perfect lashes that any woman would pay big money for.

"How you doing?" he asked.

I thought he was talking to me, but Bianca answered, "I'm fine, how about you?"

He looked at her and back at me. Then his friend approached me and got all in my face. Disappointed, I tried to pay attention as the friend of the cute guy began asking me questions.

"What are you about to do?" he asked

"I'm going home." I turned to leave but he caught my arm.

"Can I call you?" he asked.

"I have a boyfriend," I said, looking at my watch.

"I can be your special friend," he said, smiling.

"No," I said.

"How about breakfast?" he asked.

"No. I have to get up and work tomorrow."

"Where you work at?"

"I'm a stylist at Unique Designs."

"Really? My man, John Simmons, owns that spot," he said.

"Oh, okay," I said, as I looked around him for Bianca. *Yeah, whatever,* I thought. Everybody wanted to be down with John. John's brother used to be a boxer, and he gave John the money to start the salon. Dude was not worth giving my number to, so I told him I'd be right back. I pulled Bianca to the side and told her I was ready to be out. She said she was going to breakfast with the cute guy so I went home alone.

I drove home in my milk-colored Honda coupe, listening to one of my mixed CDs. Our apartment was in a converted old school building and I loved it. Once inside, I hurried to unlock my apartment door. I hated coming home alone. I went straight into my room. I had an oak sleigh bed and matching nightstands. As I undressed I found myself wishing that my man, Chris, was here. We could be all nestled under the covers. But he lived three states away. I met Chris in this big warehouse nightclub in D.C. called Dream. Bianca's girlfriend went to Howard University and she invited us down there for homecoming last year. He was deejaying that night. I walked over to him and requested a song. He asked for my number, and called me that same night. Instead of thinking there was something wrong with him for calling so soon, I knew there was something right with him, for wanting to get with me so soon. After leaving the club, Bianca and I went to IHOP and he met us there. Bianca was like "Look at you and your boyfriend, already." The next weekend I was in D.C. visiting him. We fell in love instantly.

This month we'd celebrated our one-year anniversary. One year in a long-distance relationship is difficult, but he's so worth it. In the beginning, it was hard to trust Chris because he was so far away. I used to call him at all times of night just to see if he was home. I even went on the road with him a couple of times with different groups. At first it was fun going to different cities and attending album release parties with him. But after a while it lost its luster. I'd just dozed off, with visions of my boo in my mind—he looked so good, with his six-three diesel hard body and skin the color of hot cocoa—when I heard a loud moan. I sat up and listened intently. I didn't know if Bianca had made it home or not, so I grabbed the bat I kept by the bed and went into the hallway to investigate. The moans got louder as I got closer to Bianca's bedroom door. I almost gagged as I heard her say, "Ah ah, ah. Oooh baby. Ah, ah, yeah, like that! I can take it, Daddy." That nasty little freak. I wondered which guy she ended up leaving the bar with. I went back to my room and turned my television up loud to keep out the noise. I settled back in my covers, put a pillow over my head, and then the covers over that. But I could still here a faint "Oh, baby." It was like they were having a sex marathon. I had to have a talk with her. The television covered the moaning, but it didn't do anything for the vibrating and slamming of Bianca's bed against the wall between our bedrooms.

After an hour, the noise stopped. I was on my way back to a restful sleep when I was awakened by the phone ringing. I reached over to my nightstand and grabbed the phone.

"Hello?"

"Hey. How you doing? Uhm, I think I met you tonight."

"Excuse me?"

"Yeah, I'm sorry. I think I met you. Your friend gave me your number."

"What?" I said. The nerve of him, calling me at four in the morning and not knowing who he was calling. I hung up on him and turned off the ringer.

The next morning I awoke late and sleepy. Between staying out too late and listening to Bianca's noisy sex, I didn't get any rest. I need eight hours of sleep and if I don't get it my whole day is off. I called the shop to see if any of my clients had arrived yet. The receptionist Annette said I had three ten-thirty appointments but no one had arrived yet.

I was about to take my shower when I realized my shower cap was missing. Bianca was always borrowing mine so I walked to her room to look for it. I knocked on her door and she didn't answer. I knocked again and opened it a little to peek in to see if she was asleep. I was stunned by the room's condition. Bianca's lamp, alarm clock, and jewelry box were on the floor. Her dresser was bare. Her perfume, earrings, and necklaces were strewn all over the place. Her room looked like a crime scene. I immediately returned to my room and called her cell phone.

"Bianca, are you okay?" I anxiously asked.

"Yeah, why wouldn't I be?"

"Because your room looks like a crime scene," I said, as I walked back toward the bathroom.

"Hold on. My supervisor is coming."

I put toothpaste on my toothbrush. I looked in the mirror and started brushing my teeth.

Bianca came back to the phone. "Yeah, so what's up?" she asked.

"I can't believe you made it to work," I said, as I tried to talk and brush my teeth at the same time. "Why does your room look like that?"

"That guy Khalil from last night. He was a beast!" she said in an excited whisper.

"A beast? So what happened?" I asked.

"He is so wild. He just kept flipping and spinning me all over the room. I know you had to hear it."

"Yeah, I did. You kept me up all night."

"I wasn't going to fuck him, but then he ate me out while I was on his shoulders. He's got an anaconda in his pants."

"Really?"

"Yes. He made me cum like five times! He knows how to work the middle girl."

"Okay, now you're getting too graphic. I don't want to know all that!"

"Well, you asked. He is the best piece I ever had and he got his own business."

"What does he do?"

"He has a tow truck company."

"Really?"

"Yeah. Well, I got to go before I don't have a job."

"Talk to you later," I said, and finished getting ready for work.

CHAPTER 2

7 have been a stylist at Unique Designs Barber and Hair Salon for three years. There are two barbers, Ty and Chuck, and three other stylists, Stacy, Janea, and Deon. Janea is little miss petite. She doesn't know how to do hair at all. She is always on lunch and still in hair school. But she goes with John, the owner, so he takes care of her. Deon's an old head, like forty, and always talking about sex. She turns everybody that walks out of her chair into a clone because she only knows one hairstyle. Stacy is the best stylist in the shop. After me, of course. She is hip and doesn't say too much. And last there is Annette, the receptionist and gossip queen.

I entered the shop with my Dunkin' Donuts bag in one hand and my latte in the other. One of my clients, Sharon, had already jumped her ass all in my chair.

"I gotta get to work, Gina," Sharon said, trying to rush me.

"I got you. I'll be right there," I said, annoyed. "Damn,

bitch. Can I breathe or eat my food?" I said under my breath.

"How do you want your hair?" I asked, as I turned on my stove and sipped my latte.

"Can you sew in a weave?" she asked.

"When you made the appointment, did you tell Annette you wanted a sewn-in? I don't do them on Saturdays."

"Well, can you just glue it in?" Sharon snapped, handing me the bag of hair she'd brought with her.

"Sure." I pulled her hair out of the bag and started splitting the tracks. I turned to my stove and noticed my ceramic flat iron was missing. "Deon, do you have my flat iron?"

"Yeah, here it goes. I borrowed it last night," she said, as she brought it over to me.

"Put my shit back after you're finished with it," I said playfully, then, "Sharon, relax. I'll have your hair finished in no time." I draped the cape around her neck and glued the tracks in as fast as I could. Every time I completed a curl, Sharon was touching it and looking in the mirror to see if I was styling her hair right. When I finished, I gave her a mirror to let her see how cute I had made her ugly ass. Satisfied with the results, she snatched the cape off and paid me.

Goodbye. One down and too many to go.

My other ten-thirty clients walked in.

"Nyree, can you start washing my client?" I asked, nodding my head toward Justine. Nyree was a part-time washer John had hired against my advice.

"Sure."

"Thanks. I got your lunch," I said, turning to prepare for

the next client. A few minutes later I noticed that Justine was still waiting to be washed. Nyree was playing around, talking to Janea.

"Nyree, can you wash my client?" I asked again. This time I watched her until she retrieved my client and walked her to the washbowl. She got the message and quickly washed and blow-dried Justine, then sent her over to me.

"Your little shampoo girl is too ghetto," Justine whispered, as she sat in my chair.

"What happened?" I asked, looking over at Nyree.

"She was on her cell phone while she was washing my hair. Then she wet the back of my neck with cold water." I looked down and saw that her shirt was soaked.

"I'm sorry. I'll be right back." I went to find Nyree. I located her in the backroom, chilling, talking on her cell phone.

"Nyree, can you come here for a minute?" I asked.

"I'll be right there," she said, as she continued to talk on her cell phone.

"No, come here now," I demanded. Nyree told whoever she was talking to that she would call them back, and walked over to me.

"Listen, what's up with you? I got people waiting to get shampooed. You wet my client's neck up. And now you are back here, running your mouth off on the phone."

"My bad. That was an accident. I'll do your other people now."

Nyree washed my clients, acting like she might have her act together. Then she sent over my next client, Sheila. I had given her a sewn-in weave because she had hair breakage in the middle of her head. I was trying to let her hair come back in. When I parted her freshly washed hair, I couldn't believe what I saw. My client's hair was all different lengths! Short, long, medium. Nyree had cut her hair off when she took out the sewn-in weave. I tried not to let Sheila know what was going on. I gave Nyree the look, and turned Sheila away from the mirror so she couldn't get a good look at her hair.

"What's wrong?" Sheila asked.

"Nothing," I said, as I started combing her hair. "You have a little breakage."

"Yeah, I noticed my hair was breaking off."

"That's all right. I'll have to give you a little trim," I said, as I tried to reassure her.

I cut her hair in a fly, feathered, layered style. Her hair was sharp when I got finished. I had avoided a major bomb. After that, the receptionist told me I had a call.

"Hello, this is Gina," I said, as I picked up the phone.

"Hey, Gina. This is Tiffany. Can I come in today?"

"What you getting done?"

"I want to get a ponytail weave."

"I'm kind of busy right now. Can you come around three?"

"Yeah. What kind of hair should I buy?" she asked.

"How do you want it?"

"Just straight back."

"Okay, I'm about to go to pick up my lunch. I'll pick some hair up on my way." I hung up the phone, and Stacy yelled across the shop, "Gina, we are out of black rinse and we need more deep conditioner."

"I'm about to go get my lunch. I'll pick it up," I said. I don't like buying supplies with my money because the owner acts like he can't reimburse me for the money I spend. He wants me to write it down and attach a receipt. Most times, I throw the receipt in the trash. But he is going to give me back my money today. I had one client under the dryer, and the other on her way. I had just enough time to run to the store.

Every time I go to the beauty supply store, it always amazes me that Black hair care products are being sold by Koreans. There were rows and rows of different textured and colored weave hair and wigs and creams to make your skin glow and make it lighter. Cocoa butter, press-on nails, callus cutters, and a vast assortment of nail polish and lip gloss. My phone started playing "My Boo" by Usher & Alicia Keys. I know it's corny, but that's my man's song. I took the call.

"Hey, baby. I called you," I said into the phone.

"I know. I'm sorry. I was in a meeting with the program director."

"What's wrong?" I asked.

"Nothing. She is just getting on my damn nerves. I keep spinning the same shit over and over again."

"That comes with the job. You coming through this weekend?" I asked.

"I'm going to try. I miss you, girl."

"I miss you too. You better come. It's been two weeks and I need a major workout."

"I got you. You know I miss your ass more than you miss me," he said.

"Yeah, all right," I said.

"I have been burning the candle at both ends. It's about to pay off, though. I got to go. I might be getting my own set on Saturday nights. That's major."

"Congratulations, baby," I said, uninterested.

"Why you sound like that?" he asked.

"No reason."

"I know you, Gina."

"I want to see you. I'm ready to come down today," I whined.

"You know you can't do that. We will spend all next weekend together, all right?"

"Okay," I said, ending the call. I can't wait to see my baby. I miss him in the worst way. I need to get a rubdown and tuned up. Bianca's got wild beast in her bed while I'm sitting here waiting for mines to come to town. Sometimes life is not fair.

I went back to the shop. The bootleg man came in with a duffel bag full of CDs and DVDs. I bought a few CDs. Then the costume jewelry girl came through. After that, my girl Reeva showed up with all these Juicy Couture jeans, in my size, size 6. She always came to my station first. She knew I would hook her up. I don't know how she got the real stuff. I didn't ask.

As I finished up with Tiffany, my last head for the day, she told me she overheard Nyree talking shit about me, saying she was about to quit. That was the final straw. I thought about all the drama that Nyree had caused today and decided I had to fire her ass. I couldn't wait to dig in Nyree's ass. Unfortunately, she had already left for the day. Okay, no problem, I thought. I'm going to call her cell phone. After Tiffany left, I dialed Nyree's number. Right after the first ring, I got her answering machine.

"You've reached the N-Y-R-E-E. It's Nyree. If your number is blocked, I will not answer the call. Leave a message and I'll holla."

Little stupid bitch, I'll show you.

"Yeah, Nyree, this is Gina. I heard you are about to quit on me. Don't bother coming back. There have been a lot of complaints against you. You have just not been on your job. So I got to let you go. And you can come and get your couple of dollars." I ended the call. *Now I got to find me a new shampoo girl,* I thought.

I came home tired from the day's events. All I wanted to do was get in the shower. When I entered the apartment all of the lights were off. I walked to my bedroom, undressed, and put on my robe. As I walked into the bathroom, I walked in on a naked guy, peeing. Khalil.

"My bad," I shouted, backing out of the bathroom.

Bianca came running out of her bedroom. "What's wrong?"

"What's wrong?" I snapped back. "Let a bitch know when you got company so I won't walk around in my robe," I said.

"Yeah, you bad," Khalil said, as he walked his bowlegged

butt back into Bianca's room. I went into the bathroom. Though embarrassed, I did get a good look at Khalil's ass. It was tight. His legs were well developed and he had a huge, thick, cucumber-size dick. Bianca was not exaggerating at all. All I can say is, damn, she got that? I wish I did. I need a piece of that. I should have stepped to him. He could have been my "in the meantime" piece.

The next morning, I realized I only had a month to do my holiday shopping. My family didn't really celebrate Christmas. My mom and dad stopped celebrating when we were teenagers. No tree, just a gift, and sometimes it was wrapped, sometimes it wasn't. My mom and dad started celebrating Kwanzaa instead, but I still bought everybody gifts.

I wanted to go shopping in New York. A lot of people think New York is all high-priced fashion. But if you know where to go, you can get really good deals.

Bianca wanted to go shopping with me, so we decided to start at the strip where they sell knockoff bags. I've never bought a fake bag. I work in a salon and people be checking out everything, down to the zipper. But I do want to see what they look like. I remember one time Janea walked in with a fake bag, and they clowned her for a week! She had bought it for three hundred dollars.

Bianca, however, has been down with the knockoff game. Instead of completely faking, she mixes the right amount of fake with authentic. People think she has money, but really she is broke. But I make enough. I make about one thousand dollars a week, so I can afford to buy any bag I like.

We took the train from Philadelphia into New York and got a cab to Canal Street, knockoff heaven. There was every kind of "fake" bag and name brand you could imagine. The sidewalk was crowded and the wind was whipping. It felt like it was ten degrees colder than at home.

"We should take some of these home and sell them," Bianca said, as she held up a replica of a blue Coach embroidered bag. The bag looked real and it was only twenty-five dollars. I negotiated with the vendor and got three bags for sixty bucks. I was going to take them back to the shop and sell them.

"Look at these earrings. This is where Reeva be getting all her shit! I gave her twenty dollars for this set, and look, this shit only cost three dollars!"

"Everybody got to make a dollar," I said, as I looked over the jewelry.

After shopping we had lunch a the Shark Bar, hoping we'd run into someone famous, just so we could go back and tell everybody who we saw.

"We should come up here for New Year's Eve and watch the ball drop. Then go try to find P. Diddy at his restaurant, Justin's," she said, as she ate a fried shrimp off her plate.

"I thought you got over that whole Puff Daddy crush."

"I thought I was over it too, but I think I still love him," Bianca said.

"You are so silly. Well, sorry, but my boo and I are going to be somewhere cozied up on New Year's Eve, sitting back, drinking champagne, and toasting."

"Your imaginary man. Chris, right?" she asked, like she didn't know him.

"What? My man is real."

"I don't know how you deal with that shit. I need to see my man."

"I get to see him enough," I said self-consciously.

"Well, if it works for you, fine. I just know I couldn't go for that."

We caught a cab to Penn Station and boarded our train. I put my bags underneath the seat, and settled back for the ride.

"When I get back I don't know who I'm going to get with," Bianca said.

"I'm going to get with some sleep," I said, hoping Bianca would realize I'm not in the mood to talk.

Minutes later her cell phone rang. She tapped me on my shoulder. Smiling, she whispered, "It's Khalil, the anaconda." She answered the call, saying, "Me and my girl Gina are coming back from shopping in New York. Yeah, I got you something. Uhmm hmm, yeah, maybe," she said softly. "I'll see if she wants to go out with us. All right, I'll call you when I get to town." She disconnected her phone and asked, "You want to go out with us?"

"No. I'm going to chill," I said. I turned back around and stared out the window as trees passed by. As Bianca got back on the phone making her hookups, I wondered what I was going to be doing. Nothing. I think Bianca could be right. I don't have anything to do but go home and go to sleep. I'm ready to give up on Chris. He is too far away. I need to have someone right now in my life. I always dream that we will get the opportunity to be together, on an everyday basis. People who have that don't appreciate it. It's one of the simple things. I get phone calls and flowers, but I would love to hug my boo and be in his arms anytime I want. I just want to wake up and see him beside me.

CHAPTER 3

Cold winter mornings remind me of growing up and getting ready to go to school. My mother loved a chilly house. She was good for telling me, if I was cold, to put on a sweater. Now I am grown. I turned my heat all the way up to 90 degrees if I wanted to. The weather makes me reminisce about when Chris and I first met last year. Back then, he had a lot more time for me. Now he has to schedule me in. Men always do whatever they need to do to get you. But once they've got you, forget about it. This kind of weather is for snuggling under warm covers, watching football on Sundays, black leather jackets, cute shoes, and hot cocoa.

I am going to visit Chris in D.C. I can't wait to see my baby. I'm going to tear him up. I usually go down on Saturdays after work and come back Monday evening. I left Bianca a note on the refrigerator telling her to clean up the apartment, and to smoke her cigarettes outside. I'm starting to see burn marks on my sofa. She didn't buy my furniture so she is not going to fuck it up.

Most times when I go to visit Chris, we drive to Georgetown for dinner and drinks. Our favorite restaurant is the Seafood Grill on M Street. There are pros and cons to having a favorite spot. The cons are, you always have the same meal and drink. The pros are that you know what to order and you get to know the staff. Chris promised me he would change our routine. So this time, he was cooking dinner for me. Because we only see each other a couple of times a month, I always make it my business to look good. As I pulled up to his apartment I looked in the vanity mirror and lined my lips with my nude gloss. Once I looked perfect I called his phone.

"Boo, I'm downstairs."

"I'll be right down," he said.

In less than a minute he was at my car door to take my bag from me. As I set the alarm on my car, I admired his loose-fitting jeans, slippers, and black T-shirt. His hair was cut low with light waves. Damn, my boo looks so good! We embraced and kissed, and then walked to his apartment. It was so cozy. His fiber sectional was hunter green with green-and-white-striped pillows. His bench press and weights were in one corner. In the other corner, he had a makeshift office. Yellow Post-it stickers were on the wall above the desk. He had CD cases and magazines on his coffee table. I heard a slow beat, with a drum, guitar, and light scratching coming from his room as we sat down on the sofa.

"What's that playing?" I asked.

Chris got real excited and said, "That's hot, isn't it?"

"Yeah, it sounds good," I replied, thinking he wasn't this excited when he met me at my car.

"It's a group from Dayton called Rizeup. I want to break this song on the radio. I was just arguing with my program director about it. She doesn't want to play it."

"Why not?"

"Because it's not commercial enough. It's too slow. She wants to keep playing the same songs, over and over, like everybody else."

"Well, y'all will figure it out. Where is my dinner you promised me?" I asked, changing the subject.

"In the kitchen," he said, as he walked me toward the kitchen. He squeezed and hugged me from behind, and kissed me again.

I lifted the lid off the pot to see what smelled so good. "You going to give me the recipe?" I asked, after sampling a little with a spoon. He shrugged his shoulders, playfully acting like he didn't know the recipe.

"You don't want to tell me? I'll remember that later," I joked.

"My mom would kill me if I gave out her secret."

Dinner was delicious. My boo knew how to cook. We ate by candlelight at his iron and cherrywood dinette. He poured me a glass of white wine.

"Here, I picked these up for you." He handed me a gold Godiva chocolate bag. I loved Godiva chocolate, but would never spend my own money to buy it.

I gave him a hug.

"You deserve it, baby. I'm mad because I don't get to spend as much time with you as I would like." He poured me another glass of white wine, then began to massage my feet. He rubbed the arch of my foot with his thumbs, and let his knuckles soothe the rest.

"Boo, I left my other bag in the car. Can you go get it?" I asked, taking the last sip of my drink.

"Where are your keys?" he asked, as he put on his slippers. I pointed to the coffee table. He picked up the keys and left. I wanted to change my clothes while he was gone. I was going to look sexy by the time he got back. I went into the bathroom, changed, and made sure my stuff was still in place. I had to make sure no other chicks had been coming over. My deodorant was still next to my douche, tampons, and pads. I left them there just for show.

When he returned, I was lying across his bed, dressed in a white lace negligee I had just bought at Frederick's of Hollywood. It had a cutout for my breasts and a slit in the bottom for him to enter without taking anything off. I was posed with the bottle of wine between my legs.

"You ready for me?" I asked.

He pounced on me, took the bottle, and placed it on the floor. He gently kissed me, then teased my nipples with his tongue until they perked up. Then he kissed and nibbled his way down my body. When he began kissing my pussy, greedily, I put my arms behind my head, grabbing my hair. I could barely take the pleasure he was producing between my legs, and I began grinding my hips closer to his face. He parted me with his hands, and slid his tongue through several times. It felt so good. The one thing that was good about not seeing my man regularly was that it was always so good. I was so turned on, I wanted to be his whore, his nasty girl.

We switched positions so I could take my turn to service him. He held my hair as I took all he had in my mouth. I licked up and down. Then I slurped side to side in a swirling motion. I looked up to see that his eyes were closed tightly and he was breathing heavily. I sucked harder and Chris's body tensed up like he was doing sit-ups. He almost let out a burst, but he held it back. I released him from my mouth and rolled over onto my stomach. I put a pillow underneath me. My ass was in the air as he gently pressed his muscular body into mine. I bounced back on him, our bodies swaying into each other. I flinched and shook as he smothered me with his dick. He started forcing his body farther into mine, banging again and again until I lost my balance and fell flat on the bed. I was too tired to get up, but it didn't matter. He pulled me in tighter to him, and pushed into me faster until I screamed out in ecstasy. Then he jerked and released himself into me. Anytime I think about leaving this man, times like this remind me why I should stay.

My weekend was perfect. I drove home thinking about Chris. He was everything a woman could want in a man. I just wished he lived a little closer. As soon as I walked in the apartment, all my happy feelings fizzled away.

I saw a strange woman sitting on my sofa, smoking a cigarette. Some niggah was lying on her. They were watching television, and when I came through the door they both looked at me like "Who the fuck are you?" I placed my keys on the coffee table and my bag on the floor.

"What's up, Gina? You have fun this weekend?" Bianca asked as she came out of her bedroom.

"I told you to have this place clean when I got back," I said, as I looked around my messy house.

"Yo, come on now. Get it together. I pay rent here too! Don't be walking in here all crazy."

"But it's not your place. It's mine." Bianca's female friend looked at me, then turned to Bianca and began to laugh.

"What? Hold up. Bianca, let me talk to you for a minute," I said.

But she wanted to act like she was tough. I pulled her into the kitchen and tried to reason with her. She kept trying to be hyped, getting all loud. Then she walked away. I stood there looking around the room. I got a niggah on my sofa, and some bitch smoking cigarettes. Bianca must have thought I was sweet.

I was walking toward my room when I heard Bianca's friend say, "That bitch came in here on some 'I'm your mom' shit."

"What did you say?" I asked, as I headed for the living room.

"Ain't nobody talking about you," Bianca said. Her friend started laughing again.

I turned around to her and said, "Bitch, this shit ain't funny."

"I didn't say it was," she said.

"Don't be talking about me in front of me, in my house," I said. I couldn't believe I was getting disrespected in my own house. Without even thinking twice, I turned to Bianca and said, "Yo, Bianca! Dig this, right? Get your shit, take your friends, and get the fuck out!"

"What?"

"You heard me. Get the fuck out of my house."

"What? I ain't going nowhere," she said, as she walked over to me.

I backed up a little. I was ready to swing if I had to. I looked her straight in her face with my hand on my hip. I said, "Bitch, don't fucking play with me. Get your shit and get the fuck out."

"But, I already gave you my rent for this month," she shouted.

"You're paid up until today!"

Her friend stopped laughing. I wasn't playing with Bianca anymore. She had crossed the line. I knew she wasn't going to do anything but pack her shit. She couldn't fight. And if she tried something on me, it wouldn't work. Twenty minutes later, Bianca and her friends were gone.

CHAPTER 4

*T*uesdays at the shop were usually slow days, so I took off. I wanted to get my locks changed. Bianca was mad that I kicked her out. She probably would try to come back and steal some of my shit. She was vindictive like that, so I called a locksmith to change the locks on the door. As I sat watching *The View* on television, I thought about riding back down to D.C. to see Chris. But who knew what he was doing today. I called his phone and got his voice mail. I left him a message, then called my brother, Mike. He said he was going to get me a new cell phone. I wanted to get Chris and me those picture phones so we can send each other flicks.

After the locksmith came, I got dressed, and drove downtown to Mike's job. Mike is a manager for Cell One. He was behind the desk, on the phone with one of his soon-to-be babies' moms, as the other one stood and looked at phones. My poor brother went from having no kids, to having two on the way. And the awful thing is, I don't think he is in love with either one of the mothers. Sheena is having baby number one, for him, and number five for herself. Why he would pick a woman with four kids to have his first baby with is beyond me. Why did he have sex with her raw? He knew her ass was fertile. We used to laugh about it. Kyra, on the other hand, was the gold digger. She had a whole bunch of dirt under her nails. She was always getting money from my brother, and he didn't know how to say no to her.

"Hi, Kyra. When are you going to have that baby?" I said, as I approached her and felt her stomach. She was tall, thin, and barely showing.

"In about another week or two."

"Wow, you are doing good," I said. I was amazed that the only weight she gained was in her nose and mouth.

As soon as Mike hung up the phone, Kyra went over to him and held her hand out. Mike dug in his pocket, counted a few twenties out, and gave them to her. Kyra gave him a kiss on the cheek, said goodbye to me and walked out of the store.

"Look at you," I said, as I gave my brother a hug.

"Man, it's hard work. Kyra's up here getting money from me, and then dumb-behind Sheena is on the phone asking dumb-assed questions."

"Like what?" I asked.

"She wanted to know what would happen if they both have boys. Which one would get to be the junior? If they go into labor at the same time, which one am I going to see first." It wasn't funny, but I had to laugh at him.

"Let me ask you. What made you get with Sheena?"

"Man, only a man would understand. When the lights are out, and the mood right, she knows how to handle her business," he said as he held up his hands.

"And evidently you don't know how to handle yours. You are so nasty! When are you going to tell mommy?"

"Never. She is going to go off and disown me." I laughed at him more.

"I did tell Chanel though," he said, scratching his head.

"Why you do that? Now you know Chanel can't keep anything to herself."

"No, she promised she wasn't going to say anything." Our older sister, Chanel, had the biggest mouth in the world. She'd been telling on us since we were kids. We discussed Mike's dilemma some more as he helped me buy two cell phones on his discount.

I returned home, put my mail on the end table, and turned the television on. It felt so good to be Bianca free! No more dishes in the sink and I could walk around naked if I liked. I was so happy that bitch is gone. People always say you never know someone until you live with them. That is the truth.

I sat on the sofa and opened a letter addressed to Chris. It was from the Vernés Hotel in Atlantic City. We'd stayed there over the summer. Inside the envelope was a coupon for a New Year's Eve special. It was for a dinner and massage for two, a bottle of champagne, and a deluxe room, all for three hundred dollars. I picked up the phone and made reservations. I planned to call Chris next and tell him not to make any plans, but before I got the chance to call him he called me.

"Hey, baby. I just got your message," he said.

"Guess what, Boo?" I said all excited.

"What?"

"I just made reservations for us for New Year's Eve."

"Really? For where?" he asked.

"The Vernés. The place we stayed at over the summer."

"Okay. That's going to be expensive, Gina," he said.

"It's not. They sent a coupon for champagne and the room, dinner, and a massage for three hundred."

"That's not bad. We got a couple of weeks to think it over. I might have to work," he said, unimpressed.

"And I bought us the picture phones today," I said.

"You going to send mine down with pictures of you on it?"

"Yeah, I'm going to mail it today. Why didn't you answer your phone earlier?" I asked.

"I was trying to record a promo for this party. Matter of fact, I'm going to call you back. I love you."

"I love you too. Bye," I said, as the phone disconnected in my ear. As soon as we get in a good conversation he always has to go. That shit makes me sick. I sat on the sofa and sulked a moment. Then the doorbell rang. I peeked out the window. It was that dude, Khalil. What was he doing here? He looked better than I remembered.

"Hey, how you doing? Is Bianca here?" he asked.

"No, she moved," I said.

"Really, damn! She ain't even tell me. Well, what's up with you anyway?"

"I'm cool," I replied.

"Can I use your bathroom?" he asked.

"Yeah, sure," I said, after I thought about it. If Khalil was a murderer, he would have already killed Bianca. I let him use the bathroom. As he was leaving, he said, "I know you're glad she is out of here."

"Why you say that?"

" 'Cause she is a broke airhead. But you got it going on. I like women that make their own money."

"Thank you," I said, a little confused that he would talk badly about Bianca.

"You know she is jealous of you. She's always talking about you. That you think you better than everyone 'cause you got a place and a nice car."

"She said that?" I asked, stunned.

"Yeah. I asked her why she was hating on you," he said, as he took a seat on my sofa.

"Is that right?" I said. He had to be lying. But then he started dropping major jewels. Like how my man lives in D.C. and how he be playing me. That I'm cheap as shit. That my dad drinks all the time, that my mother is crazy.

"I gave that bitch somewhere to live when her mom kicked her out. I can't believe she would say that about me. I gave that bitch a home," I said, as tears began to form in my eyes.

"Yeah, she ain't shit."

"I know that. But why are you really here?" I asked.

"I've always had a thing for you," he said, looking over at me.

"Yeah?" I said. I twisted my lip, as if to say "Whatever."

"You know I wanted you that night I met her. I was looking at you. But when I said, 'How you doing,' she stepped up front. I knew she was easy, so I hollered at her. I wish I could have talked to you that night, and by now you'd be my woman."

"I doubt it. I have a boyfriend."

"I heard about the dude. He's no threat. I'm a threat to him," he said confidently.

"How you figure?" I asked.

"I'll show you," he said, grabbing my hand. Just the touch of his soft hand made me flinch. I had to shake it off. He noticed and asked me if I was cold.

"No, I just got a chill."

"Yeah," he said, as he bit his lip and looked me over. "So, miss, what is your plan for the rest of the day?"

"I don't know yet," I said, as I walked him toward the door, hoping he would get the hint to leave.

"Don't make any plans. I might want to take you out."

"No, that's okay. I'm cool. Thank you though."

"Here, take my card, and tonight when you are all alone, lying on your lavender sheets and watching television, think about me."

"How do you know what kind of sheets I got? You my stalker?" I said, surprised.

"No. But I told you. It was you I wanted," he said, as he handed me his business card.

"Goodbye," I said, as I opened the door.

"When the lights are out and you wish somebody was there with you, call me, okay?"

"Whatever," I said, as he exited. After I closed the door, I looked down at the card and smelled it. It smelled just like him. I had just spent a beautiful weekend with my man, a good man. But in the back of my mind, I was curious about Khalil. I knew he knew how to throw it on you. Damn. Momentarily, I imagined how Khalil would feel inside my body. I wanted to get back at Bianca for talking shit about me. I already knew he's got the biggest package I've ever seen. I couldn't believe I was even letting my mind go there! People say the moment you meet somebody, you know whether or not they could get it. I don't agree with that. I think you just need the right time and space.

I put Khalil out of my mind and called my brother, Mike.

"What's up, daddy-drama?"

"Nothing. What's going on?" he asked, sounding a little impatient.

"I want to ask you a question," I said.

"Make it quick. I got somebody on the other line."

I told him how Bianca and I were on Khalil at the bar, but Bianca was more aggressive and hollered at him first. Then I mentioned how she and I had a heated blowup.

"Now you know you can't live with anyone. I don't know why you let her move in in the first place. Continue," Mike said.

"So he came over here. He said that he really liked me and wanted to get with me."

"Are you stupid? That's so much game."

"No, he said and knew things that he would know only if Bianca told him."

"Gina, he is trying to play you."

"You think so?" I asked, confused.

"Yes."

"He said he liked me. Why would he say that?" I asked.

"He is using the oldest trick in the book on you."

"And what's that?"

"Get with her girlfriend. You talk to her and get all the info you can on the one you are really interested in. Then you dump the first one. You then have the ammunition you need to get with her girlfriend. Y'all run y'all mouths, so chances are, he knows everything about you."

"He said he likes a girl with her own money. He said he likes a woman that is independent, and he likes that I got my own shit."

"He was trying to stroke your ego. It is a game. It don't matter what you got. He is just trying to fuck you. To be honest, looks ain't everything. I'll take an okay chick with a great body and—"

"I already know," I said, interrupting him.

"Shut up and let me finish. One, I can't believe you are going for this. I raised you better. Two, he is going to say and do whatever it takes to get you. But hey, don't listen to me. Do your thing. I got to go; I got baby-momma-drama."

"Which one?"

"Sheena."

My Boo

"Next time wear a condom."

"There won't be a next time. I'm getting snipped. Bye."

So what do men want? A cute girl or a girl with her own money. I don't know. Sometimes you see a cute guy with a busted chick, but she got money. Then you might see an okay-looking chick and she got somebody doing everything for her because she looks half decent. I don't know if men like independent women or not. I told everybody in the shop about what happened with Bianca, and how Khalil came to see me. Everyone had a different opinion. My survey was unscientific, but out of the five people I asked, only one person told me to get with Khalil. I would love to get with him. If the shoe was on the other foot, I know for a fact that Bianca would do it to me. But I'm not Bianca and I have a man.

CHAPTER 5

*M*arcia, a client of mine that I'd gone to high school with, looked in the mirror and grimaced. "Gina, these curls are too tight."

"Trust me. After you get out of the shower your curls are gonna drop."

"But what if they don't?" she asked.

"They will. I promise." Marcia was my last customer of the day, so I thought I was just about done. I was so wrong. As Marcia was leaving, Sharissa, a woman I'd worked on the previous day, walked into the shop looking like she got attacked. She walked over to me, and the only thing I could say was, "Girl, there is a patch of your hair missing."

"Yeah, I know, girl. He be pulling my hair out bad," she said, as if it was normal. I looked a little closer and saw that her eye was bruised.

"What's that? A black eye?" I said, as I touched her face.

"He thinks I'm cheating on him. He said, 'You think you cute 'cause you got your hair done.'" She started crying. "I don't have anywhere to go. He is looking for me."

Janea walked over and asked her if she told him where she was going. She said no, but we still locked the door and pulled the blinds shut. I walked over to Sharissa and made her have a seat.

"Listen, you should call the cops, and then I can drop you off somewhere," I said, as I tried to remain calm. We all looked up at a loud knock on the door.

We all knew it was Sharissa's boyfriend. Janea called the salon owner on her cell phone. I called the cops on the shop phone.

Janea went to the door and peeked through the blinds and said, "May I help you?"

"Yeah. Tell Sharissa to come on out!"

"There isn't anyone named Sharissa here," she said.

We were all quiet, hoping that he would just go away. But he didn't. He said to Janea, "I see her car and I'm about to put it on fire. If you don't want to get involved, tell her to bring her ass out."

"Okay, listen," she said. "This is my shop, and Sharissa ain't here. She got her hair done yesterday."

"Well, if you see her, tell her her man is looking for her."

"Okay, I will do that."

He left and we were relieved when the cops came. Sharissa filed a report, and after the cops left I tried to do something with the hair she had left. I thought the drama was over until Annette told me I had a call.

I picked up the phone and said, "Hello."

A dark voice responded, "Are you the bitch that got my baby looking like a ho?"

"What?" I said.

"You're covering for her. I know she messes with one of those barbers in there."

"We don't have any barbers," I lied, trying to calm him.

"Yes you do, and I'm sure this white Honda is the dude's car she is messing with."

"That's my car. Please do not touch my car!" I screamed. Everybody turned around, and we all ran for the door. But it was too late. He'd flattened all my tires. I called the cops again. While we waited for them to return, I thought, like, do you know how much my tires cost? Sharissa must have read my mind because she pulled out two hundred dollars and gave it to me. We didn't ask her to, but she gathered her things and left.

"I knew I had to have my car towed to the shop. I immediately thought to call Khalil. I dialed the number off his business card. He answered on the first ring and I blurted out, "Hey, this is Gina. All my tires are flat. Do you think you could come tow my car to the shop?"

"Damn, you in a rush. Where are you?" he asked.

"At the shop on Fortieth and Spring Garden Street."

"I'll be right there." Khalil arrived fifteen minutes later, wearing a tan construction jacket, tan boots, and a black skull cap. He smelled like he just got out of the shower. His hair was lightly greased and his waves were aligned in perfect *S*'s. His facial hair was trimmed just right. Everybody in the shop did a double take, like, Who is that? He walked up to me and asked for my keys. I gave them to him. He loaded my car on a lift and told me not to worry. He would get it fixed.

He brought my car back two hours later and told me the cost of the repair was on him.

"Well, I really appreciate you getting my tires fixed," I said, as I walked him to the door.

"You can call me for anything you want, tow-related or not," he said, stroking his chin.

"Okay, I will."

"Look, I know you got a man, but how about us being friends?"

"I got enough friends," I said.

"We'll see," he said, as he eyed me over. "Can I call you later on? Maybe we can talk."

"Talk about what? Bianca?" I asked.

"No, talk about us," he said with an attitude.

"Whatever. It's cold out here, I have to go," I said, as I walked back into the shop. As I stepped inside, I could hear Janea yelling, "Who is that?"

"That's the one I was telling y'all about. That's the one Bianca said was the best piece ever," I answered.

"Oh, see," Deon said. "She couldn't be my friend, I would be like, oh really, let me find out for myself." She stood in the middle of the floor and poked her butt in the air. Everyone laughed at her ass.

"You know I'm faithful," I said, placing my hand over my heart.

"Where your man live at? Where, D.C.?" She put her hand up to her ear, waiting for my response. "While he in D.C. doing who knows what, I would be in Philly doing *him*," she said, nodding her head toward the door. "What's his name, Mister Tow Truck Man? Shit, give me his card," she said, and snatched it out of my hand.

"I know that's right," Stacy and Janea said. I took the card back from Deon and we all laughed.

"Look what the wind blew in," Annette said. I turned around to see who she was talking about. It was Nyree. Everyone said hi to her and asked how she was doing. Everyone except for me. She came over to me and said, "Can I please have my job back?"

"Girl, we hired somebody else. Sorry," I said, playing with her.

"Well, you got to fire them because I need my job. I already know how to do everything and you're going to have to train the other person," she said, trying to plead her case.

"It is easy to train somebody," I said.

"No it's not. Please take me back," she begged.

"Why should I take you back?" I asked.

"For real, Gina. I promise I will get my act together." She knelt on the ground and looked up at me with imploring eyes.

I gave her a real hard look that said she'd better not make me regret giving her another chance. "Nyree, you can start back tomorrow," I said.

She was so happy she got off the ground and hugged me. She just didn't know how bad I needed her back. My arms and back muscles were hurting from bending over the wash-bowl.

"Thank you so much. I will not fuck up again. I promise," she said.

"Watch your mouth," Deon said.

"My bad okay. I'll be here right after school." Nyree hung out for a moment, then left.

CHAPTER 6

7 was in the house by myself and Chris was on his way from D.C. I hoped he'd make it before the snowstorm came. We both agreed that the newscasters didn't know what they were talking about half the time. I called him to make sure he was on his way.

"Chris, are you still coming?" I asked.

"Baby, it is snowing down here bad. It is going to be a nor'easter," he said.

"So, does that mean you're not coming?"

"Gina, what do you want me to do?" he asked.

"I want you to come and be with me. I want you to be here."

"You want me to get stuck? I can't fly to you. I want to be there with you too."

"No, you don't."

"Yes I do. Stop acting like a baby."

"Stop acting like a baby?" I screeched. "I cancelled all my clients for you today. Now you want me to stop acting like a baby? Fuck you." I hung up the phone, then picked it up and called Khalil. "Hey, this is Gina."

"What's up?"

"Nothing. I just wanted to see what you were doing," I said, nervously.

"I got a couple of tows scheduled. It is supposed to get really nasty out today. You should take a ride with me if you're not doing nothing."

"All right. Come and get me," I said.

He said that he would be at my apartment in half an hour. I threw on an old bra with grandma panties, so I knew I wouldn't give him any. It always worked. I put my knee-high Timberland boots on and my black hooded Roca Wear coat. I waited by the door until I saw big lights and heard the sound of a throttling engine approaching. Khalil pulled up in his big tow truck and I closed and locked my door. The snow outside was about six inches deep already. I couldn't believe it was coming down the way it was.

"I didn't know it was going to be this bad."

"Yeah, I know. This is kind of a surprise storm. They are talking about twelve to fifteen inches now." I climbed into the truck, moving aside receipts and a clipboard. The scanner went off, and Khalil picked up the receiver and said, "I'm right on it."

"Who is that lady on dispatch?" I asked.

"That is my aunt." Khalil maneuvered the truck effortlessly through the snow to his first call, a man who had a car accident.

The driver was taken away in an ambulance. We towed his car to the garage. I soon realized that bad weather created brisk business for Khalil because his aunt sent us to almost a dozen locations to tow cars that had been in accidents or help people get their cars out of snow.

After four hours of constant towing, Khalil called his aunt to have someone take over for him.

"Now that I'm done working for today, do you want to get something to eat?"

"No, I'm not hungry."

"Do you want to get snowed in together?" he asked, not even bothering to look over at me.

"No, I want to go home," I said.

"Why? You think you can't control yourself?" he said, finally looking over at me.

"I can control myself," I said, while giving him a look like *Please*.

"I don't think you could. I'll take you home. Let me just get out of these wet boots first," he said, as he pulled the truck up in front of an apartment building. I assumed he lived there. "You can sit in the truck. It should only take a few minutes."

I waited for Khalil for over thirty minutes before I called his cell phone to tell him to hurry up. I waited another few minutes for him, then I took the keys out of the ignition, got out of the car, and walked up to the apartment I'd seen him enter. I knocked on the door. "What is taking you so long to get changed?" I asked, when he opened the door.

"Here I come. You can have a seat. I don't bite," he said, as he walked around in his towel.

"Put some clothes on," I said.

"I'm about to." Then he changed subjects on me. "How about your girlfriend. She keeps calling me," he said, as the phone rang.

"For real?" I felt nervous. I felt like she knew I was over there. I hadn't talked to her since she left my house.

"Won't you tell her to stop calling my phone?" he said.

"You tell her. What I look like?" I said, with an attitude. He hit the speaker phone button to answer the call. I heard Bianca, all hyped and desperate, saying, "What's up, Lil? When you going to come and get me so I can hit that?"

"What you going to do to me?" he said, and she fell right into the trap.

"First I am going to suck your dick so hard you are going to come two times in my mouth. I'll swallow it, and let it run down my lips," she said, laughing. I cringed. I couldn't believe she was playing herself like that, telling him how she wanted him. Then she said, "I don't have to spend the night. Just let me come over. Please, Khalil," she begged. That wasn't even her man and she was talking about putting his dick in her mouth. She is so disgusting.

"Please, Lil, come get me," she begged again.

"No, I'm cool," he said, then hung up on her.

"I told you your girlfriend is a freak."

"That's on her," I said.

"You know you about to get stuck in here with me," he said, approaching me from behind.

"No I'm not," I said, hoping my nervousness didn't show.

"What happens if you do?"

"I won't," I said. I was so attracted to him. I could feel his breath on my shoulder as he said, "So when you going to stop playing?"

"I'm not playing."

"You ready for me then?" He wrapped his arms around me and pulled me back against his chest.

"Ready for what?" I said and took a deep breath. He smelled so good. His arms were defined with just a few traces of light stretch marks. I'd wanted to cuddle in his arms. I just needed to be hugged and caressed.

He moved so that he was standing in front of me, then knelt and slowly pulled down my pants. He removed my grandmom panties and began licking over my pussy, fast and ferociously. He was like a kitten licking its paw. I held my coochie lips open so he wouldn't miss a spot. He was wobbling his neck and head, moving it from side to side. Soon, my pussy had a heartbeat of its own, and it was racing fast. I grabbed the back of his head as I came.

He sat back with a satisfied expression on his face. He shook his head and said, "You look so good. Now I want you to sit on my face."

I was a little uncomfortable with his request. I didn't want to squat over his face, but he pulled me toward him until I felt his nose, lips, tongue, and mustache circling the length of my vagina to my buttocks. It was so thrilling that I grabbed my own breasts. They needed to be touched. He snatched my hands off them and made me touch my clit. I stroked as he ate until I came again and collapsed on him. But he wasn't done yet. He entered me, and I savored the feel of my skin slapping against his. I heard myself make puppy noises I've never made in my life. He fucked me harder than I had ever been fucked in my life. It was good, but once it was over I was confused. How could I be with Khalil and Chris?

"Can you take me home, Khalil?" I asked, as I got dressed.

"There is twelve inches of snow, outside" he responded.

"I need to get home."

"All right. Listen, how about we order something and relax."

"No, just take me home," I demanded. I had just had the best sex of my life, but I felt horrible. And when Khalil finally dropped me off at my apartment I wanted to tell someone about what just happened, but I had nobody to call and tell.

CHAPTER 7

I was at the shop, and it was the end of the day. It had snowed the entire day so I had a lot of cancellations. Me and the other stylists were all sitting around doing nothing. I decided to clean my station. I sprayed it down with some Fantastik and wiped my mirror and everything down with a towel. I wanted to go home, but I was scared I might run into Khalil. I'd been avoiding him hard for like a week. He'd been stopping by my house and blowing my phone up. I didn't know why he didn't show up at the shop. I was determined to ignore him. If I didn't, he would try to turn me out. Then I'd be on his answering machine just like Bianca, leaving nasty messages.

I don't think so. The man has some kind of magic stick and his tongue game is amazing. And I don't want any parts of it. I love my man and I don't want to lose him. And that's exactly what's going to happen if Chris finds out about all of this. I'm not risking my relationship on him. I want to build a future with Chris, not Khalil. Plus, I don't even know him like that. With all that said, I am still drawn to him and I don't know why. His body ain't better than Chris's, he don't look as good as my boo, but his ass is sexy as hell. There's just something about him. My musings were interrupted by Annette screaming that I had a call. I walked over to her and took the receiver. "Hello."

"Gina."

"Yeah, who is this?"

"This is Bianca."

"Bianca," I said, surprised.

"Yeah, hey, girl."

"Hey," I said, wondering why the fuck she was calling me.

"So, how you been?" she asked, like I just didn't kick her out a few weeks ago.

"I'm fine. What's up?"

"I just wanted to say that I think we been friends for too long to let something like this interfere with our friendship. You know what I'm saying. We grew up together." She paused, waiting for me to say something, so I said, "Oh. Well, I got a client. So I got to go." I hung up right in her ear. I couldn't believe that bitch was trying to be my friend. Imagine that, us being cool again. The only reason she was trying to call me was because she didn't have nobody to go out with. Nobody liked her ass. I was finished cleaning my station and was getting ready to leave when Stacy said, "You going out with us, right?"

"Going where?" I asked.

"We're taking Janea out for drinks for her birthday."

Damn, I had forgot—they had asked me last week. I was

tired and I wasn't dressed. I had on old boots and a big coat, plus I hate to go out when it snows. I told Stacy and Deon that I would go with them, even though I didn't feel like it. I turned and looked in the mirror to check my appearance. I brushed my baby hair down and pulled my hair up into a ponytail. Then I put on some blush, lip liner, and aqua-colored eye shadow. I changed my shoes, and I was ready for the bar.

We went to Scotty's, a bar near the shop, and took turns buying Janea a drink. After downing my watermelon jolly rancher shot, we all got on the dance floor, dancing and singing, "Go, Janea, it's your birthday! We going to party like it's your birthday!" Janea got out in the middle of the dance floor and put her hands over her head. She was swaying, popping, and shaking her hips.

"Give her another Woo Woo," Deon yelled. We were having fun dancing and joking. We were having a good time and had a soul train line going on when I saw him. Khalil. I tried to hide, but he walked straight over to me and whispered in my ear, "Where have you been hiding, Gina? I came by the shop for you. Your receptionist told me where to find you. Why have you been avoiding me?"

"I haven't been avoiding you," I said.

"Yes, you have. It's cool. I know how to take a hint. If you don't want to be bothered, just tell me."

"It is not like that. I've just been busy. I got a man and what we did that night was a mistake."

"You sure about that?" he asked, as he grabbed his chin.

"Yeah, positive," I replied. He said okay, nodded up, and walked away. I continued to dance and took down shots of Janea's drinks. She didn't need them. She was passed out in a chair. I looked for Stacy and Deon. I couldn't find them, so I assumed they were in the restroom. I was walking to the restroom to check when I noticed Janea and Khalil dancing. I was about to go stop them before Janea's boyfriend, John, walked up in here and fucked her up, but changed my mind. I figured Khalil was trying to get me jealous, so I let him have his fun. I got another drink, sat down, and pretended like I didn't see him grinding up against Janea. After the song ended, he stopped dancing with her and came and grabbed my hand to pull me toward him. I was so close I could feel his abs pressed up against my stomach.

"Why are you playing with me?" he said, close to my ear so I could hear him above the music.

"I'm not playing," I said, and I turned away.

"You are coming home with me tonight," he stated.

"Okay," I said.

"Go tell your friends. Right now. We are leaving." I walked over to the girls and told them I was out. I tried not to care that they knew I was going home with somebody that was not my boyfriend. I tried to make it look innocent, saying, "He is just driving me home. I'll see y'all tomorrow."

I realized how drunk I was when I got in the backseat. Khalil started the car and then got in the back with me. "Why you back here?" I asked.

"Rob is going to drive us home," he said, as he yanked my

pants down. I tried to protest a little, but he got on his knees and started kissing and nibbling all over my pussy. I couldn't believe he was in the car, in the parking lot, doing this. His friend Rob got in the car, and he didn't stop. I saw Rob looking at me in the rearview mirror. I was feeling so good and flirty, that I blew him a kiss. He licked his tongue out like he was next. I closed my eyes and imagined Rob grabbing my breasts, and fucking me as hard as Khalil did. Khalil brought me back to reality by inserting two fingers into me, twisting back and forth until I trembled and came all over his fingers.

We reached Khalil's place. I walked into his room, undressed, and lay across the bed. For the moment I put Chris from my mind. He wasn't here and I needed something hard and firm planted between my legs, regularly, and Khalil's long, hard dick would do. Khalil walked in the room, and behind him I saw Rob. I covered my naked body.

"What are you doing?" I asked, nodded toward Rob.

"Nothing. You want him to stay?"

I thought about it for a moment. Why not? Why not have both of them pleasure me? I thought about it some more, though, and declined Khalil's offer. He pushed Rob out of the room and came over to me.

"You made the right decision. I don't like sharing my woman."

I haven't decided what I am going to do about Khalil. I like him, the sex is good, but I don't know if that's all we have together. After leaving the bar with him I spent the entire night at his apartment. The next morning I called Annette to cancel my appointments so Khalil could take me out to breakfast and then to the mall. We spent the day together just shopping and chilling. It was real nice to be with him, having all of his attention. I felt like I was falling for him. I didn't know what I was going to do. He was saying and doing all the right things, bringing me lunch at the shop, sending me flowers, and texting cute messages. Chris hasn't even missed me or caught on yet. He only called once in three days and left a message saying that he would be up Monday for my mother's Kwanzaa dinner. I had forgot all about the dinner. I'm glad he remembered something. I decided to call my mom to check in.

"Mom, just wanted to see if you needed anything."

"No, I have everything covered. Just make sure you get here on time."

"I will Mom, don't worry. So, what is Nana doing?" My grandmother lived with my parents and was always doing something comical.

"Your father took her to the Senior Center to get some fresh air." She sighed dramatically.

"Mom, Nana is not that bad."

"Humph, you try living with her. Well, see you tomorrow, sweetheart."

CHAPTER 8

$\mathcal{T}$he following evening I dressed up for my mother's Kwanzaa dinner. Chris was supposed to be here already, so I called him to make sure he was on his way.

"Baby, where are you?" I asked.

"I'm getting ready now. Look, I have something to tell you."

"Like what?" I said curiously.

"I'm about to quit my job."

"Why?" I shouted.

"Because I'm going on tour overseas with Rizeup. Remember the group I was telling you about?"

"For how long?" I asked.

"Three months."

"Three months! What am I going to do while you're away for three months?"

"It's not concrete yet. I wanted to talk to you first before I made up my mind."

"This is crazy. You are tripping. What am I supposed to do while you're on the road?" I asked.

"Wait for me, baby," he said.

"Wait for you. You sound real stupid!"

"Look, I'll see you when you get here." I was furious with him. He was not thinking about us, he was thinking about himself. Why quit a radio station job to go on tour with a no-name rap group?

I finished getting dressed and went to my parents' home. When I arrived, my uncle Rich and Dad were outside fixing my dad's silver Ford Astro van. I gave both of them a kiss and went inside. My parents' home is a big corner house with four bed-rooms. The large living room is decorated with African sculp-tures and paintings. My nana was sitting on the big burgundy sofa under the picture window. I gave her a kiss on her cheek. My mother came downstairs and hugged me.

"Go dish yourself up a snack. I'll meet you in the kitchen shortly."

I was making my way into the kitchen when I heard my nana scream out, "Somebody went in my room and stole my damn pearls! Who got my shit?" My sister, Chanel, came over and whispered, "Nana tripping again." Nana walked right past me with her cane and went up the steps in search of her neck-lace. My brother, Mike, came up to me and hugged me and we both started laughing at our crazy eighty-five-year-old grand-mother. That lady was crazy. We had to find her pearls for her or she would drive us crazy the rest of the night. Everybody stopped what they were doing and began searching for her missing necklace. My mom came over, gave me a kiss, and said, "See what I got to deal with."

"Remember when we were kids and she used to accuse our friends of stealing?" Chanel said, laughing.

"Yeah, I remember," I said, as I joined in the search for my nana's pearl necklace. We all looked around for about an hour. Mike found the necklace under her pillow. As usual, she had misplaced it. She was always hiding shit from herself, blaming everyone else, and never apologizing to anyone. This time was no different. She put her pearls on and went and had a seat on the sofa.

After the hunt for Nana's pearls, Mike and I sat at the kitchen table and began fixing our plates. My mother had the table decorated with kente cloth, and red, black, and green Kwanzaa candles were in the centerpiece. She had a tray of my favorite dish, banana pudding. She also had cooked salmon, duck, cabbage, yams, turkey, mashed potatoes, macaroni and cheese, and stuffing.

"Where is Mr. DJ?" Mike said, as he put mashed potatoes on his plate.

"Home. He is coming up to get me, and then we are driving back down."

"That should be nice," Chanel said, as she sat down with us.

"Where is Harold and the kids?"

"They went to the movies," she said, as she loaded her plate. Then she turned to Michael. "Has Sheena had her baby?"

Michael whispered, "Not yet. And Kyra hasn't had hers either."

None of us realized that our dad was behind us, eavesdropping, until he said, "Wow, you know a lot of pregnant women, son." He laughed. He had no idea they were both his son's babies. We looked up and laughed it off with our dad.

"He should know them. They both his kids," Chanel said.

"What?" my dad shouted. "Two women pregnant! Michael, what's going on?"

"Chanel, mind your business!" Michael said, as he stood up. Chanel said she thought everybody knew.

"Michael, you have two women pregnant?" my dad asked again. I thought Michael would lie, but instead he said, "Yeah, I do." Uncle Rich came up behind my dad, shook his head, and said, "All right, now. Player player." He tried to give Mike a pound but Mike stepped aside. Then my mother walked into the kitchen. "What is this I hear about a baby, Michael?"

"Mike got a baby on the way, Mom," Chanel blurted out and put her head down.

"Lord have mercy," my mother said, as she sat down. Everything stopped. We waited for her to say more. Finally, she said, "I dreamed about fishes a long time ago. I thought it was Chanel, or you, Gina. But it's you, Michael."

"Yeah, I was going to tell y'all," he said nervously.

"Well, when you going to bring her to meet us?" my mother asked.

"It's a 'them,' Mom," Chanel put in. This time I gave her a look to cut it out.

"Huh? I'm confused. What do you mean it's *them*, Chanel."

"Look, I don't have anything to do with this," she said.

"Joan, Mike got two different women pregnant," Uncle Rich said.

"Is that right, Mike?" She said as she looked over at him. He nodded yes and then she said, "Well, bring them both over," and got up from the table. I heard her mumble, "God does have a sense of humor. Instead of having one, you have two!" She went to tend to Nana and get ready for the candlelighting ceremony. My mother took the news way better than I expected. Mike shook his head and Chanel got up from the table because she knew she was dead wrong.

Turning to Mike, I asked, "You okay?"

"Yeah, I'm fine. If anything I'm glad that's over with," he said, as he wiped imaginary sweat from his forehead. "So what's up with you? Now that I'm outed, I'm ready to put somebody else on blast. What's going on with you with that dude that Bianca was seeing?"

"Nothing."

He looked over at me and said, "You sure?"

"Yeah, I'm sure," I lied. I didn't want to tell him what was going on.

"I don't want to hear it," he said. "Don't call me saying he hurt me. He played me. Then I'm going to get on the phone with my boy Chris and tell him what's going down."

"No. For real, everything is cool. I'm not seeing him," I said, as I started to clear the table. I walked into the kitchen to help Chanel do the dishes. I didn't want to talk about Khalil, and decided to lecture Chanel about telling Mike's business. She knew she was wrong, but before I could say something to her Chris called my cell phone.

"You almost here?" I asked.

"No, I'm caught up at the radio station. Can you catch the train down? I'm going to have one of the interns pick you up, okay? Then we'll sit back and chill."

"Chris, I don't want to catch the train. I want you to come pick me up like you promised," I whined.

"I can't leave, Boo. I miss you. I want to see you real bad. Don't be mad at me, okay?" he said.

"It's going to be hard not to."

"Are you going to get on the train?"

"Yeah, I'll get on the next train. Bye," I said, and ended the call.

I told everybody goodbye. My mom wanted me to stay and light the candles, but I didn't have time. Reluctantly, I caught the train to see Chris. As soon as I got on the train, I felt cramping, like my period was coming on. That was a relief. I didn't have to have sex with Chris. Chris knew the only thing I wanted him to do when my period was on was rub my feet and stomach. I didn't know what I would do if he tried to have sex with me. He probably wouldn't guess I'd been with somebody else. But even if he didn't know, it just wouldn't have felt right. I arrived at New Carrolton Station just outside of D.C. He sent one of the station interns to come and pick me up. He was a tall brown-skinned kid with braces.

"Hi, I'm Jules," he said. "Burner sent me to get you."

"Chris," I said, laughing. I never called him Burner, his DJ name. Jules took my bag, got on his cell, and called Chris, and we drove to the radio station.

The station was in the middle of nowhere, I guess to keep crazy people away. The giant antenna and power lines towered over the small building. We entered through the side door. Plaques and posters of artists lined the walls. Chris was on a commercial break so he came out of the studio booth and gave me a kiss. He said he had to stay until the other DJ came in. She was three hours late already. I took a seat and listened as he answered the request lines. There were kids calling in, asking did they win tickets and could he play an Usher song, and young ladies excited to give a shout-out to their men on lockdown. It was all real funny. An hour later the other DJ, Chi, came in with her daughter and apologized for being late. I was ready to go home and get in the bed and relax with Chris.

As we left, Chris said, "We got to make one stop."

"To where?"

"I told you, we have to go to the Club Enya. I just got to stop in for a little bit. They're paying me five hundred dollars."

"What club? You didn't tell me about no fucking club, Chris," I yelled.

"I did. You must not have heard me."

"You said you were at the station and to come down so we can sit back and relax. What are you talking about? You're lying for no reason."

"I'm not lying. I thought I told you. We can use the money I earn to pay for the room you got for New Year's."

I sucked my teeth, got in his car, and slammed the door.

I escorted Chris to Club Enya. Even though I was half asleep, he tried to introduce me to people in the club. I was unresponsive and he could tell I was upset. He looked at me and said, "It is not always going to be like this."

"Yes it will. Baby, I need to see you when I want you. I'm tired of this long-distance shit."

"So what are you saying" he asked with an attitude.

"I don't know," I said, as I hunched my shoulders.

"Maybe we should take a break. Because I need somebody a little more understanding," he said with a pout.

"Maybe we should," I said, folding my arms unsympathetically.

Two hours later we finally made it back to his apartment. He had an attitude, and so did I. I decided that first thing in the morning, I was getting out of there. Chris can DJ the rest of his life and go overseas and do whatever he wants. I don't care. He slept on the sofa while I slept in his bed. The minute I saw the sun, I jumped up and called a cab. He heard me on the phone with the cab company.

"Why are you going home?"

"Didn't you say maybe we need a break? You don't consult me about things going on in your life. Then you say you're going away for three months. And then after all that you lie to me about having to spin at another club. I'm fed up. I can't take this anymore."

"You're fed up. What about me? You know what, fuck it." He threw his hands up. "Do you want me to take you to the train station?"

"No, I'm catching a cab," I said, as I walked passed him. He grabbed me and said, "If you don't want me to go on tour, I won't go."

"No, I want you to do whatever you want. Don't stop following your dreams for me."

"You are a part of my dreams, Gina." He tried to hug me, but I pulled away from him and said, "I used to believe that, but now I don't. You are the one who needs some time to think. I'm going home." I grabbed my overnight bag and walked out of his apartment. He didn't stop me.

CHAPTER 9

On the train on the way home, I wondered what was going to happen between me and Chris. We were growing apart because of the long distance between us. My thoughts were interrupted by a call from Khalil.

"Why haven't I heard from you?" he asked.

"I didn't know I had to check in with you," I said.

"Damn, what's up with the attitude?"

"I don't have an attitude."

"Have you been thinking about me?" he asked.

"No, I been busy."

"Well, I have been thinking about you. Can I see you?" he asked.

"I'm on the train on my way home."

"Can I pick you up?"

"If you want to, but my friend is in town."

"I don't care. I just want to see you. What time does your train get in?"

"At three thirty. Meet me where all the cabs are. Bye."

After Khalil picked me up, we stopped, got something to eat, then went to my apartment. I walked straight to the bathroom, took a shower, and put on nightclothes. When I came out of the bathroom Khalil was already in my bed.

"Excuse me. I see you have made yourself mighty comfortable," I said, as I entered the room.

"Come. Lie down."

I got in the bed and he pulled me closer.

"Don't this feel good?" he asked, as I lay beside him. He pulled the covers over us and we turned the television on and went to sleep cuddling.

The next morning I awoke, and Khalil was still asleep. I took another shower and was drying off when I heard a knock on the bathroom door.

"Your phone was ringing," he said, smiling as he held my phone up in his hand.

"Who's on the phone?" I asked, confused.

"You know somebody named Chris?" he asked.

I looked at Khalil like he was out of his mind, then snatched the phone out of his hand. "Hello," I said, hesitantly.

"Who is that answering your phone?" Chris screamed at me.

I disconnected the phone. I couldn't deal with Chris right now. Right now I had to deal with Khalil.

"I know you didn't answer my phone," I snapped.

"It was ringing. What?" he asked, acting like he didn't know what he had just done. I threw my pillow at him.

"You knew what you were doing. Why you trying to blow my situation up?" I yelled.

He grabbed me, and put his arms around my waist. "Why do you even bother with that dude? You don't want him. He's not treating you right. You want me."

"Well, the only reason you want me is because I didn't leave him yet," I said, as I broke away from him.

"Why are you fighting it?" he asked.

"I'm not fighting anything, Khalil. Yes, we are sexually compatible, but what else do we have going on?"

"I make you smile and laugh," he said, trying to make me laugh. But I didn't smile at all.

"All you are going to do is drop me when I drop Chris. I'm not stupid."

"How long have we been seeing each other? If I wanted to drop you, I would have done it already. I know what you are scared of. You can't take the pressure."

"The pressure of what?"

"A man ready to give you everything that you want and need," he said.

"It's not that."

"You sure?"

"I'm positive. I know what I want," I said as I shook my head.

"I don't think you do."

"Why me? Why do you want to pursue me. I mean, there are a lot of girls out there. Call one of them."

"That's not what I'm looking for. I want you. I want to settle down and see my lady after a hard day."

"I mean, look at the circumstances how we met," I said.

"So. That's not important. How I feel about you is. Tell me you don't feel anything for me."

"How can you feel something for me and it has only been a few weeks?" I questioned him.

"Time doesn't matter. I know that you are different."

"Well, I don't know what I feel. I think we should talk later."

"So you putting me out? All right, I'm tired of playing games with you. When you get your shit together, get with me." He left and I made sure the door was locked.

Khalil had a lot of nerve. I didn't disrespect him. I never answered his phone or looked through his phone numbers. And he wants to play me with my man? I sat thinking how I was going to get out of this mess. Chris kept calling me back. He would alternate between the house and my cell phone. I didn't want to speak to him. I didn't know what to say. I love Chris, but he doesn't make me happy. He is not around enough to make me happy. A relationship takes work, and it is impossible for us to make this work with him living so far away. I dialed Chris, but before I could get what I needed to say out of my mouth, Chris was screaming at me. "So who was that Gina?"

"A friend," I said.

"A friend, huh? Why was he over your house?" he said suspiciously.

"Chris, come on. He's just a friend."

"You take a shower while your friends are over? I don't know about you," he mumbled.

"Baby, I can't do this anymore," I said.

"Can't do what?"

"I can't do us."

"What do you mean?"

"I mean, you are too far away from me. Sometimes I want to hold you, and touch you, and I can't."

"You know I love you, Gina."

"I know, but your love does not have arms that can hold me at night. If I feel like I want you, or I get real hyped and want to run to you, I can't. All I can do is call you. I can't even drive to you. Chris, you are miles away. You are always working. I want more. I deserve more." I cried.

"Stop crying, Gina. I love you, girl. Things are about to pop out here for me."

"I don't want to hear that shit. I got to go, Chris."

"So, we are over. Just like that? One year of my life for nothing, huh, Gina?"

"Chris, I've got to go." He was not going to make me feel bad for wanting more. I need someone who's in the same city as me, someone that is willing to do whatever it takes. Hopefully that someone is Khalil.

I drove to Khalil's apartment in less than a half hour. I knocked, but he didn't answer. His car was there, so I knocked again. He still didn't answer so I dialed his number. The phone rang and rang. I got out of the car and banged on his door three times. Finally, he came to the door.

"Gina, what are you doing here?"

"I left him," I said, looking like a lost puppy.

"You did what?"

"I left him," I repeated.

"Come in," he said, and extended his arms out to me. I walked into his apartment, and for the first time I had no attachments. I was free to do whatever I wanted. As soon as I entered, Khalil pushed me to the sofa. He kissed me intensely, and then we sat down.

"You made the right choice," he said, as he tilted my head up toward his.

"I know I did." We began to kiss again, and remove each other's clothes. Naked, I knelt in front of him and took his dick in my mouth. He gasped as I licked all around the outside and the top of its head. His dick became hard and long as I took it in and out of my mouth. I looked up at him and his eyes were closed and he was biting his lip. When he couldn't take it anymore, he stood over me and positioned my body like I was about to take off in a race. He pushed my ass on his dick, and plunged his massive dick deep into me. Then, with four fast pumps, he was done and I was out of breath. He got up and got me a washcloth.

"Why you do that?" Khalil asked as he handed me the washcloth.

"Do what?" I asked.

"Make me cum so quickly."

"I don't know," I said, smiling. I sat on the sofa beside him.

He tapped me and said, "What are you doing New Year's Eve?"

"I haven't given it a lot of thought," I lied, thinking about the plans I'd made with Chris that needed to be canceled. "I'm probably going to be doing hair or something."

"I want you to take off. I want to take you somewhere."

"Somewhere like where?" I asked.

"We can go to Vegas."

"Las Vegas?" I asked in disbelief. "When?"

"Tomorrow. I'll give you the money and you can go to my travel agent."

"Are you serious?"

"Yeah, we can bring in the new year right."

The next morning I went to Khalil's travel agent and she reserved us a room at the MGM Grand hotel. We were leaving December 30 and returning January 2. Our trip came to twenty-three hundred dollars because we were booking it so late. Khalil had given me three thousand and told me to spend the rest on myself and I did. I had never been to Vegas and I wanted to look good. I couldn't wait. I called the shop and canceled all my appointments. Janea said she would take them. I had to get my nails and feet done and finish preparing for my trip. A month ago who would have thought I would be bringing in the new year with Khalil instead of Chris?

After getting my nails done, I went home and packed my

bags. I was spending the night with Khalil because we had an early flight. As I was walking out, I saw Chris's number on my caller ID. I was tempted to answer it, but I knew he would try to convince me to get with him. I had been with him a year and he hadn't taken me anywhere. Here I had been with Khalil less than a month, and we were on our way to Vegas.

Khalil's friend Maurice drove us to the airport the next day. It was the longest flight I had ever taken. I'd never been to the West Coast and I was a little nervous about flying nonstop for five hours. Khalil went right to sleep. I looked out the window into the clouds, thinking about Chris.

"Are you okay?" Khalil asked when he woke up.

"Yeah, I'm fine."

"What are you thinking about?"

"Nothing, I just . . ."

Before I could get it out, he stopped me midsentence and said, "Listen. We are cool. We are not rushing. We are coming out here to have a good time. Whatever you decide to do when we get back is totally up to you. I know that your man had a good thing and didn't know how to appreciate you." I felt a little more relieved, like I had made the right decision.

We took a cab from the airport to our hotel. The MGM Grand was huge! There were grand chandeliers, shiny marble floors, and loudly ringing slot machines throughout the ground floor. Everything was so busy. In a matter of five minutes I saw three brides walk by, and one Elvis impersonator. People were already walking around with New Year's shiny glasses and hats on. We followed the bellhop as he took our luggage up to our suite. Khalil tipped him and we got settled.

"There is so much to do! Are you going to gamble?" I said, as I placed what I was going to wear on the bed.

"No, I don't want to go anywhere near the casino. Once I get started, I can't stop."

"That's going to be hard. There is gambling everywhere."

"I know, but I didn't come here for that. I came here to spend time with you," he said, as he pulled me close and kissed me.

We walked down the Vegas strip. The weather was cooler than I expected. It was about 60 degrees, but it still felt good. There was a roller coaster and a replica of the Statue of Liberty across the street from our hotel at the New York–New York Hotel & Casino. We walked a few blocks, taking in the sites. Sex was everywhere. There were big billboard signs with naked women up and down the street. A man gave me a flyer with porn on it. I gave it to Khalil, and we laughed at it.

After our stroll, we returned to the hotel and ate at the Rain Forest Café. It was like a rain forest with mechanical birds and animals.

"What do you want to do next?" I asked Khalil.

"We can go to the pool, go back to the room and relax, and then go out tonight. Order me a burger and fries," he said, as he got up to go to the bathroom. When he left the table a man came over to me. He looked normal, but he asked me was I working the track. I told him I didn't know what the track was. He looked at me strangely and left. Khalil returned and I told him what the man had just said to me. Khalil laughed and said that the man was a pimp. He was trying to get me to work for him and I'd had no idea!

After lunch we went swimming in the heated indoor pool. I felt comfortable in my cute white and yellow bikini until some big-chested bitch came walking past. *It must be the law to get breast implants in the state of Nevada,* I thought. Everyone, even regular moms and black girls, had big Pam Anderson–looking cleavage. Khalil did a double take. She had light brown skin, a big curly weave, and wore the skimpiest string bikini I'd ever seen. She had a magazine, beach bag, and two drinks in her hand, and conveniently dropped her magazine. Khalil, jumping out of the pool so fast he almost hurt himself, walked up to her and said, "Here, you dropped this."

I watched in disbelief. Not only did he follow her to her chair, he began having a lengthy conversation with her! I thought he might notice me, as I got out of the pool to dry off. He didn't even turn around. I was pissed as shit. I couldn't let it show though. I just continued to dry off and left. I was in the room, fuming mad. I wanted to cuss him out so bad. A half hour later, as I was getting out of the shower, I heard Khalil enter the suite.

"Listen. I know I'm not your girl, but I am not going to tolerate you flirting right in front of my face!"

"What are you talking about? I'm just having some fun," he said, as he sat on the bed.

"You're having fun? Huh? You are funny. Did you get her number?" I asked, steaming mad.

"No, but I could have. Why you tripping?"

"I'm tripping because we are here together," I said, as I got in his face.

"I know we came here together, but you are not my woman. Listen, don't get serious on me by putting handcuffs and shit on me." Khalil began searching in the drawer for something to wear.

He was right. We were just friends. I was here with him. He had brought me to Las Vegas, not the chick at the pool. Not Bianca, but me. There was something special about me. So I let the pool episode roll off. I regained my composure and said, "What do you want to do next?"

"You," he said. We ordered room service, and for the rest of the afternoon we went at it multiple times.

We awoke around ten and listened to the radio to see where the hip-hop clubs were. We took a cab to the club with the biggest party. There were big bouncers outside the club, as well as lots of foreign sports cars. The club was playing hip-hop music, but the crowd was not what we expected. It was diverse, but the atmosphere wasn't right. We were the only black couple in the club. Khalil went to the bar to get a bottle of champagne and we made an early New Year's toast. Two girls came over to our table and asked if the seat next to us was taken. I said no. One was a blonde, the other had dark hair. They both had on bright red lipstick, were barely dressed, and teetered on stiletto heels.

As soon as they sat down, Khalil and I got up to dance. We were having fun, making the best of the club. We came back to our booth to see the girls kissing each other. Making out! I tried to look away. I couldn't believe they were all over each other. Khalil looked over and said, "Okay. Let's not disturb them." We went back to the dance floor again. After about five songs and four drinks, Khalil asked if I was ready to leave. I told him I had to go to the restroom first.

I went to the restroom, and as I came out, I saw Khalil sandwiched between the lesbians, kissing the dark-haired one. The blonde was feeling all over his butt and legs. He saw me and didn't bother to stop kissing her. I ran out of the club and got the bouncer to flag me a cab. I was so drunk that when I got back to the hotel, I fell on the bed with my clothes on and went to sleep.

When I woke up on New Year's Eve the sun was shining and Khalil wasn't there. My head was on fire. I didn't know where he was, but I knew one thing. I wasn't staying in Vegas with Khalil to get disrespected like this! I packed my shit and took a cab to the airport.

CHAPTER 10

During the ride to the airport, I kept asking myself if I was doing the right thing. Khalil invited me on this trip. Then he had the nerve to act like this? I wasn't his woman. We were "just friends." That's why he should be on his best behavior, because I wasn't his woman yet. I should have known better. This motherfucker had me three thousand miles from home, and then started tripping on me. I was mad at myself for having a nasty hangover, falling for Khalil's shit, breaking up with Chris—all of it. I called Mike as soon as I got out of the cab.

"Mike, listen. I'm in Vegas with Khalil. He is being so disrespectful. He's been flirting with other women the whole time, right in my face. Then, when we were in this club last night, he started kissing a lesbian. I left, and he never came back to the room." Tears ran down my face.

"Stop crying. He's tripping. Does Chris know where you're at?" Mike asked.

"I broke up with him."

"For Khalil?" Mike said, surprised.

"Not really, but I wanted to go on this trip without reservations, to see how it would feel."

"What are you going to do now?"

"Get a flight home."

"Call me as soon as you get a flight so I can see how you made out."

"I will. I got to find a flight first." As soon as I disconnected, my phone began to ring. It was a blocked number. I was scared to answer it. It was probably Khalil, trying to find out where I was. Fuck that niggah. If it is him, I'm going to cuss his ass out.

I answered my phone. "Hello."

"Gina, where are you?" a voice asked.

"Chris?" I said, taking the phone away from my ear in disbelief.

"Yeah, it's me. I'm in Philly. Where are you?" he asked. I didn't know what to say. Before I could respond, he said, "I went by your place and checked the hair salon. They said you went on vacation. Where are you?" I didn't know what to tell Chris, so I just started to cry. He hated to see or hear me cry.

"I took a trip with Bianca to Las Vegas. I don't want to stay here with her. I want to come home to you! I'm sorry. I miss you, I miss you," I cried.

"Get a plane home."

"I'm trying. I'm sorry, Chris, I miss you, I was wrong."

"I know, I know. You're at the airport?" he asked.

"Yes, I just got to the airport."

"Do they have any flights?" he asked.

"I'm trying to see now. I'll call you back." I tried to calm myself down. I had to get out of Vegas and get back home to my man. I went to the terminal to see if there were any flights to Philadelphia. I didn't care what time it left. Anything was better than spending my New Year's Eve with Khalil in Vegas, or by myself.

I walked up to the information desk. The woman, in her late sixties, was on a call, giving someone directions. I waited until she finished and got her attention.

"Hi. May I help you?" she said.

"I need to find a flight back to Philadelphia. Today."

"Today? I don't know. Most flights to the East Coast are booked. You see that red phone over there? Pick it up, and somebody will try to help you." I thanked the woman and walked over to the phone. I picked it up and the operator asked what I needed assistance with.

"I don't care what airline or price. I just need to get out of Vegas!"

"Can you fly into New York or Newark?"

"Newark is good enough." She found me a red-eye, arriving at nine in the morning. I wanted to leave right now so I asked her was she sure there weren't any other flights. Then she said, "Hold up, there is another flight with Frontier Airlines. It's leaving in forty-five minutes to Reagan International. It would get you into Washington, D.C., at seven P.M. You lose three hours going back to the East Coast, and the flight is four and a half hours."

"Okay, I want it," I said.

"The only problem is they are about to start boarding in fifteen minutes. You still need to make it through security and you're going to be cutting it very close."

"I'll take the chance. I want the seat," I said.

She took my credit card information and booked the flight. She told me that I could pick up my ticket at the Frontier counter. I hung up the phone and ran to the ticket counter.

"Excuse me, sir, my flight is about to leave. I need a boarding pass." He took my identification and printed out a boarding pass. He said, "You'll never make this flight, but here is your boarding pass. Have a nice day."

I took my pass from him, put it in my bag, and ran up the escalator to security. When I reached the top I saw a security line with at least a hundred people waiting. I looked down at the time on my cell phone. I had exactly twenty-five minutes to make it through security. I got the attention of a security person and begged to jump to the front of the line. "I need to make my flight; it leaves in twenty minutes. Can you please let me go to the front of the line?" I forced my ticket into his hand.

He glimpsed at it and walked me to the front of the security gate. I made it to my flight just as they made the final boarding announcement.

Once I was settled in my seat I hurried and called Chris before the flight took off. His voice mail answered so I left him a message. "Chris, this is Gina. I got a flight back home. I'm flying into Reagan International. I know you are in Philly, but can you meet me down there? I arrive at seven P.M. Flight 1016

Frontier Airlines." I turned my cell phone off, fastened my seat belt, and prayed to God that Chris would take me back.

The plane landed and for the first time in my life I wasn't the first person off the plane. I wasn't pushing people and sighing when they didn't move fast enough to get off. I was taking my time because I did not want to face the reality that Chris might not be waiting for me. I was optimistic that he still had feelings for me, and that's why he'd looked for me and called my cell phone. I hoped he got my message, or else I'd have to find my way home from Washington. But anything was better than being stuck in Las Vegas with Khalil.

My phone rang and I fished for it in my bag. I saw Chris's number on the screen of my phone. I answered the call.

"Yo, did you make your flight."

"Yes," I said.

"Where are you? I'm at the terminal waiting for you," he said.

I sighed with relief.

"I'm about to walk outside." I walked over to the curb as his tan Chrysler 300 pulled up. He unlocked the door and I placed my bags in the backseat and got in. His car smelled like strawberry air freshener. I was scared to look at him. I could feel his eyes on me.

He said, "I don't care who you were with, what happened, or any of that."

"I'm sorry." I sniffed as I tried to keep my tears in.

"All I care about is right now. I love you and I know I don't want to ever go through this again. I haven't slept in two days. I couldn't stop thinking about you. Look at me. I look a mess," he said, as he held his arm out, pulling on his shirt. I stretched over the car console and hugged him. I was crying, but I felt overjoyed that I was with my boo. Our reunion was interrupted by a cop telling us to move because there was no waiting at the airport. Chris started the car, turned on the radio and drove us to his apartment.

Once we were inside he told me the plan for the night.

"Gina, I got to deejay tonight at H20. I want to stay here with you and bring the year in, but they already paid me. So, you can stay here if you like. I have to go." He walked in the bathroom and I followed him. I said, "Baby, I know that's your job and I want to go with you."

He had to be at the club in an hour, so he undressed and got in the shower. I took off my clothes and joined him. The water was hot, but felt so good after my long flight. I stood behind Chris and just held him as the water ran down our bodies. He turned around and squeezed me tight.

"I even missed your smell, girl," he said, as he kissed me. He took his washcloth, lathered it up with soap, and knelt on his knees and began to wash me up. He started with my feet and worked his way up my legs. He slid the soapy cloth between my legs and moved it gently back and forth. I grabbed my boo's hardness and stroked it in a circular motion. He then lathered my breasts. He rubbed his dick against my clit, teasing her, then picked me up and told me to wrap my legs around his waist. We thrust in unison until we both were satisfied.

*   *   *

It was ten o'clock, two hours away from the new year. Chris was already dressed and waiting on me. My hair was still damp from the shower so I took a headband out of my bag and brushed my hair and wore it wild. It looked how I felt, sexy and carefree. I had on an ocean blue asymmetric dress that hugged my body just right. Although we didn't plan it, Chris and I wore the same colors. He had on a white and blue striped collar shirt and blue slacks, with black hard-bottom shoes. I applied shimmering light blue eye shadow and wore dangling gold earrings and a matching bracelet. My shoes where multicolor gold and blue pointy stilettos. I was ready to go.

With Chris working for the night, we didn't have to wait to get into the club. Chris's intern, Jules, was deejaying until he got there. We walked to the bar, passing people who already had drunk too much. People had on party hats and colored aluminum streamers were everywhere. A girl I didn't even know blew a party whistle in my face and said, "Happy New Year." I said the same as I followed behind Chris. He purchased a big bottle of champagne and handed me a glass. Then he shook the bottle until the cork popped, making a loud noise.

"Happy Near Year early, baby," Chris said, as he poured the champagne and it overflowed my glass. I smiled and sipped it down. He hugged me and we walked over to the booth so Chris could take over. Jules took the headphones off and they shook hands. Chris gave him a glass of champagne too. Then we all toasted and I joined Chris behind the booth, grinding against him to the rhythm of the music. He had one hand on the equipment and the other hand on me.

The new year was almost here. At eleven fifty-eight Chris stopped the music and screamed, "Okay, the year is almost over. Make some noise."

The crowd of over a thousand people screamed at the top of their lungs.

Chris continued, "I'm going to bring Jules to the ones and twos and he is going to spin y'all into the new year."

Jules got behind the booth and put on a hyped collage of high-energy songs. The club went crazy with excitement. Chris grabbed me and we walked over to a quiet hallway off the main room. Chris hugged me as Jules called out the official countdown. Everybody began to yell in unison, "Ten-nine-eight-seven." At six I held Chris tighter and screamed along, "Five-four-three-two-one. Happy New Year!" Streamers fell from the ceiling as Chris and I kissed. The new year meant a new beginning. It wasn't a New Year's Eve filled with high rollers and bright lights, but I couldn't imagine a better way to bring in the near year than in the arms of the man I love.

The next morning I awoke to find Chris on the computer.

"Why are you up so early?" I asked.

"I'm looking for a job in Philly."

"You are moving?"

"Yes. I almost lost you last year. And it's not going to happen this year. I love you, baby." I sat on his lap and helped him look through the job listings. I was so happy. My man was moving closer to me.